The
Vanishing
Tide

The Vanishing Tide

HILARY TAILOR

LAKE UNION PUBLISHING

Text copyright © 2022 by Hilary Tailor
All rights reserved.

Published by Lake Union Publishing, Seattle

www.apub.com

Amazon, the Amazon logo, and Lake Union Publishing are trademarks of Amazon.com, Inc., or its affiliates.

ISBN-13: 9781542036580
ISBN-10: 1542036585

Cover design by Emma Rogers

Printed in the United States of America

For my mother, Gill.

"O Mary, go and call the cattle home,
And call the cattle home,
And call the cattle home,
Across the sands o' Dee."
The western wind was wild and dank wi' foam,
And all alone went she.

From 'The Sands of Dee' by Charles Kingsley

Prologue

It is always the same. The sun is setting and there is no sign of her yet. She sits on the sea-wall, back to the lagoon, kicking the heels of her sandals, waiting for Clare. She has developed a quiet patience for her sister's timekeeping, but the baby will be awake soon and she must get back. Her gaze tracks the cockle wagon as it trundles down the long stretch of sand, the men sitting on the edge with their rakes and buckets, their legs dangling and swaying as they laugh and joke. Their voices become faint and begin to recede into the wail of the seagulls and the advancing tide. She squints into the sunset as it suddenly stops: a solitary man leaping from the back, tearing into the water.

This is when the shouting begins.

The wagon becomes alive with men, jumping onto the sand and sprinting through the sea, kicking up foam and stone like so many wild horses. They surround the object of their disquiet. One of them, still a boy, turns and vomits into his hands. She sees them gather a dark shape and heave it clear above the water. It is only when that beautiful hair falls back into the waves like an inky waterfall that she knows Clare isn't coming back.

Chapter One

Isla, March

Sliding the key into the lock was harder than she thought. Isla had waited almost ten years to enter this house and now she didn't need Astrid's permission, she still felt like an intruder. A salty wind stung her skin as her wrist angled itself against the doorknob, a complicated sleight of hand only three people, now two, could perform to get the key to turn. A click gave way to a groan as the door swung slowly in.

Isla put her rucksack down, hung her coat on the only hook in the hallway and considered her inheritance. The old leather armchair was still there in the sitting room, but the floor was uncluttered by the mess she remembered as a child. It had never been this tidy when she was growing up. The air didn't smell as if it had been sealed up against the world and there were no strands of tobacco scattered across the coffee table; the bowl containing Astrid's Rizlas and her carefully wrapped chunks of resin had gone. It could have been an ordinary room where a normal family might live an unremarkable life. The deception was unsettling. The only thing that looked familiar was an enormous metal shelving system running the length and height of the wall. Hundreds of art books, hurled together and threatening to topple at the lightest touch. She looked at the titles and recalled that several of them had once been aimed at her head, one after another, whizzing by in a blur of colour.

She opened the door into the dining room, quickly averting her eyes from the painting above the fireplace – a habit from childhood she could not shake off. It had always given her the creeps. Maybe she would have liked it more if somebody else had painted it, somebody nicer. It was worth more than the house, she knew that, and the house was worth a fortune. You weren't allowed to build this close to the shoreline any more and the view to the sea was stupendous. Astrid had regularly fended off estate agents who came knocking. The building, more than a hundred years old, needed renovation and was ripe for profit. She never let them down kindly. Upsetting people who wanted something from her was a sport in which Astrid excelled. Now it was Isla wandering through the rooms like a prospective buyer, noting the jobs that needed to be done, the cracks that had to be filled. It wasn't too bad. The white weatherboard on the beach side was peeling, but the skeleton of the house had endured. She would enjoy doing something with her hands while her mind considered what to do with the absence. Loving Astrid had been a burdensome task. London was too far from here to make social calls, especially when you knew you weren't welcome. Although Astrid seemed to tolerate a phone conversation once every couple of months, it was always Isla who made the call. Astrid had never courted anyone's company but her own.

The house felt unnaturally cold. A damp breath of wind snaked around her neck, stirring the curtain drawn against the window, making her shudder. Spring came late this far north, and she cursed herself for leaving her warmest jumper behind. She had spent almost two decades of her youth here and on the few occasions she'd returned, it was always in the futile hope that the weather would be as warm as the capital. She'd forgotten how the cold crawled into

4

your bones and squatted there till summer. Isla peered back into the hallway to see if she had left the door open. It was shut.

The last time she'd visited, she had brought wine and flowers. It had been a significant birthday for Astrid; Isla had felt there should be some acknowledgement, even though Astrid had not remembered Isla's birthday for years. Astrid had given her a curt nod of appreciation when she'd handed the flowers over. There were only eighteen years between them. They should have been more like friends. But, just as before, she'd found herself cold and alone for the weekend while Astrid painted in the studio. Isla had used the time to brood. She was past forty and still with no family of her own. She didn't want to be here. Astrid didn't want her here. No wonder she couldn't hold down a relationship – she had never been shown how to care for anyone else. Astrid was all she had, all she would ever have. Isla was suddenly floored by the understanding that this would never change. She had lost her opportunity to make her own family; she'd been too busy moping over the mess she'd left behind in this house.

Two days later, when she saw the flowers lying on the kitchen countertop, wilting in their cellophane, something inside her snapped. This would be the last time. If Astrid wanted her company, she would have to ask for it. The request never came, and when the time stretched between them it had been more a relief than a heartbreak. As Isla looked around the place, remembering that weekend, it struck her that Astrid had always been incapable of nurturing the living, and she had passed this affliction on. It was probably the only thing they had in common.

A faint chemical scent she couldn't put her finger on drew her to the foot of the stairs. There was a large circular stain on the oatmeal carpet, pale grey in colour – not what she'd imagined. She crouched down and touched it, conscious of being close to something very profound. It was dry and crisp and when she drew her hand back, a fine white powder coated her fingertips. She wondered who had taken the trouble to do this. It must have been hard to clean.

She stood. Using the stairs would be difficult without thinking about Astrid's last moments, but even so, as she stepped over the stain, a small seed of excitement began to grow in the pit of her stomach. Maybe the information Astrid refused to provide when she was alive could be prised from this house now she was dead. Astrid had always delivered the truth like an unwanted meal. It didn't matter if it was unpalatable to the recipient; you were to eat it all without complaint. If Astrid had wanted to tell Isla about the circumstances surrounding her Aunt Clare's death, no doubt she would have taken delight in frightening her with the gory details. But to refuse to talk about it at all – well, that was something else. The story of Isla's father had been repeated like a folk song throughout her youth: *He was a waste of space, he didn't care, he's gone, gone, gone.* Astrid could have used his death to curry sympathy, but she didn't. It was the women who mattered in this family. Men added a layer of complication. It was a lesson Isla was still trying to unlearn.

As she reached out to steady herself, she noticed the finial at the end of the balustrade. The tip was missing, broken off by Astrid's fall. Isla touched her own head and winced at the thought. She had felt fine about coming alone, staying here by herself. It hadn't crossed her mind to book into the only hotel in the village, but when she started to walk up the stairs she felt a resistance, the flex of a muscle, willing her to go back down. Halfway up she paused, unsure what to think. Astrid was gone. Isla would never again bear the brunt of her disapproval. But the house was charged with friction. She could feel it gathering round her like mist rising up from the sea.

She said out loud, 'This is my house now.' The words sank through the air like stones through water and before she finished saying them, she knew it wasn't true.

6

Chapter Two

ISLA

The rooms at the top of the house were even more light filled than the ground floor, offering a panoramic spread all the way out to the islands and beyond. As Isla considered the view that had inspired her name, she wondered once again how Astrid had lived with it. Missing Clare was the only vulnerability that Isla ever detected in her considerable armour, and she struggled to understand how Astrid could bear to paint the very thing that took her sister away.

Isla stood in the hallway and contemplated the only door she knew would be locked, wondering where the key was kept. She tried the handle, smeared with years of dried paint, the ghost of Astrid's thumbprint recorded on the Bakelite. Bracing herself for the loud shriek as it rotated, Isla knew it couldn't be this easy. Sure enough, it wouldn't budge.

'Hello?' a woman called out from below.

Isla frowned.

'Isla, is that you? Are you up there?'

She recognised the voice of Penny Walton, the only human being Astrid called a friend.

'Yes, it's me. Coming.' Isla turned away from the door, crossed the landing and tramped down the stairs. A weather-beaten face waited for her at the bottom, strong brown fingers worrying Astrid's spare keys between swollen knuckles. Her denim espadrilles avoided the stain, her expression betraying the fact she was wondering whether to deliver gentle sympathy or a stiff upper lip. If it hadn't been Penny who had found Astrid at the bottom of the stairs, hours cold, Isla would have cut the meeting short. But she was Astrid's oldest friend and had handled the police until Isla could be found. Isla acknowledged the debt and made herself be kind.

'Would you like a drink? Tea?' Isla said, walking past her into the kitchen. 'I'm sure I can find something somewhere.' She rooted about in the same larder she had opened as a child, in the same vain hope that something of use might be found. Amongst the mouse droppings, an elderly jar of something clouded and pickled crouched next to tins of food she would never want to open, the prices indicating the state of their contents. 'I'm amazed she didn't poison herself. When did they abolish the halfpenny?' Isla inspected a packet of suet and threw it in the bin. 'I need to get some traps – it reeks in there.'

'It's OK. I brought you something. Here.' Penny proffered a cotton grocery bag, an armful of bangles clattering against wrinkled skin.

Isla took it gratefully. She had forgotten the nearest shop was a half-hour walk to the village and would probably be closing soon. 'I don't understand,' she said, shutting the larder door. 'The rest of the place is spotless.'

'The police made such a mess . . . well, they added to the mess. I needed something to do. I didn't want you coming back to . . . you know . . .' She stopped and considered something privately. 'I . . . when I was waiting for the police. After I found her. I

8

took her things. From the table in the sitting room? I didn't want the police to find it and think the worst of her. She didn't smoke that much anyway. I hope you don't mind.'

'No, I don't mind.'

'You can have it back if you like. I kept it safe.'

'It's yours. I don't want it. I never took to that stuff. Makes you paranoid.'

'Fair enough. You'll want this though.' Penny put her hand in the pocket of her dress and withdrew something on a thin black chain.

'What is it?' asked Isla.

'She had it on when she died. I kept it because I didn't want it getting lost. It was important to her.'

Isla examined the pendant. It was flat, made from filigree metal that had once been painted in the centre. She could see flecks of azure and white clinging to the recesses. 'Did she make this? I don't remember her wearing it or seeing it in the house.'

'I don't think she ever took it off these past few years,' Penny said quietly. 'She always wore it under her clothes.' She touched her clavicle briefly with her fingertips as she remembered.

'It looks like an upside-down flower head.' Isla tipped the pendant towards the window so it caught the light. 'It's got a design on it. Something in the middle.' Isla squinted at it, trying to make it out. She wondered what she'd done with her reading glasses. They were new, a depressing reminder of middle age, and she wasn't in the habit of wearing them on top of her head like other people did. She spent most of her day looking for them instead.

'It's a hamsa,' Penny explained, frowning.

'What's one of those?' Isla asked, aware she was missing some kind of point.

Penny gently took the pendant and turned it the other way up. 'It's a hand, not a flower.'

'Oh. Now I see it. What's that thing in the middle?'

'It's an eye. It's supposed to . . . protect.'

'Protect? From what, exactly?'

'I don't know. Bad spirits, that sort of thing.' Penny looked uncomfortable.

Isla tried to stop herself from laughing. 'Astrid was no hippy. Why on earth was she wearing this?'

Penny gave a shrug. 'No idea. But she would want you to have it.'

'Really?' said Isla, puzzled. 'Why?' Then she remembered the feeling she'd had, climbing up the stairs. She thought about how Astrid had died and she felt the disquiet that rose in her chest like a tide. 'Let's have that tea, shall we?' she said, putting the pendant round her neck.

Isla filled up the kettle, her fingers familiar with the heft of it, the angle needed to close the lid, the pressure required to depress the switch. They sat at the kitchen table, the comforting ritual of tea-making filling the air. It was almost cordial. But Penny had always been Astrid's ally and Isla regarded her with a wary reserve.

'We sat here, just like this, the day before she died. If only I'd known . . .' Penny muttered.

'How can you predict something like that? Nobody could know.'

'It just seems so . . . meaningless, falling down like that. And unfair.'

'Being fair wasn't Astrid's specialty, though, was it?'

'Unless . . .' Penny paused, looking bothered.

'Unless what?'

'This last year. There was something going on with her.'

'Like what?'

'She seemed more shifty than usual. Vague. I didn't see her so much.'

'You don't think she had dementia, do you?'

'No. Not Astrid. Her memory was as sharp as a tack. Better than mine.' Penny shook herself, rubbed her arms. 'I don't know. It was just a feeling. Like I'd caught her by surprise sometimes. Like something wasn't right. I wondered if there was something troubling her.'

'She was always in some kind of a mood,' Isla said. Then under her breath, 'Troublesome wasn't the word.'

'I know she could be troublesome. That's not what I said. Being troubled by something and being annoyed are two separate things. This was different from one of her moods. She seemed out of sorts.'

'Are you saying . . . she did this to herself? On purpose?'

'No . . .' Penny shook her head and shrugged. 'I don't know. Ignore me.'

'She would have left a note,' Isla ventured. 'You know Astrid, she wouldn't have been able to resist leaving a note.' And there are better ways to end your life than hurtling down the stairs, she supposed.

Penny nodded. 'You're right. Her balance was dreadful and getting worse, but she wasn't ill. She would insist on wearing that long cotton robe, though.'

'The djellaba. I remember it. She lived in it, practically. It must have been on its last legs. The hem was always coming down.'

'The inquest will confirm it, I suppose. Tell me,' Penny said, putting her mug down, 'are you still down in London doing . . . what were you doing?'

'Accountancy. Tax, to be specific,' Isla replied. 'Yeah, I'm still there. Though at my age I think I've outstayed my welcome.'

'Don't be ridiculous, you're young by today's standards. You have everything to celebrate.'

'Penny, I turned fifty last year. That's not to be celebrated.' This wasn't strictly true. Her birthday had been marked with the few

11

friends she'd managed to salvage from college, but they had already receded from her life and only a handful turned up. The evening was spent discussing things she knew little about. Teenagers, mainly: which universities to make them apply to, how to get them to clean up after themselves, how to curb their addiction to social media. They talked about how glad they were they had left London. How much better the air quality was on the commuter belt, the low crime rate, the price of a house. The contrast to her own situation was so great it went unmentioned, an elephant standing silently in the corner of the room. Her friends had made something permanent for themselves. They had found partners, made children, bought property. It was as if they had all been given a manual for life and, for some reason, she had missed out. At the end of the evening, she'd returned to her empty flat feeling cheated.

'What was the area you were living in? It had a funny name as I recall,' Penny asked, breaking into her thoughts.

Isla smiled. 'Crouch End,' she said, 'north London.'

'Doesn't sound like London to me. Sounds like the back of beyond,' said Penny, wrinkling her nose.

Isla raised her eyebrow and gestured to the view beyond the window. 'Like this, you mean?'

'As long as I can walk to get a pint of milk and a loaf of bread, it does for me. Astrid, too.' Penny imitated Astrid counting on her fingers. '*Grocer, doctor, bank and baker. That's all anyone needs*, she used to say. Whenever anyone put in a planning application for a new shop in our village, she'd oppose it. I never dared ask her about all the fancy art galleries in London she used to sell through, or the fact she popped into Atherton's, the art supply shop, every five minutes.'

'Do as I say . . .'

'. . . Not as I do.' Exactly. That was Astrid alright. In fact, a gallery opened up here not long ago and she refused to set foot in it. The work was inferior and the owner full of pretensions, or so she thought. She had a fine time fulminating about it at any rate.'

'She was in a good frame of mind, then? When you saw her last?'

'As good as it ever got for Astrid. I'm going to miss her a lot.' Penny sighed. 'Partly because she was better at making roll-ups than me.' They both laughed. Astrid's fingers had the dexterity of a magician.

'Penny.' Isla took a breath. 'I want to go into the studio, but the door's locked.'

'Why do you need to go up there?' Penny frowned.

'You must have heard the rumours.'

Penny seemed surprised. 'What rumours?'

'There've been some reports in the press that she hid some of her work, some important pieces. Diaries, that sort of thing. I don't care about the paintings, but I'd like to read her diaries if the rumours are true.'

Penny looked upset. 'You can't do that. Diaries are private things. Astrid would hate that.'

'She's not here to object any more, is she?' Isla tried not to sound impatient. Astrid was her mother, but she was painfully aware it was Penny who knew her best. Even after death, Astrid could still make her feel like a failure.

'I keep forgetting she's not coming back.' Penny shook her head as if to dislodge a thought. 'Astrid always closed the studio up. When she wasn't working on a painting, she locked the door.'

'Where's the key?'

'No idea. It was unusual . . . a funny shape, but I haven't seen it for years.' She cast Isla a concerned glance. 'Will you be alright here on your own? I know you didn't see eye to eye, but all the same . . .'

Isla tried to smile. 'At least I don't have to carry on wondering if we'll ever like each other. We both know she wasn't the mothering type. She was a . . .' She paused, hunting for words. 'Christ, I don't even know where to begin.'

'She loved you.' Penny's sympathy was genuine.

'She had a funny way of showing it. I can't ever remember her putting me to bed, or helping me with schoolwork, or any of the things a normal parent gets involved with. She spent her life continually pushing me away until I eventually got the message and left home.' Isla sniffed and looked down at her hands, bunched in her lap. 'The ridiculous thing is I would have come back, you know, if she'd asked me to. All she had to do was ask. It's been nearly ten years since I saw her.'

'She was a highly unusual person. You can't judge her by normal standards.'

'I can judge her by standards of decency and she would be found wanting, Penny. I think we both know that.' Isla felt the old resentment stirring up. 'I had to walk down to the village to buy myself an alarm clock when I was seven so I could wake myself up in time for school. I stole the money out of her purse. She never even noticed. What kind of mother treats her child like that? I thought it was normal until I went to school. Then I met everyone else's mothers . . .'

'Yes, well. It's difficult.' Penny's face closed up.

'I'm not having a go at you, Penny. If it wasn't for you sending me a birthday card every year, leaving food on the doorstep . . .'

'Ah,' Penny said, 'I didn't think you knew about that.'

'Who else would it be? You were our only neighbour. Astrid wasn't interested in food when she was working. It was me who took it off the doorstep and ate it. Astrid would have left it there until she starved.'

'I should have done more, I suppose. A birthday card and a bag of groceries every now and again isn't much.'

'It was better than nothing,' Isla said. 'Do you know, I loved going to school. Because they fed me. They were *kind* to me.'

An uncomfortable silence stretched out between them. Isla left the table and dumped her cup in the sink. She didn't feel like talking any more and hoped Penny would go. When she heard the chair scrape on the floor behind her, she felt a rush of gratitude for not having to ask her to leave.

'Knock if you need anything. We're neighbours now.' Penny embraced her on the doorstep and Isla inhaled a nostalgic mixture of patchouli and rolling tobacco. Tears stung her eyes as she nodded and turned back into the house.

Maybe she had made a mistake in coming back here, Isla thought. She had spent the last few years not knowing what to say to her mother, but now that it was too late to ask, she could feel questions rising up like a flood tide: questions about her childhood here, the way it was between them, and why. Like driftwood washed up on the beach, cured by salt water to a strength beyond its natural state, time had hardened the past to a density that seemed impossible to penetrate.

Chapter Three

Penny

If she allowed herself a moment of honesty, Penny liked to think she owned the bay. Between them, she and Astrid had explored every nook and cranny. As they grew older, they avoided it during the day. Neither of them much liked the tourists with the noise and rubbish that came with them. They preferred it all to themselves. When the warmth disappeared from the sky and the sun readied itself for descent, that's when Penny and Astrid re-established ownership. As soon as the beach was clear, they met on the sand and walked. If someone had asked Penny to recall their conversations, she would have found it difficult. Astrid wasn't talkative unless something had particularly displeased her that day. Most of the time they walked in silence and that was just fine. If they did speak, they never conformed to the stereotype thrown at people their age. They never discussed the past. Astrid had taken care of that. It was an arrangement that Penny had been conscious not to break.

Now that Astrid was not there to walk with her, Penny crossed the sand alone and thought about the hours they had spent together with so much unsaid. It had been a relief to talk to Isla about Astrid's state of mind before she died, but, now the words were out, it was impossible to unsay them, and Penny began to worry about her indiscretion. Astrid would have disapproved of them sitting at her kitchen table picking over her private life. Penny had come away from the house feeling disloyal, even though she hadn't been as forthcoming as she might. Astrid *had* been different over the past year, in particular, but it had started long before then. Two years ago, Penny began to notice the spotlights in the studio roof were on regularly, after Astrid had told her she wasn't painting any more. Penny could see it lit up like a beacon over the water. Over the last year, Astrid's face looked more harried than usual. Pinched and lined. Not the usual lines you would expect approaching seventy, but something else etched permanently into her skin. Occasionally, on their walks, Penny would point out something interesting. The family of seals that had taken to breeding here, perhaps, or the black-tailed godwits digging for worms, or something bizarre washed up by the tide. Astrid used to be very keen on the seals, but the last couple of breeding seasons, she had seemed to lose interest. Maybe she was winding down after all. Sixty-nine was considered young for death, but old age took people differently. And what a life she'd had. It was bound to have an impact, all that sorrow.

Even though it was a cold evening, Penny wanted to take her shoes off and feel the sand under her feet, but there was nothing to hold on to and she was afraid she would topple over if she tried. The idea of falling here didn't bother her; it was the indignity of needing a stranger to help her get up. She and Astrid often grabbed each other's shoulder or arm to steady themselves, usually without even asking. Now Penny felt rudderless and alone. Astrid's death had caused her to think about her own life, what was left of it. She hadn't realised how much she valued having Astrid down the lane, even if she didn't see her for days at a time. It was a comfort to know someone else was there. Jacob would ask her to move in with him if she didn't snap out of it. It was a conversation that circled round rarely, once a year at most. At least the villagers had finally accepted the situation and stopped asking when they would marry. It had only taken them thirty years.

The evening used to be her favourite time of day. The night tide would come in and sweep the sand clean, preparing to receive their footprints. Now it was a single set that marked her route and, today, the lack of company depressed her. She looked around her, unenthusiastic about continuing. It was getting dark. Penny turned back and headed home.

She entered her house, flinging her coat in a practised arc onto the bannister as she moved across the hallway. When she approached the threshold of the sitting room, she stopped short. The door to the drinks cabinet was wide open. The change in atmosphere was swift and palpable. Penny paused, unwilling to enter her own lounge. She detected a familiar density in the room, a smell of something old and briny and knew it would not go away.

'It's too early for a drink. I was going to have a bath first.' Her voice sounded braver than she felt.

A faint breeze sighed and tipped the glass door open a final few degrees. It reached the extent of its hinge and squeaked.

Penny muttered to herself and crossed the threshold. 'Not again,' she said, and her heart began to thump a little harder as she recalled the conversation with Isla. She bit her lip and tried to remember exactly which details she had given away. Pouring herself two fingers of whisky, she reached for an oblong tin on the mantelpiece that once held old-fashioned mints. Half a roll-up lay amongst the shreds of tobacco and cigarette papers. She picked it out carefully and lit it with a match before settling herself down on the armchair by the fire. Her hand tremored as the flame caught the old ash and she drew in the smoke as it came alive, comforting her like the embrace of an old friend. She cast the spent match into the dying coals of the fire. It flared briefly and settled to embers.

'You didn't tell me . . . I wasn't expecting to feel sorry for her.' Penny shook her head. 'I wasn't expecting that.' And then, more under her breath than anything else, 'You didn't tell me a lot of things.'

A thin curl of flame rose up among the coals. It hovered there for a few seconds, anchored to nothing. Penny watched it flare briefly and die.

'I defended you,' she continued, her voice firmer now. 'I will always defend you. But you can't keep on like this. You're frightening me. I never know what I'm going to find when I come back home. Do you understand?' Penny took a sip of whisky. 'This is my house, not yours.' The defeat in her voice betrayed the defiance of the words.

A faint creak of wood against nail sounded in the corner of the room. Penny tried to ignore it, but found she could not. Her eyes swivelled to follow the sound.

'You know what she'll do, don't you?' Penny said. 'She'll turn that house upside down. It's only natural. I can't stop her from doing that. I hope to God she's not right about those diaries. I told you not to write anything down.'

A soft click sounded from the kitchen. Something in Penny's chest leapt painfully.

'If you've left anything lying around . . . it won't be my fault. You didn't prepare me for this. We didn't discuss it.' Suddenly, Penny softened and slumped back in the chair. 'Why wouldn't you talk to me about it?' she asked, looking up at the ceiling. 'Isla's right about that necklace. You never used to be superstitious. What were you afraid of?'

The hush in the house felt like velvet; even the sound of the tide fell away. Penny knew she was being listened to. 'You must have known she would come back here eventually. It's only natural to ask questions. I can't keep her at arm's length. Anyway, I like her.'

Penny took a last drag from the roll-up and felt a curling breath at her face. She threw the stub in the fire and watched it blacken. Her vision blurred momentarily as the tears came. They usually did at this time.

'I miss you,' she sniffed. 'It wasn't right, what happened. You didn't deserve it. Any of it. But can't you see? She's asking me questions and I'm torn. My loyalty will always be with you, that doesn't change. We've been through so much together it counts for something, doesn't it?' Penny traced her fingers round the rim of her glass. 'I just wish . . . I wish we could have talked about it, that's all. Because she's a nice girl, Astrid. Doesn't she deserve to know?' A tear tracked its way down her cheek and she wiped it with the back of her wrist. 'I don't know what to do. You always had the answers. Ever since we were little. You and Clare. You always knew what to do.'

The weight in the air suddenly lifted and the house became hers once more. It happened like that. Like a switch. Penny heaved herself from the chair and crossed the room to draw the curtains.

The moon was clear tonight; it cast a cold light on the beach below. The tide was coming in again, she could hear the sigh of the waves approaching. Penny could just make out her own footsteps marching away up the beach. They were slowly disappearing into the saturating sand. Her return appeared higher up, further from the water, near the wall of the lagoon. The impressions were clearly visible, plodding towards the steps that led to her house. Right alongside, there was something else. A third set, lighter in tread than her own and narrower, tracking her footsteps, following her home.

Chapter Four

ERIN

Erin shifted in the hard plastic seat. The waiting room was stifling and the flickering strip light had begun to give her a headache. The woman next to her reeked of a scent that reminded her of dying lilies. She began to feel sick. She looked down, breathing through her mouth, and studied the hard rubber tiles beneath her feet. A faint pattern of snaking lines in varying shades of blue emerged and receded. They looked like varicose veins.

What am I doing here? she thought. She gathered her coat, shouldered her bag and made for the door.

'Erin Baker?' The doctor appeared, confounding her escape, and ushered her into his room. 'You looked like you were about to leave back there,' he joked.

'Oh. I thought I'd forgotten . . . something,' she mumbled, failing to match his mood, unable to think of a reasonable excuse for leaving.

He gestured for her to sit down. 'How have you been getting on since I last saw you?' he said, leaning back in his chair. They could have been sitting in a cafe together, old friends, catching up.

'Fine,' Erin replied automatically. A stupid answer that wasn't true.

'Sleeping?'

'Not really.'

'Appetite?'

'Not much.'

'OK, let's do the basics, shall we?' He motioned for her to roll up her sleeve as he opened the hard case containing the blood pressure monitor. He fastened the cuff around her arm and pressed on a black rubber bulb to inflate it. Erin closed her eyes, waiting for the unpleasant sensation to begin. It felt like a kind of suffocation.

'Is your daughter still waking in the night? You mentioned last time she had trouble sleeping.' He removed the stethoscope from his ears.

'No, she sleeps through now. She can't sleep beyond five-thirty in the morning, though. No matter how late I put her down.'

'How old is she now? Francesca, is it?'

'We call her Frankie. She's just turned six.' Erin brightened. 'She's in school now. Loves it, thankfully.'

'That old already? Doesn't seem like five minutes since you were starting IVF. You had a bit of a time with that, didn't you?' He looked into his computer and clicked through the medical reports that failed to articulate just how awful the whole process had been. Three miserable years. Four embryos and Frankie had been the last; frozen in the darkness, quietly waiting her turn while her siblings lost their grip, one after another, in sad succession, like the slow tolling of a funeral bell. The set of circumstances that had conspired to keep Frankie hanging on still made Erin draw breath.

The doctor turned away from the screen and looked at her pleasantly. 'How are things at home?'

'A bit better,' she admitted. 'We've just hired a part-time manager to help. Mark's still working too much, though. The hospitality industry is pretty relentless.'

'Ah, yes, I know all about that. Late hours,' he sympathised.

No you don't, Erin thought. The incessant domestic drudgery that came with running a hotel, even one as small as theirs, demanded every waking hour of their attention. When she'd first met Mark's parents, they'd been careful it was a part of hotel life she was not introduced to. She thought back to her student days, sitting at the honesty bar drinking wine with the guests, unaware of the deluge of small emergencies that flooded the hotel on an hourly basis.

'And you?' the doctor said. 'How have things been since I saw you last?'

She fought the impulse to tell him that she felt like leaving her husband at least once a week, but the idea of failing at marriage and motherhood was unthinkable. She thought about telling him that the sense of loss she carried inside her felt like a physical sickness. She tried to keep her voice neutral, light. 'I just need something to help me sleep, or to help me feel . . . better,' she said.

'We've discussed this before,' he said kindly. 'Medication isn't a cure-all. It can throw up a lot of other problems.'

'I know.'

'Have you tried meditation? Exercise? We talked about it last time. I'd like you to go down that route first.'

'I just . . . haven't had time. Everything's always so frantic.'

'Your daughter's at school now, though? Maybe you have a few minutes in your day to take a break, try and relax?'

Erin thought about the guests who passed through the hotel and the torrent of inconvenience they brought with them. Blocked toilets. Food allergies. Thieving. 'I suppose,' she said, resigned to another wasted visit. She resolved to book an appointment with one of the other doctors in the practice next time she came.

'I have in my notes here that you were thinking about relationship counselling. Did you look into that?'

'We can't afford it. Besides, we can't both leave the hotel. Someone needs to be there all the time.'

'There are NHS options. I can try and—'

'We'd both be retired by the time that came through.' *Or divorced. Or dead.*

'Are you able to take a holiday? Even for a couple of days. You mentioned another manager. Maybe they could help lift the burden? Close the hotel for a week during a quiet month?' He looked up, head cocked on one side.

Holiday.

The word skipped in the air. She hadn't had one of those since before Frankie was born. Without warning, a deep yearning opened up in her for the remote beach in the north of England she had visited as a child. Wide skies, the screech of gulls, the sharp smell of the sea. A horizon far enough away to blur into nothing but shades of grey. The warmth of sunlight on cold skin. She remembered the texture of her hair, thick with salt. Waking with the grit of sand in her bedsheets. A satisfying fatigue in the late afternoon.

They had gone to visit an elderly aunt – long dead now – but the memory of that holiday had endured, bathed in the golden tint of nostalgia. In a rare lapse of formality, her father had taught her how to catch crabs with bacon. There had been a huge, sweeping sea-wall that enclosed a sort of lake. A *lagoon*. That was the word the locals had used. A mysterious word she had repeated to herself, like an incantation. She had insisted that they walk on top of the wall from one end to the other. It was just wide enough for two people. Her father had held her hand. Her mother had followed, pointing out how the stone wall slid under the water in a gentle curve, green with algae and crusted with limpets. Even at that age, she had been conscious of straddling a division that separated the murky depths of the lagoon from the bright, sandy bay below. The thought that everything would be levelled by water when the tide came racing in had thrilled her.

All at once, Erin wished she was a child again: free of responsibility, free of the worry that her life constantly generated. She thought about her own daughter. Frankie had never seen the sea. That fact alone made her want to weep. As she left the surgery, empty-handed, she made a promise to herself that she would find that beach again and take her daughter there for the sake of her own sanity. With or without her husband.

Erin walked back, even though she knew it would take a long time from West Kensington. She had not changed her GP surgery since Mark had inherited the hotel and had no intention of ever doing so. It was her last link to this place: there was no other reason for her to be here. She deviated from the route home and turned down the quiet tree-lined road, unable to shake the feeling she was trespassing. The flat was about halfway down. It was a typical Victorian build like the rest of the street but even now, years later, it was still the smartest.

They had been so happy here. Both of them in jobs they loved, in a place they could finally call their own after years of shared housing and grotty student digs. Erin remembered the satisfaction of sleeping late and eating breakfast in bed at the weekend, opening the windows and hearing polite clapping coming from the Queen's Club tennis tournament every June; dancing in Soho with Mark until the early hours and sobering up in Bar Italia. Having a family was far enough away to enjoy the here and now, but near enough to savour. A baby was the next jaunty step on a path strewn with good fortune. She had no idea they were living on borrowed time, that the happiness was finite. As she stood on the pavement outside her old front door, Erin remembered the bidding war. Three couples had wanted her home. It had been sold for nearly thirty thousand pounds more than the asking price. When the estate agent rang her to deliver the good news, Erin had wept for the rest of the afternoon.

The two bay trees on either side of the front door had grown and somebody had threaded fairy lights around their foliage. The white shutters were open, and she remembered the light at this time of day; it would just be slanting into the sitting room, warming the varnish on the floorboards they had sanded down together over a bank holiday weekend. Erin was pleased the owners had kept the door colour, a rich blue, almost black. She stopped in front of it and still regretted not unscrewing the knocker and taking it with her. It was an elegant fox's head in polished brass, its narrow nose pointing down to the matching letterbox. There was nowhere she could have put it. She didn't have a front door any more, not really. It belonged to the carousel of guests that passed through her personal space every five minutes. She imagined how the flat might look now, wondering how it had come to this, how she had ended up standing on the wrong side of that door.

Chapter Five

ISLA

Isla knocked, even though Penny's door was open. When she got no reply, she walked round to the beach side of the house and found her sweeping the patio with an ancient besom broom. As Penny turned and smiled, her grey curls caught in the wind and raised up, snakelike.

'What are those jobs called – a Greek name, I think – that means they're never-ending?'

'I have no idea,' Isla said, amused.

Penny straightened up. 'Sisyphean. That's it. A Sisyphean task, this is.' She nodded at the stone beneath her feet. 'This'll be covered with sand again tomorrow. Don't know why I bother. Whole house would disappear if I didn't, though.' She looked at Isla. 'Everything OK?'

'I came to apologise,' said Isla. 'I think I was rude to you yesterday.'

'Ah.' Penny shrugged. 'It's a sad time. I wasn't offended.'

'You were closer to Astrid than I was. I hadn't thought about that. You're grieving too.'

'Yes,' Penny conceded. 'This place, these houses . . .' She looked at her own and then gestured to Astrid's down the lane. 'They make people close.'

'Yeah. Probably because they're so isolated.'

'Not just that. Did Astrid ever tell you about what happened in the years after they were built?'

Isla reached back in her mind and couldn't catch hold of any memory of Astrid talking about the houses.

'It's a good story,' said Penny. 'Here.' She fished out a small hip flask and pointed to a lichen-covered bench crouched out of the wind in a corner of the patio. 'Sit yourself down and I'll tell you all about it.'

Penny handed her the flask. Isla took a sip and a peaty, warming liquid slipped down her throat. She didn't drink much and certainly never in the afternoon, but something about being here, occupying a space between the land and the sea, meant ordinary rules didn't apply. They sat side by side, looking out onto the restless ocean, passing the flask between them as they talked. The tide was high, partly submerging the islands, and the water licked the steps that led from the beach up to the patio where they sat.

'Does it ever come over the steps?' Isla asked, nodding at the water.

'Sometimes. The powerful storms begin in the autumn. See that line there?' She pointed to a tidemark that crept two inches up the wall of the house. 'That's the worst it's ever been. It's never come inside – the doors are set high into the house – but the whole of the patio was underwater.'

'That must have been scary. Did you leave?'

Penny snorted and took a sip from the flask. 'No.' She gave Isla a sideways look. 'I can't believe Astrid never told you about what happened to the other houses.'

'What other houses?'

'There were five houses here, originally.'

'Five?' Isla's eyes followed the spit of land that extended into the sea. 'I can't imagine how on earth they fitted five on here.'

'Silly. The land used to be a much longer peninsula, stretched out almost to the first island. Must've been connected at some point, I suppose. They were built in a line, see?' She pointed to her own house, 'One . . .' then her finger turned to Astrid's house, 'two . . .' and then it moved beyond the lane and into the waves, pausing on each number to locate the phantom houses. '*Three . . . four . . . five.*'

Isla shivered. 'What happened to them?'

'They were gobbled up by the sea. One by one. The land just . . . fell away.'

'And the families who lived there?'

'Oh, they knew what was coming. They all left well before the storms finished them off.'

'Did you ever have to leave?'

'This wasn't in my day, Isla. It was the time of my grandparents and your great-grandparents. The Waltons and the Jarsdels. They made a pact to stay and it bound the two families together for life. We're survivors.'

Isla heard the pride in her voice and felt a tug of sadness that she had never had this conversation with Astrid.

Penny continued, 'After the third house was taken, they took bets in the village that our houses would go too. But they didn't. They held fast. Have done ever since. Some say the rock is stronger here, closer to the land. Some say the houses are protected.'

'By what?'

'Oh, I don't know.' Penny took a sip and passed Isla the flask. 'Some kind of magic.'

Isla looked at her, eyes narrowed. 'You don't believe that, do you?'

Penny paused and looked out to sea. 'This little finger of land is a Thin Place.' She turned to Isla. 'Do you know what that means?'

'No.'

'It's an old Celtic saying. It means a place where the walls dividing us from this world and the next are so thin you can feel the other world pressing in.'

'A Thin Place. Huh.' Isla tried out the words. Penny handed her the flask and she took another sip. 'So you think our dead ancestors are looking out for us, then? And because the walls are thin here, we can feel them? Is that it?'

'I didn't say anything about looking out for anyone. I just said *this place*,' Penny jabbed her finger on the bench slats between them, 'is close to *other places*. Be that the space we occupy after death, or a different time, a different dimension, I couldn't say. All I know is that you can feel things sometimes and they can't be explained easily.'

'Feel what?'

Penny made an impatient noise. 'I just said it can't be explained easily.' She shifted and pulled her cardigan closer. 'I've lived here all my life. I've learned not to rule anything out. There's one thing I'm sure of, though. They develop loyalties, houses. Especially ours. There's never been another family here but ours.'

'Oh come on.' Isla began to laugh, but Penny was serious.

'Three generations. They've seen all sorts. It seeps into the stone. Gives the house its character. Have you never walked into a house and felt something? For no reason? Doesn't have to be a bad something. Just a feeling.'

Isla remembered the resistance she'd felt when she entered Astrid's house. The sensation that she wasn't welcome. 'I suppose,' she said, 'but that's more to do with how it's decorated, isn't it? The furniture, the people inside it. Memories.'

'Exactly. It's the people inside that make the house. And when the same bloodline lives in the same house, the house can't help but absorb their traits. When the people are gone, you can still feel them, even when they're dead.'

Isla looked at Penny. 'Do you think that's why Astrid wore that necklace. The hamsa?'

'Possibly.' Penny motioned for the flask and took a swig.

Isla touched the hamsa around her neck and wondered if her mother had done the exact same thing when she thought about the dead. An idea occurred. 'Can you feel her? Now that she's dead? When you go into her house?'

'Astrid was too big to be contained in that house, Isla. She's everywhere.' Penny looked beyond the lagoon and past the cliffs, her brow furrowed. A breeze wound itself through the marram grass, stirring the tall stalks and making them sigh.

'If walls could talk . . .' Isla said as she watched the sand move across the patio in little eddies.

'Exactly. They'd have plenty to say.'

The drink made Isla reckless, and she blurted out, 'Do you think they'd tell me why Astrid never spoke about Clare's death? Why was it such a big mystery?'

After a long pause, Penny said, quietly, 'People deal with a death like that differently. Some want to talk about it all the time and some just . . . clam up. Do you know what I think?'

'What?'

'I think she buried Clare in her paintings. She did all her grieving privately.'

'Did she ever talk to you about her?'

'Clare died a long time ago, when I was barely twenty. It's not something that came up in everyday conversation between me and Astrid. I was always careful not to open old wounds with her.'

31

'It's just that . . . I remembered the house to be messy. Packed with stuff. She must have kept something of Clare's. She was terrible at throwing things away.' Then Isla had a thought. 'You didn't throw anything away, did you, when you tidied up?'

'No! Of course not. I would never do that.' Penny was indignant.

'Sorry. I didn't mean . . .'

'Did you get into the studio yet?'

'No. That's my next job.'

Penny looked uneasy.

Isla grinned, tried to make a joke. 'Thin Place or no, I'm going to get into that room if I have to hire a locksmith.'

The wind picked up. Penny didn't laugh. 'Astrid wouldn't like that. Having her studio forced open like that. Nobody was allowed up there. Not even me.'

'It sounds like you're afraid of her, Penny,' Isla said gently.

Penny stared out beyond the marram grass to the islands beyond. 'Like I said. This is a Thin Place, and Astrid can't be contained. She couldn't be contained in life and she won't in death.'

Isla stood up, woozy and defiant from the contents of Penny's hip flask. 'Well, that house is mine now, and I want to see what she's squirrelled away up there. I'll find that key eventually. It's got to be somewhere.'

A fierce gust of wind blew a wave of fine sand back onto the patio and Penny rose with her broom to fend it off. 'I think it's time you went,' she said. 'Oh, and read that. I saved it for you.'

Isla turned to where Penny was pointing. There was a newspaper folded underneath a large stone on the patio table.

Isla picked it up, turned it over.

'Page fifteen,' said Penny. 'Take it home. I don't want it back.'

Chapter Six

ISLA

Isla kept the newspaper folded until she reached the house, where she spread it out on the kitchen table and hunted around for her reading glasses. It was a broadsheet; one she didn't usually bother with. She turned to page fifteen and was confronted with a large black-and-white photograph of Astrid and a full-page article about her life. The photograph had been taken several decades ago. Isla recognised it as one that was habitually pulled out whenever anyone published anything about Astrid. Astrid refused to sit for portraits and this, taken at one of the only art openings she had attended, captured her in profile, still youthful, confronting one of her own paintings. She seemed to be unaware she was having her photograph taken. She certainly wouldn't have agreed to pose for it. The piece was part obituary, part biography. There was the usual speculation about Clare's death and the effect it might have had on Astrid as a young woman. Her subsequent work was well documented. There was some attempt at decoding some of the symbolism in Astrid's paintings and relating them to her sister, but Isla was at a loss as to whether there was any truth in it. It was all guesswork. Two-thirds of the way down, her interest was piqued:

When an artist of this calibre dies, particularly an artist with a penchant for secrecy, there will always be questions about surviving work. Astrid Jarsdel was well known for making copious notes about her paintings, sometimes incorporating text into her imagery, or referring to childhood diaries for inspiration. There is anecdotal evidence from several collectors that she kept these notebooks, known to have documented her development as a painter. There has even been speculation about paintings and drawings that never saw the light of day. But the rumours are unsubstantiated. Jarsdel died, age 69, on the same isolated peninsula in the far north of England that she was born on, and the small community there is as protective of her privacy in death as she was in life. With outsiders, the locals are notoriously tight-lipped about the tragic drowning of her sister, Clare, which happened on the same stretch of sand that Jarsdel's house and studio overlook. When I visited after Jarsdel's own sudden death, I was given short shrift by the neighbours I approached for comment. Whatever secrets Astrid Jarsdel had in life, she has surely taken them to the grave.

So it was true. The diaries had existed. Isla re-read the article. It had taken Penny a while to get in touch with her after Astrid had died. She had written a letter, asking Isla to call her. Isla had not found the letter for a couple of days; it had been lost in the jumble of the shared mail basket by the front door. The journalist would have arrived before she had managed to get here. It must have been Penny or the villagers who had turned him away. It was curious there was no mention of her. It was as if she didn't exist. Isla wondered if this was an oversight: shoddy journalism. Or was it because Astrid had never mentioned her to anyone else? Isla scanned the words once more. The journalist had devoted a fair chunk of the article to reflecting on Clare's death and the wall of silence that surrounded it. It seemed her aunt's story was as compelling to strangers as it was to Isla. Whenever she tried to broach the subject with Astrid, the conversation was shut down. It was true, her mother was a private person, but, within the walls of the house, when it suited her, the rule of silence fell away. Astrid summoned Clare at will like a medium summoning a spirit. Her death was used as a weapon to keep Isla in line when she was little, but the comparisons began when she grew older, a constant presence trailing her like a shadow. Clare had been twenty years old when she died, and the nearer to that age Isla got, the more she felt the weight of her aunt's virtues upon her. Clare was brave, inventive, funny, charming. All the things Isla was not, could never be, in Astrid's eyes. Would Astrid have loved her more if she were more like the sister she lost? It had always been an unvoiced question, tracking through the fabric of her life like a pulled thread.

On occasion, she had been stopped in the street by someone who had known Clare. Uninhibited by sorrow, they had held her face in their hands and sometimes cried at the loss of a woman Isla would never know, but was somehow reflected in her own features. Maybe Astrid had done the same. Maybe she had seen her sister in Isla's face too, but that was where the resemblance ended. Maybe living with Isla was like living with a badly forged painting and Astrid couldn't stand it.

Isla thought about the usual way writers ended their obituaries. The last line should have read: *Astrid Jarsdel is survived by her daughter, Isla.* And that word would have been apt. She had survived Astrid. But that was all she had done. She hadn't lived or thrived. *Survived* was the most appropriate word she could think of.

Isla studied the image of her mother as a young woman at the beginning of a successful career. She had never understood Astrid, and, judging by the article printed underneath, neither had the journalist. *Who were you, really?* Isla wanted to ask. *What were you thinking about when you looked into one of your own paintings?* They had shared this house for seventeen years, but she had never really known the woman behind the work.

Isla took her glasses off and sat back in her chair. Penny had hinted at something, a feeling that things weren't right. Isla had sensed it herself in the house, a latent discord she couldn't shake off. Again, she experienced a flood of questions rising around her and wondered if it was possible to be overcome by doubt; that if she didn't start finding some certainty soon, she might sink under the weight of it.

Chapter Seven

ERIN

Erin approached the hotel, looked at her watch. Frankie would be home from school soon and then the day could really begin. As she mounted the steps to the large double doors, she quietly scolded herself for being so negative about the hotel. Although it had been a gut punch to sell the flat, she had loved the idea of running a hotel with Mark. They had been good at it. Together they made a formidable team. It had been frayed with age when they had taken it over and now it was stylish and modern, something to be proud of. She remembered the first year they had moved in, Mark still grieving for his parents. The horrible realisation of the debt they had inherited. Every night, they went to bed and lay side by side like dead people, glassy-eyed, too tired to sleep.

Eventually, Erin had thrown herself at his mercy. 'Mark, please *please* can't we sell the hotel? It would solve all our problems. We can start again . . .' The vision of going back to her old life was so bittersweet she felt her throat ache.

Mark was steadfast. 'This hotel has been in my family for generations. I won't be the one who fucks it all up.'

'This isn't about looking good for the dead relatives, Mark. It's about our future. When I think about what lies ahead, I'm scared shitless; I don't mind telling you.'

'Erin, do you remember when you first came to the hotel when we were students? How glamorous you thought it was? How you loved staying here?'

'Yes.' She remembered those weekends like snatches of a movie: down-filled duvets, red wine and bowls of olives, showers together in endless hot water.

He moved towards her. 'Let me make that happen for you again. I know I can turn this around. Please. It's all I ever thought about growing up and I can't do it without you.' His hand sought hers in the gloom. Erin squeezed it hard, remembering they were in this together. There was a long, fine crack across the plasterwork. It feathered into a damp patch she had not noticed before. She screwed her eyes shut and kissed him.

'I'll help you as long as I can go back to work when we start making a profit,' she promised.

'Well, I don't know . . .'

'Once we've cleared the debt. We've already had to sell the flat. I don't want to do this forever. I want to go back to the job I trained to do.'

'OK,' Mark said.

'And there's something else.' Erin pressed, sensing she had an advantage that wouldn't last for long.

'What?'

'A baby. We should have one now, while we're both effectively working from home. It makes sense.'

'Hotel work is pretty full on, Erin. We can't hire anyone else to help when you get pregnant.'

'It can't be any worse than what I've done before. Event management is long hours, don't forget. I'm used to getting up early, staying up late. Other people manage.'

'I'm not sure it's a good time . . .'

'We should do it before I go back. It'll be harder then. I can't manage an event on the other side of London if I'm supposed to be breastfeeding a baby. But I can do it here while we turn the hotel around. I know I can.'

There was a silence and Erin crossed her fingers in the dark.

'OK,' he whispered eventually. 'It's a deal.'

Erin took over with steely determination. After three years of backbreaking work, they still hadn't cleared the debt. After four, they began to turn a small profit but not enough to hire extra staff. The years had raced by with no baby in sight. It had been in the back of her mind, a niggle of worry, but she put it down to the frantic pace of the hotel. It had a habit of swallowing time and energy. When she finally admitted to herself that things weren't right, Erin consulted doctors, scrolled through endless blogs and made ovulation charts that clung to the fridge. After five years, she realised that the baby she bargained for that night in bed with Mark should have been at school by now and she should have been back in her old job. It would be impossible to go back now. Everyone she knew in her industry had moved on and she would be considered too out of touch to enter at the same level she had left. The idea of starting again, with people much younger and less experienced, nearly made her weep. A desperate phone call to her parents confirmed everything she had always suspected: they did not understand her, they would never understand her, she had only herself to blame. They couldn't afford to pay for IVF, and her parents wouldn't lend them the money, but their local hospital gave them one cycle free of charge. With the four embryos this allowed, transferred one at a time in an agonising orbit of pregnancy and miscarriage, Francesca – Frankie – had been their last chance.

It should have been the making of them. The hotel was beginning to do well and Erin felt herself enveloped by the same kind of euphoria she had last experienced in their old flat. She began to look forward to their future together, and, even though they were both tired, they talked into the small hours in the same way they had done when they were new to one another. After her twenty-week scan, her belly nicely rounded, the baby moving like a pendulum inside her, Erin felt as if she and Mark had scaled a mountain. Now they were at the summit, they could pause and enjoy the moment together, their lives mapped out below them.

Erin could pinpoint the moment they were split apart. Although it was technically Frankie who precipitated disaster, it was Mark Erin blamed. It happened in the middle of an afternoon, an ache in her back that had been nagging her all morning. When the cramps started, she knew it was too early. Mark had been checking in guests. She'd had to wait until the queue was gone before she could tell him.

'Are you sure?' he said.

She could see he didn't want to believe it. She wasn't due for weeks. Faisal, the manager he'd just hired, was still working out his notice in Glasgow.

'How can I be sure?' she replied. 'I've never had a baby before.'

He made a decision. 'You should go to the hospital. You need to get checked out.'

The *you* hurt. She knew he couldn't leave the hotel. There was no one else. Even so, she felt let down. She hailed a cab in the street, feeling foolish, but by the time it pulled up outside the hospital the fear had set in, and she began to cry.

They examined her. She could tell she was right to come by the speed with which other people entered the room. She'd had a birth plan, it was all typed out, with a list of music she wanted playing in the background. It was in a plastic folder with her notes in the holdall she had packed specifically for this event. The holdall was at the hotel. She felt the injustice, keenly. She'd had a hard time conceiving. She deserved a break over the birth.

'The baby – she can't come now,' Erin sobbed to the midwife holding her hand. 'I haven't bought a cot yet. I don't have any nappies.'

'If baby comes soon, we'll look after her for a bit,' the midwife said, winking. 'Give you some time to sort things out. Besides,' and here she looked less cheerful, 'she'll be too small for a cot.'

When the baby came, she *was* too small. Too small to be called Francesca, the name they had carefully chosen. Too small to come home. In the Special Care Baby Unit, Frankie looked how Erin felt: raw and bewildered. Mark had not been there for the birth. It had happened too quickly. In a panic, he had called her parents. Although she could understand his reaction, Erin could not forgive him for sending her mother in his place.

When Frankie eventually came home from hospital, their world split in two. Mark focussed on the hotel. They needed the income, he insisted. They needed a roof over their heads. Erin thought his focus should have been on Frankie, or at least his wife. *If not now, when?* she asked herself. The answer came to her, clear as a bell: *Never.* Overnight they stopped working as a team and existed in opposition.

Pregnancy was the first thing she had failed at. Erin felt there was a debt to be paid. She hadn't been able to keep Frankie safe, but when she was allowed home, still fragile and far too small for the Moses basket Mark had hastily bought, Erin made a vow to do everything in her power to make up the loss. She watched Frankie while she slept, afraid she would stop breathing if she slept too. She carried on expressing until her milk dried up, refusing to switch to formula so Mark could share the feeds. She insisted on using the steriliser well past the recommended time. Nobody but Erin was allowed to feed her, change her, comfort her. She needed Frankie as much as Frankie needed Erin. She imagined herself conjuring a spell around her daughter to keep her safe. To leave her for any length of time would break it. To share her daughter with anyone else would dilute it. Erin poured everything she had into Frankie. When Frankie finally caught up with herself at the age of two, Erin didn't stop there. Out of principle, she never referred to Frankie's corrected age like all the other mothers at the premature baby group. Her daughter wasn't going to be defined by her early arrival; she would be given all the help Erin could muster.

Now, as Erin pushed open the heavy doors to the lobby, she could tell that Mark had been waiting for her and that something had happened.

'Where have you been?' he asked, agitated.

'Doctor's appointment, I told you. Why?'

'The school phoned. They want us to go down there.'

She felt panic rise in her chest. 'What's the matter? Is Frankie OK?'

'I think so.'

'You *think* so. Didn't you ask?' The panic turned into a surge of annoyance.

'They just phoned and said can we stay behind when we pick her up because they want a word.'

'So she's not ill?'

'Don't think so.'

'I'll phone them and find out.' She plunged her hand into the depths of her bag to locate her ancient mobile phone, cursing herself for forgetting to switch it on after her appointment.

'We may as well go now. By the time you've finished talking, we'll have to leave anyway.'

The clock above the reception desk told her he was right. 'It's OK, I'll deal with it. You stay here.'

'I'm coming. Faisal has already arrived for his shift. He can hold the fort for an hour or so.' Mark did not usually insist. Something in his voice silenced her rebuttal. Besides, he already had his coat on.

Chapter Eight

ISLA

From the moment the search for Clare began, Isla was thwarted at every turn and she began to think Penny was right about the house having loyalties. Drawers would not open – she had to find implements to prise them free. Knife blades and screwdrivers broke, lodging themselves in the wood, bruising and breaking her skin. Each liberated space yielded nothing but the most pedestrian of objects – final demands for art supplies more than a decade old, tangles of misshapen paperclips, several magnifying glasses scattered throughout the house, dried-out pens and dirty lengths of string. A huge collection of masking tape prompted Isla to wonder if Astrid had ever finished one before starting another.

It didn't surprise her that there was little evidence of her own existence in the house, but Isla couldn't believe Astrid hadn't kept anything that related to her beloved sister, Clare. Isla remembered the stories in the village from her childhood: how loved Clare was, how close the sisters were. Clare had been a constant presence in the community ever since Isla could remember: mentioned often by the old folk, reminisced over, memorialised. They never spoke to Isla about her death. The secrecy surrounding it, the image of a life cut so brutally short, built up in Isla's young mind and developed into a fascination that never left her. In the house, Clare was a ghost that Isla was not allowed to acknowledge. But she was there every time Astrid paused at the window and looked out to sea, a certain expression on her face; she was there when Astrid flinched when Isla mentioned her name. She silently inhabited the space left by all the things that couldn't be said or done. She couldn't have been swept away so thoroughly.

Isla dug through cupboards that had swollen shut, feeling the stubborn resistance of the house confounding her attempts to find anything out. The more she looked, the further away Clare receded, and her absence loomed larger and larger, until it became so conspicuous that Isla began to feel her history had been purposefully excised from Astrid's life. But why? Isla touched the hamsa, still hanging round her neck. She lifted it towards her and picked out the outline of the eye in the centre of the palm with her thumbnail. This was an ancient symbol. She knew it had survived for hundreds of years, thought by several different civilisations to protect and ward off evil. Astrid wasn't religious and Isla was pretty sure she would have called it claptrap. Why then, would she never take it off? It was the burden of the living that they would be left with questions only the dead could answer.

Isla reorganised the bookshelf out of spite, taming its contents into alphabetical order; something she knew her mother would have disliked. After three days and several plasters, she realised that if there were any secrets to be prised out of Astrid's death, they would lie in the studio in the roof of the house. But where was the key?

Digging through the airing cupboard, her hands found it before her eyes did. Later, when she tried to remember exactly what had happened, she thought she felt the atmosphere change before her fingers found the shape of the box, tucked in between threadbare towels. But it was possible she felt the air condense around her after she closed her fist around the long, slim shape and drew it out. There was a smell, she was sure of that. Something salty and old. It filled the dark space like smoke in a room and, for a moment, she found it hard to breathe. As soon as it appeared, it suddenly vanished, as if she had conjured it up herself. But the density of the atmosphere remained. It felt saturated with something that wished her ill. Heart beating hard, she moved into the hallway and opened the box. There it was: an elegant silver key, secured against velvet by thin elastic. Isla remembered the first – and last – time she had touched this key and the sharp slap across her six-year-old cheek. Now, she reached out, wanting to trace the ornate AJ entwined at the head and her fingers recoiled. The metal was hot. Blinking, she swore loudly and tried again, wrenching it out of its moorings. Then, quite suddenly, the metal cooled against her skin; it felt like a live thing in her hand. Just as quickly, she dismissed the thought. The key had been hidden next to the hot water tank. It must have stored the heat and rapidly released it when she opened the box. She held it up to the light and saw that the surface was worn to a dull shine by her mother's thumb. It was a beautiful, fragile-looking object, commissioned by Astrid and crafted by a local silversmith – a rare bit of indulgence. Full of trepidation, she climbed the stairs and put the shaft gently into the lock. It turned as easily as if it had just been oiled.

The narrow staircase before her was flooded with daylight, illuminating the dust motes stirred up by the shifting air. It climbed steeply, turned sharply, and suddenly opened out into a large room the width of the house. Glass ran along the exterior wall, bringing the ocean inside. Slanting skylights above her head drew in the heavens, creating a seamless horizon of sea and sky, but it wasn't the view that seized her. It was the walls. They were covered in paintings, applied directly to the plaster. Her mother's pain, articulated in beautiful, sinister seascapes, flowed all around her, a raging storm covering every spare scrap of space. Isla could see that words were scribbled, frantically, illegibly, over some of the artwork. She tried to read some of them and ascertained they were notes on technique, but could decipher little else. The whole room submerged her as she stood, rooted and motionless, trying to absorb a life she had not been party to. She thought back to the conversation she'd had with Penny and felt foolish for dismissing her superstitions. Her mother was right in this room, and she felt so close Isla could almost feel her breath on her face. The paint – oil, she assumed – was so thick in places she could trace the savage line of the rocks with her fingertips. Angry swirls of sea foam held small fragments of dust and grit, immortalised by her mother's hand. Here was a strand of hair, long and black and tangled, held fast in the paint by a threatening wave of grey. Here was a cliff, arching into the blackened sky, a smudged figure standing at its peak.

She shivered at the memory of her childhood self, the tangible fear she felt in the presence of Astrid's work: lurking, indistinct forms moving darkly around her peripheral vision, nothing genial on which to anchor her thoughts. The waves concealing the abyss. She thought about the picture two floors below, dominating the fireplace, a swirl of menace framing a ghostly face. Those feelings, so easily recalled, were never far from the surface of her life. As she stood in that room, the smell of dried-up paint and spattered varnish lingering in the air, they reared up and confronted her like spectres.

Isla looked around uneasily. Like the rest of the house, this room was uncharacteristically tidy. On the rare occasions she had defied Astrid's instructions and snuck up here, the floor had been covered in the flotsam and jetsam of Astrid's labour: screwed-up bits of paper, pencil stubs, a canteen of dropped palette knives. The edges of the room had always housed her canvases, leaning against the walls or flat upon the floor. A few of them would be pristine and newly stretched, but most of them were covered in the beginnings of something, still incoherent; sinister stories only half told. The long wooden table running the length of the room habitually groaned under a riot of scribbled notebooks, dried-up palettes, well-thumbed reference books and inky sketchpads. But the floor had been swept and the table was clear except for ancient drops and smudges of paint that had solidified into an historical document of all the colours Astrid had ever used. Isla thought back to the conversation she'd had with Penny in the kitchen. The worried look on her face. The word suicide hadn't been mentioned, but Isla knew it was common to want to get one's affairs in order. It was also something her mother did when she started a new piece of work. *What were you preparing for, Astrid?* Isla wondered. *The beginning of something or the end?*

Isla walked across the floor, remembering the drawers under the table. As she slowly pulled each one out, the sound of wood sliding against wood made her feel like the room was drawing breath. All but one was empty; the third drawer contained a single, enormous magnifying glass, the handle smudged with paint. Isla presumed it was used to incorporate detail into the canvases Astrid was working on. But where were those canvases? The journalist who'd written that article seemed certain there was missing work. If it wasn't here, where was it?

Isla frowned. This wasn't just her studio; it had been a vessel for the contents of Astrid's head and heart. Where were her personal things? What had happened to all those screwed-up bits of paper, the notebooks and the canvases? They had contained her private thoughts; Isla knew that as sure as she knew the tide would keep on turning. Painting was Astrid's whole life, and, judging by the state of this room, there was a big chunk of it missing.

Chapter Nine

ISLA

Isla had not understood Astrid's talent until she was about eight years old. The act of painting and the rages it provoked were an unquestioned staple of her childhood. Artists set up easels under the sea-wall every summer; she had always assumed that most adults practised in their spare time. When she was too small to be left alone, Isla would play with her mother's paints and Astrid tolerated this if she kept to her own canvas and didn't touch hers. But the misery of producing what Isla saw as a meaningless jumble of smudged and blackened colour become suffocating and soon she learned to avoid Astrid when she painted and made her own pictures away from the tumult of the studio. She knew that art was Astrid's job, for she never went out to do any real work and a man periodically came to the house to collect the canvases, returning with a cheque or an envelope filled with cash. Isla sometimes saw him from afar, but never up close. He was a cloud of dust as he drove up the lane when she returned from school, or a clanging letterbox and a shadowed outline as he dropped envelopes onto the doormat. Sometimes Astrid told her to leave for the day when she was expecting him, and Isla always complied. But one morning it was different.

Curled up on the sofa with an invented illness that had got her out of school, scribbling on the back of a notebook, her concentration was broken by a knock at the door. Astrid was up in the studio, unreachable. Isla answered to a stranger whom she guessed must be the man who bought her mother's work and delivered the money.

'She's upstairs.' Isla pointed to the staircase. 'You can't go up there, no one can.'

'What about you?' he enquired kindly.

'No one's allowed, not even Penny and she's Astrid's best friend.'

'You call her Astrid? You don't call her Mummy?'

'No.' The very idea was alien to her.

'Can I wait inside? I've come a long way.' He smiled at her.

Isla shrugged and showed him into the sitting room.

'These are very nice.' He gestured to the doodles on her notebook as he sat down. 'Looks like you've got your mummy's . . . er . . . Astrid's talent. Do you paint too?'

'No. Not like she does. I just make pictures.' Isla glanced up, beyond the ceiling.

He nodded to himself and gave her a look she couldn't fathom. She had an intense desire to run out of the room, but he might think her rude and she liked this man with his kind eyes and questions. 'I know how to switch the kettle on if you want . . .' Grown-ups always drank tea, as far as she could tell.

'What a good idea. I have a packet of biscuits in the car. Do you like custard creams?'

They sat at the table, he drinking tea, she with a glass of milk, splitting custard creams. Years later, she could still recall the sensation of the delicate yellow paste curling softly against her tongue as she carefully scraped the biscuit against her teeth.

'What's Talent?' she asked him, 'You said, *you've got Astrid's Talent*. What is it?'

'Your mother – Astrid – is not just good at painting, she's astonishing. Better than almost anyone else I know. She has a talent, a special ability . . .' he gestured like a conjurer, plucking the words from the air, '. . . a gift, which means she can make paint look like magic when she puts it onto canvas. Have you seen her pictures?'

'Yes.'

'What do you think of them?'

'I don't like them.'

'Why?'

'Because they look scary. And angry.' Then she said in a small voice, her toe tracing an arc in the dust on the carpet, 'When Astrid paints, she gets angry sometimes.'

'True.' He bowed his head thoughtfully. 'But she paints the sea like no other artist and that's what makes her so special.'

'In the summer, there's people like her on the beach! They paint the sea – more nicely than Astrid. Happy pictures. I can show you them if you like.' She gestured beyond the window.

He shook his head and laughed. 'None of them can match your mother. She's unique.' He smiled at Isla's confusion. 'There's no one else like her. That's why collectors want to buy her paintings. If you talk to the people on the beach, I bet they don't sell paintings for the price your mum does.'

Isla absorbed this new information with surprise. 'Is she rich?'

He laughed again, 'I have no idea. She asks me to sell a painting when she needs to pay for stuff, that's all I know.'

'She has loads of paintings! Why doesn't she sell them all and be rich?' Isla looked at the packet of custard creams, imagining what it would be like to eat them on a regular basis.

'That's a question I ask her all the time.' He smiled ruefully and they both fell silent as they each considered a private alternative reality. The moment was broken when Astrid entered the room.

'Edward!' She looked alarmed at the scene before her. 'I wasn't expecting you. What day is it?'

Isla knew better than to remain in the kitchen, so she eavesdropped from the stairs. It was hard to make out what they were arguing about, but she could tell he was trying to get Astrid to do something she didn't want to do. Try as she might, Isla couldn't get to the nub of the disagreement. All she could hear were his patient tones reasoning with her shrill voice. Knowing what the outcome would be, Isla skipped out of the house and ran to the chip shop. She knew if she hung around long enough, she would get some freebies. Later, when she returned, full and greasy-fingered, the nice man with the custard creams was gone and she never saw him at the house again.

Chapter Ten

PENNY

Penny stared out of her window and onto the beach below. It was empty because high tide was coming in fast and the locals knew to leave or risk being caught out. She watched the water devouring a ridge of crushed shells and stones it had deposited only a few hours earlier; a long, snaking wrack line that roughly mimicked the arc of the shore. Looking up, she could just make out someone walking on the cliff path above. Penny loved the cliffs because they prevented anyone else building on the beach and they made access for casual visitors difficult. The high bluff towered over the bay, casting a shadow over the large tidal lagoon. The wall that separated the lagoon from the beach was made of local stone and was wide enough and flat enough to walk upon. When high tide advanced, it lapped over the top of the wall and the lagoon slowly sank beneath the waves like a mirage. Penny's house was elevated enough that she could see this happen every day and she never grew tired of it. Today, she watched it with less pleasure than usual because she missed Astrid and she had a creeping sense of unease about the arrival of Isla Jarsdel.

Although Penny lived alone, she hadn't quite cut herself off in the same way her friend had done. She had known Jacob for as long as she had known Astrid, first in the classroom and then when he returned to the village as a GP, years later. Penny was seldom ill, but on the rare occasions he had cause to make a home visit, they had rekindled something they both assumed had died with their childhood. But the idea of giving up her family home was anathema to her. Village life was too claustrophobic; Astrid was always saying so and Penny supposed she agreed. Jacob argued he could not contemplate living in such isolation, especially with a practice the whole village relied upon. The track that ran behind the houses to the road beyond was an unlovely affair of stone and weed and it was hard to get a car down it in the finest weather. In the winter, when the snow fell, it was often impossible. So they drifted into a routine of weekends and occasional evenings. It suited them both, eventually. The pressure to bow to convention: to marry and move in together slowly ebbed. When Jacob retired and was free of the surgery, it was too late to change. They had grown to cherish a rare kind of intimacy and neither of them wanted to ruin it. But recently, Penny had begun to wonder how much of their separation had been for Astrid's benefit. It had surprised Penny that she couldn't remember the last time all three of them were in the same room together. Astrid had never called round when Jacob stayed. She only ever contacted Penny when he was gone. When he was here, Penny walked with Jacob in the day, with Astrid at night. It was only now, with the benefit of hindsight, that Penny saw the lengths she had gone to to please her friend. Penny always told herself she would never move from here because it was where she belonged. But if Jacob was in his own house, as he often was, who did she have now, close by? Isla was almost twenty years her junior. There was only so much understanding they could have between them if she chose to stay. With Astrid on one side and Jacob on the other, Penny had felt stable, sure of herself. But now, with Astrid gone, she felt the imbalance and she wondered if time would put it right.

'Penny for them, Pen.' Jacob looked out from behind his newspaper.

She continued to stare out over the lagoon, the top of the sea-wall now tracing a curve in the water. 'I don't know. I worry about that girl. She has a look of Astrid about her that I don't like.'

'She doesn't look anything like Astrid. And she's not a girl any more.'

Penny made a noise of annoyance. 'Pedant. You know I don't mean that. I mean her ways. She's aloof. Cut off.'

'Come on, Penny. She's just lost her mother, she's bound to be under par.'

'She's not had one friend visit since she arrived. There was nobody from London at the funeral. She doesn't leave the house. It's not good for her. She's taking on Astrid's life and leaving her own behind.'

'I think you're reading too much into it. She's grieving, she's probably got a lot to sort out over there, and she doesn't feel like company. Leave her be.' He shook the creases out of the paper and continued to read.

'I should have done more when she was little.' Penny frowned. 'When I think back to how Astrid behaved, I should have helped out more. But we were all so young.'

Jacob put his paper down. 'Astrid didn't maltreat her, did she? Was she abusive?'

'I don't know about that. But she neglected Isla. That's just as bad as physical harm. I'd see her out alone at all hours, all weath-ers. Astrid, locked in her studio, completely oblivious. If I'd had kids of my own, or even a sibling, maybe I would have known what was right and what was wrong. That child needed someone, a confidant.'

He scratched his beard in thought. 'You're not responsible for her, Pen. That was all a long time ago. She's lucky she had the life she did. If it wasn't for the fact that these houses are so isolated, somebody else might have intervened and she would have been carted off to some children's home. Astrid did the best she could, under difficult circumstances.'

'She's come here looking for answers. And if she's anything like her mother . . . She's already trying to get into the studio.'

'Well, what's the big deal? She's entitled, isn't she?'

'Astrid doesn't want anyone up there. It's private.'

'It's not up to Astrid now, though, is it?'

'It should be left alone.' Penny turned back to the window.

'Astrid's dead, Penny. It's Isla's house now. I know you miss her, but there it is.'

'She's looking for diaries, Jacob. It's a violation. She's trying to get inside Astrid's head, find out about the past.'

'You mean find out more about her father?'

Penny shook her head. 'There's nothing to find out, more's the pity. If he'd been a local, things might have been different. But once he was gone, she only ever had Astrid.'

Jacob grunted and turned back to the paper. Penny continued to stare into the sea, wondering how deep Isla was prepared to dig, afraid of what the truth might bring.

Chapter Eleven

ERIN

They had never picked up their daughter from school together and Erin felt self-conscious. This was her territory and normally she made small talk with the other parents at the gate, but Mark's presence made her feel shy. She shoved her hands deep into her pockets and racked her brains for something to talk about so they could look normal.

Frankie's class emptied out slowly and Erin craned her neck to see into the classroom, but there was no sign of her daughter. When Mr Samuel was finally freed from the swarm of parents and their offspring, he ushered them in and made them sit on plastic chairs several sizes too small.

He laughed, looking at Erin's face. 'Don't be alarmed, she's fine. Frankie's choosing a reading book with the teaching assistant in the library. I thought we could have a few moments together before she comes back.'

'What's happened?' Erin asked, wide-eyed.

'Nothing untoward. I wanted to ask your permission to . . . deviate from the pattern of learning I usually map out for kids in my class.'

'I don't follow you,' said Mark.

Mr Samuel opened a cardboard file. 'I think Frankie needs a little bit more than she's been offered so far. I already mentioned this to your wife, in passing. We always do some assessments at this stage to see where the children are in their learning journey and Frankie did hers this week. You can probably guess what the results were.'

Erin felt Mark's eyes on her. *This is it,* she thought. *This is what I've been waiting for.*

'Erin?' Mark said.

'You have a fast learner, Mr Baker, that's all. Frankie's going to need some extra support while she's here.'

Mark ran his fingers through his curls. 'I know she picks up stuff quickly but . . .'

'It's more than that . . .' Erin said.

'. . . Kids can't usually read and write before they start school,' Mr Samuel continued.

'Really?' Mark's voice was riddled with confusion.

'Is Frankie your first child?' Mr Samuel asked.

'Yes,' said Mark.

'She has an unusual concentration span for someone of her age. You only have to explain something once and she picks it up.' He turned to Erin. 'Just out of interest, how much did you do with her before she started school?'

How could she tell him without looking like a pushy parent? While she had expended every ounce of energy making the best version of her daughter that she could, the promise Frankie showed wasn't all down to her efforts. The questions she asked as a toddler, they were not the kind of questions other children asked. Her remarks were full of understanding. With every page recited in the reading books she brought back from the library, for every day she took her out to learn, Erin paid the debt she owed for failing to carry Frankie full term. With every leap of logic her daughter made, Erin felt the noose of guilt loosen a little more until she could finally breathe again.

She looked over at Mark and felt a pang of regret at his discomfort. She hadn't told him any of this. After Frankie was born, there didn't seem to be time to talk. He was pulled in every direction but hers by the demands of the hotel while she stayed on a single trajectory with Frankie. She so wanted to be good at something again. Now, hearing the confirmation that all her hard work was beginning to pay off, Erin felt a surge of warmth as Mr Samuel outlined the bright future that lay ahead of the girl she had made single-handedly.

'It's early days,' Mr Samuel smiled, 'but we run an accelerated learning programme here at the school. I think Frankie would be an excellent candidate if things carry on as they are.'

'What does that involve exactly?' said Mark.

'Her timetable would be less structured than her class. AL kids get a bit more freedom to go at their own pace. We move them around the school. For example, Frankie might find maths or literacy more challenging if she joins classes higher up the school. She still needs social time here with her own age group, though. If I had one concern it's that she needs to develop her friendships more.'

Erin tried to explain that it was difficult having children back to the hotel for playdates. Other people's children were not like Frankie, Erin thought. They lacked understanding. They broke things. They brought their colds with them, their chicken pox and tonsilitis. They didn't want to sit and read a book. They wanted to explore the hotel and make a mess.

When Mr Samuel began to outline the programme the school would tailor for their daughter, Mark grew quiet and didn't speak again until they had left the building and were almost home.

Two streets from the hotel lay one of Frankie's favourite places. It wasn't the Science Museum, or the Natural History Museum, both of which were a stone's throw from their front door; it was a sunless, paltry playground hidden behind a cluster of buildings that lacked the access required to turn the space into parking lots. It might once have been a shared garden of some sort, but had since fallen on hard times. Erin could never understand why Frankie liked it so much. They lowered themselves onto a neglected bench half sunk into the ground and watched her swing from an ancient climbing frame, blistered with paint. Erin comforted herself with the knowledge that Frankie had already received her tetanus booster and settled down, listening to the muffled din of traffic rushing down the Cromwell Road.

'I felt a bit of a fool in there,' Mark said eventually. 'I didn't know what Mr Samuel was on about. Why didn't you tell me Frankie was . . . you know? Special.'

'I didn't know myself until today. Not really.' There were cigarette butts under their feet and the dirty smell of fox hung in the air, but she still felt elated. She looked up at the sky, a mean square of grey bound by rooftops. 'Every parent thinks their kid is special,' she said. 'She doesn't have siblings so I've nobody to compare her to. How could I know for sure?'

'Bloody hell, though. We've got a genius in the family!' Mark rubbed his hands together and laughed.

'Steady on. He didn't use that word.'

'*Accelerated learning.* That's what he said.'

'What can I say? We have great genes.'

'Seriously, though, you've done so much with her. Taking her places all the time. Reading together, helping her with her writing. You never stop.' He paused and twisted his wedding band. 'I . . . uh . . . you've done a great job. Really. I can't take any credit for her.' He said it without rancour and his generosity opened something in her that had been sealed for some time. She leaned into him and took his hand.

'Mark, let's go on holiday. Can we afford it?' She rested her head on his shoulder.

'A holiday? What's one of those again?' He laughed softly and stroked her hair.

'Do you remember going to Brighton for the day when we were students?'

'Do I? You stole my pants when we went swimming. I won't forget that in a hurry.'

'I don't know what you mean.' She smirked.

'I had to go commando for the rest of the day.'

She squealed at the memory. 'I thought I was going to wet myself, I laughed so much.'

'Yeah, it was fun.'

'Let's do it again. Let's take Frankie away when the weather gets warmer. There's a half-term holiday in May.'

'Where shall we go? To Brighton? Re-live the magic?'

'Too pebbly. I want to make sandcastles with her. I want her to be barefoot the whole time. And I want to get well and truly out of London.'

'Where, then? We can't afford to go abroad.'

'There's a beach I knew as a child. In the north. It's a long drive, but it's worth it. It has the most beautiful sandy bay I've ever seen. There's something about it – I can't put my finger on it. But it's so different from London.' She nudged him gently. 'I have a feeling it will be good for us. Good for us all.' As she said the words, she could almost smell it and the same sad yearning for open space she had felt in the surgery that morning washed over her.

'OK.' Mark nodded and kissed her. 'OK. May half-term. It's a deal.'

Chapter Twelve

Isla, April

A month had gone by already; the time had leaked away, unnoticed. The air in the house was heavy with damp and something else Isla didn't want to acknowledge, something closing in. A weight wrapped itself around her, dragging her into sleep. Every evening, grateful for the oblivion, she waited for unconsciousness to come and take over, like waves over sand.

When, one morning, the distant synthetic ring of her mobile phone penetrated the fog of slumber, it took a while to understand what it was she could hear, it was so at odds with the yelp of the gulls and constant low murmur of the sea. She lifted her head from the cold pillow and stumbled through the icy house like a drunk. The phone fell silent and began again, an insistent buzzing that provoked conflicting feelings in her foggy brain. First, annoyance at being pulled out of sleep so roughly and then gratitude that somebody wanted to talk to her. When she unearthed the handset from underneath a pile of yellowing newspapers, she saw it was her landlady, Nicky. Isla dimly realised she must be wondering what on earth was going on.

She had left the flat so quickly, taking a supply of clothes and toiletries, as if she were about to go on holiday. The only anomaly in her rucksack was a white conical shell. The locals called them ladder shells, the ridges stuck out like fins forming a staircase that marched around its spiral shape, converging at the tip in a soft point. When she was little, finding one had always reminded her of other children's birthday cakes. They looked like iced decorations made by a huge piping bag. But this one was different. It was much bigger than the shells that usually washed up on the sand and it was perfectly, wonderfully, intact. Often, they came to the beach broken; the top snapped off, the ridges chipped. This was whole and a pristine white, apart from a strange thing: a narrow pink stripe down the length of the shell, as if someone had taken a fine paintbrush and carefully traced a path from tip to tail. She had never seen anything like it, and she hadn't since. After several house moves and the culls that came with them, it had survived as the only reminder of the place she grew up in. There were no photographs, no cards and letters from Astrid. Nothing else that nodded to her past.

In Crouch End, Isla lived and worked in the same little flat, in a small room with a bay window overlooking a street lined with plane trees. For other people, this would have been a second bedroom. For Isla, it was her office. Nicky, her landlady, lived in the flat below with her teenage son and a partner Isla rarely saw. He was a banging door in the early morning and a taxi pulling up late at night. She could hear them together at the weekend, the usual domestic noises layered with a raised voice asking questions, cheering the football, shouting at the son. Isla imagined Nicky looking up at the ceiling from time to time and wondering at the quiet. She rarely came into the flat. When Isla had first moved in, Nicky had done a six-monthly check, nodded to herself and had never been back. The flat was sparse. Isla didn't have many possessions; she was incapable of hanging on to anything apart from the ladder shell. When Penny had delivered the news, it had been uncomfortably quick to pack up her life and leave.

'Hello? Nicky?' It was hard to get the words out. Her mouth felt foul and dry.

'Isla, I've been worried about you. I heard about your mother. I'm so sorry.'

'Who told you?'

'I read about it in the paper. I remember you saying something about your mother being a painter and you have an unusual surname so when it became obvious the flat was empty, I put two and two together. Are you there now? Your post is piling up. I can send it on. Some of it looks pretty official.'

Isla glanced at her laptop, the dust powdering the lid. Her clients. She should have emailed them before now. 'Yes. I'm up here.' She made a mental note to transfer their files to an agency before the end of the day.

'What can I do?'

'Nothing. Honestly. But sending the post to me would be a big help. I don't think I'll be back for a while.'

'Are you coming back here then? I don't want to charge you rent on a flat you aren't using, that's all.'

Was she going to go back to London? What was there to go back to? Working from home, staring at spreadsheets and data. College friends that had moved away and hadn't stayed in touch. A life that shrank a little more each year. The short forays into London to see clients had become the only meaningful social contact she had with others. Numbers were her friends. There was something very comforting about the absolute symmetry of them. Equations had to be balanced. Rules had to be obeyed. In a world where social constructs were opaque and perplexing, Isla always knew where she stood with numbers. They told her if she was right or wrong.

Her eyes sought out the ladder shell, now sitting on the mantlepiece. At the time, she hadn't acknowledged that her intention had been to bring it home. But as she spoke to Nicky and told her she should let the flat to someone else, she knew it wouldn't be going back.

'You don't need to give me notice, Isla. Just cancel the direct debit. If you like, I can box up your things for you. It won't take me very long and Sean can send it over through his work. They won't care.'

'Are you sure?'

'Yes. I'd like to help.' Nicky paused. 'To be honest, I called for selfish reasons too.'

'How do you mean?'

'Matty, our son. He's been looking for a place to rent with his boyfriend. But it's so expensive for them. If you're sure about leaving, I'd like to put them both up there. I don't think they're going to be as easy as you were, though. You've been great.'

Isla switched the phone off and looked around the house with new eyes. It was in a worse state than when she had arrived. A stale fug hung over the rooms and the carpet had retreated under the creeping detritus. She was no better than Astrid and had no one but herself to blame for the mess. She picked up the dirty dishes and walked through into the kitchen, dumping them in the sink and covering the evidence with suds. As the water slowly warmed up and snaked past her fingers, Isla thought about the newspaper article and tried to think where Astrid might have hidden her diaries. Every drawer had been sifted, emptied. Every book opened, shaken. She wondered about enlisting Penny's help and resolved to broach the subject again when she next called round. She had to know something. Penny had taken to stopping by every so often and Isla, despite her desire to be left alone, enjoyed these visits, but she was beginning to find it hard to believe the woman knew nothing. For someone who found it difficult to tidy up and impossible to throw things away, it didn't make sense that Astrid hadn't left something behind, apart from a superstitious symbol. The only place she felt she was near to finding something of significance was the studio. The image of the swept floor and uncluttered table kept haunting her. The thought that Astrid had thrown away her canvases and notebooks to prepare for her suicide surfaced once again. It would be typical of her to take her secrets to the grave. The verdict at the inquest had been accidental death, but coroners weren't always right.

Chapter Thirteen

ISLA

After the ground floor was restored to its former tidiness, she decided to tackle the bedrooms upstairs. Her old room was untouched, the single bed stripped down to the ticking. This was the room Astrid and Clare had shared as children. She had never seen it through their eyes before. It had always been hers, but now she tried to see beyond the marks she had left as a teenager; the rectangles ghosting the walls where her posters had hung, the blobs of hardened Blu Tack and sticky tape that curled and clung to the paintwork. It hadn't been decorated since she had done it herself, aged fourteen, and she had obliterated the past carelessly, with a blatant disregard for her family history. She hadn't asked Astrid's permission and Astrid hadn't commented. At the time, Isla had assumed she hadn't noticed, but now she wondered if it had hurt her mother to see the room she'd shared with Clare transformed.

The plaster had blown in several places, bubbling and flaking onto the grey carpet below. The room felt cold and smelled claggy and damp. She walked over to the window, pulled back the thin blue curtains and noticed that the double glazing had been breached long ago. A salty mist of condensation occupied the space between the two panes of glass, unable to escape.

Her memory shifted to the time she had left home. She had hidden the letter confirming her college place under her pillow. She'd been terrified of leaving and terrified of staying in equal measure. This was all she had known: the constant murmur of the sea, the vast and lonely stretch of sky. London would be closed up, busy. But she was certain the sounds would have a strange familiarity. There, too, would be constant noise of a different kind. The hum of traffic, or a low drone of voices and footsteps perpetually passing in the street. She had not feared loneliness; she was used to that. It would be a relief to go. Astrid would welcome the space she left behind.

It had taken her a long time to find the words to tell her mother she was leaving, but even then she had faltered. Astrid had passed by her bedroom on the way down from the studio and Isla had called through the open door as she sat on the carpet, her belongings strewn around the floor, a new rucksack, reeking of nylon, propped against the wall waiting to accommodate the things that mattered.

'Accountancy? You're going to be a bean counter?' Astrid had shrugged as she stood in the doorway. 'Suit yourself, I suppose. I was never very good at maths.'

'I don't have to go to London. I can study here, closer to home.'

Something in Astrid's expression softened and she had almost smiled. 'What on earth is keeping you here? You're better off down there than up here. And you'll need to get yourself a job to see you through college. The sooner you leave, the better.' She nodded to herself and left.

Isla had lain in bed that night, alert to the feeling that she was about to pass from one world to the next. She was certain her life would begin in London. Until now, she had just been treading water.

When she finally arrived after a long coach journey and a confusing tube ride to her student digs, she had unpacked her rucksack and discovered an envelope stuffed with a large amount of money amongst her clothes. Astrid had not left a note, she didn't need to. Isla knew it was the closest she would get to an apology.

Now, more than thirty years later, she felt no intimacy or affection for the room she had occupied for seventeen years. She had slept here on the odd weekend she'd come to visit Astrid, but Isla had not considered sleeping here when she'd arrived two months ago. She'd instinctively crawled into Astrid's bed, hoping to gain an understanding of her mother by some kind of spiritual osmosis. It hadn't worked. She closed the door and headed there now. The room resided in semi-darkness. She opened the blind and looked around. The floor was covered in clothes. The same backpack she had left with as a teenager lay on its side like a dirty drunk disgorging an assortment of knickers, books and screwed-up socks. She swept up the clothes in her arms and threw them into the wicker laundry basket that stood in the corner of the room, wondering if she'd been waiting to make the decision to stay before she unpacked.

She turned to Astrid's walnut dressing table, backed up against the wall, surveying the personal items left on its surface. It seemed right to clear these things away now. Isla picked up a moisturiser in a squat plastic tub. She unscrewed the lid and looked inside. It was a tender yellow, the colour of whipped butter, and there were deep indentations where her mother's fingertips had gouged out the contents. Isla pictured Astrid sitting in front of the mirror, businesslike, rubbing the cream into her face as if she were giving herself a good wash.

To the side lay a hairbrush and a heavy glass bottle almost empty of perfume; an inconsistent vanity that always puzzled Isla. She twisted the cap off and sniffed. A familiar, overpowering scent of roses filled the air. She flung the moisturiser and perfume into the little bin at her feet and picked up the hairbrush. It was a Mason Pearson. Too good to throw away. Isla dug her fingers into the bristles, soft and pliant from years of use, and teased out the remaining strands of her mother's hair. They came away easily; a tangle of silvered grey in her palm like a small, abandoned nest. Isla cupped it gently. How could Astrid's hair be here in her hands when the rest of her was reduced to dust? She knew she should throw it into the bin, but the thought gripped her so completely, something prevented her from doing it. She looked at the carpet beneath her feet, suddenly sensitised. There, threaded into the woollen fibres, were several strands of hair; silvered grey, unmistakeable. Isla retrieved her glasses from the bedside table to get a closer look and knelt down. There was another strand, then another. She became aware of a sea of hair weaving in and out of the carpet like thousands of tiny aquatic faunae.

She wasn't aware of time passing as she crawled around on the floor, her weird harvest growing like a macabre cloud. She ignored her aching knees and the creeping stiffness in her back until, suddenly, she caught the scent of roses in her throat. Afraid, she scrambled to her feet, half expecting Astrid to stride into the room and demand to know what the hell she was doing. The air thickened with suspense and she waited, paralysed, listening intently for something to happen. She had a powerful feeling she was being watched. What was it Penny had said? *This is a Thin Place.* Isla tried to shake off the feeling, rubbing the goosebumps that rose up on her arms, almost believing it.

Isla scoured the kitchen, found a clear Ziploc bag and carefully transferred the precious bundle, silently sealing the top. The plastic was soft and clean, the cloudy thickness of it reassuringly clinical. She took the bag and stored it in the back of the drawer in Astrid's writing desk, wondering if she was suffering from some kind of madness. She ascended the stairs once more, determined to finish what she'd started.

The duvet felt damp beneath her fingers and the pillowcases smelled of her own, unwashed hair. She pulled off the fitted sheet, balling it and throwing it out of the door. The mattress had probably not been changed since her mother was at the height of her career. There was a definite dip on one side and the ivory ticking had dulled to grey. Isla put the flat of her palm in the middle of the depression and felt the whorl of ancient springs. No wonder she woke up feeling exhausted every day. She grabbed the plastic handles and, with some effort, flipped the double mattress over. It gave a *whump* as it fell, skew-whiff, dislodging an oblong piece of card that had lain there, trapped in all likelihood, for decades. Isla retrieved it, turned it over and was confronted by an image so tender it made her hold her breath. Had it had been mislaid or put there on purpose? She imagined Astrid reaching for it when she lay in bed, studying the details and then thrusting it back.

It was monochrome, the contrast of long black hair against a white sunlit beach startling. Squatting on the sand, bare feet flat as only a child of a certain age can, absorbed in a private task, her name must have been called by someone she loved and she had briefly turned her head and smiled. The image was unaffected, beautiful, and filled with so much love, Isla found it hard to look at. She knew it wasn't her own face smiling out from the past, but there was a family resemblance that couldn't be denied. She flipped the card over and spotted what she had missed: *Clare, age 7,* written in faded pencil.

'Hello, Aunt Clare,' Isla whispered, drinking her in, 'we meet at last.'

71

Chapter Fourteen

Isla

Isla consulted a tide timetable and decided she had enough time to walk to the islands before the tide returned. The sea was retreating and the sand stretched grey into the distance, encircling the three sandstone reefs the area was famous for. Uninhabited and frequently cut off by the water, they were a haven for bird life. Locals knew the circuitous route that should be taken to cross the two-kilometre stretch to reach the islands. But many holidaymakers, enchanted by the idea of a leisurely walk to the biggest reef, often made the journey directly and had to be rescued. Hidden gutters and gullies, heavy with soft sucking sand, quickly filled with the incoming tide that flowed faster than a man could walk. If you didn't get swallowed whole by the sand, you would be overcome by the speed of the water.

There was an enduring tale of a horse and its rider, unable to extract themselves from one of those gullies. By the time help had arrived, the sea had done its work and all that remained above the water was the head and chest of the man, his arms submerged, his hands unable to let go of the reins. The locals took a cackling delight in re-telling this story to tourists. But ever since Aunt Clare was pulled from the water on that warm spring evening, it was never mentioned in front of a Jarsdel again. The silence that surrounded her death had originated with Astrid, but the whole village conspired to preserve her wishes.

Isla skirted around the sand, as she had done so frequently as a child, doubling-back round the south side of the smallest island before striking north to the larger isle. She considered the many times she had walked this passage, barefoot, the sand rising between her toes. She couldn't remember ever making the journey with others. Astrid discouraged schoolfriends on the grounds that they were noisy and broke things. Consequently, Isla spent the holidays alone, peering into rock pools, climbing the sandstone boulders, watching the tide rise and retreat before hunger spurred her home. She could spend several days like this, not talking to anyone. When Astrid was in the middle of a painting, she always rose early and went to bed late, fearing the loss of some kind of creative spark. Solitude was a familiar state of existence for Isla. When her mother confined herself to the roof, the only indication anyone was there at all came from the occasional creak of the floorboards above and the periodic screech of annoyance that muffled through the fabric of the house. Penny was the only friend Astrid seemed to have and Astrid preferred to walk down the lane than have her in the house. Sometimes Isla heard her mother stumbling back, late into the night, fumbling with the door catch and muttering darkly to herself as she dressed for bed.

She reached the first island in a remarkably short time. She had not made this journey for several decades and remembered it in epic proportions, but, in reality, it was a brisk half-hour walk to the first island and then a further ten minutes to the second. The islands too had diminished. There was a modest house on the largest, where a warden lived, according to the notice, and several makeshift hides in which visitors could observe the bird life. Isla resented the imposition and left as quickly as she had arrived, not wanting to meet anyone mad enough to brave the cold as she had done. They were bound to want to talk.

She turned back and made her way over the sand bars, noticing how the crushed shells became bigger and more whole the nearer she got to the lagoon. Some quirk of the tide deposited the best shells here and Isla thought about the ladder shell she'd packed in her rucksack, taken from this very spot. Ever since Astrid had mentioned to her that she'd never been able to find one intact, Isla had looked for one every time she'd walked the sand, hoping she would find the thing that Astrid couldn't. It had proved fruitless. Astrid was right: the position of the islands created fast-flowing channels of water that either diverted the whole shells from the beach or smashed them up on their journey here. But not this one. Exactly one week after her thirteenth birthday, by some miraculous turn of fate, it had survived the journey and been carried by the tide right to her feet, like a belated gift from the gods. Although much of her childhood had passed by in a blur, Isla remembered the day she found the ladder shell with unusual clarity.

She had spotted it first. She'd cried out at the sight of it; she couldn't help herself, after all those years of looking. But the other girl, kneeling on the sand at her feet had been nearer, quicker. She had followed Isla's gaze to the ground beside her and reached out her hand like a darting fish, her fist unable to close around it completely. The girl was a tourist, here for a week, and had stuck to Isla like a limpet on a rock for the whole afternoon. Isla had been filling an aimless hour alone on the sand, carving a channel with her hands for the tide to find. The little girl had stood and watched, finally inserting herself into Isla's labour by helping her dig with her spade, decorating the edges of the narrow gully with stones. Isla noticed that the spade was wooden, with a red metal handle and blade. It separated her out from the rest of the tourists

74

who usually bought their kids the cheapest plastic they could find. Isla could tell this had been bought as an indulgence. It was cared for, like the girl who owned it. She wore a pretty dress that looked clean and new and her hair had been carefully plaited in a French braid that fell down her back. As the afternoon wore on, the girl had become bossy, filled with her own self-importance. Because she was younger, Isla had found her amusing. Until now.

'I saw that first,' Isla said, gesturing to the shell. 'Hand it over.' As she held out her hand, she felt a flash of anger at the look of triumph on the little girl's face.

'It's mine,' she said, pushing a loose strand of hair from her face with her free hand. 'I'm the one that picked it up.'

'Only because I saw it. You would have missed it if it wasn't for me.'

'Finders keepers.' The little girl shrugged, putting the shell in the pocket of her dress and resuming her dig.

All afternoon Isla worked her ire into the sand and thought of a way to retrieve the shell so she could present it to Astrid. She knew what the tourists did. They took things off the beach and forgot all about them as soon as they pulled onto the motorway. The shell would be abandoned in a bag or left in the car. Maybe it wouldn't make it out of the pocket of her stupid dress. It would go straight into the washing machine and break into pieces. Isla put her spade down and stretched her back. She made sure the little girl was watching and did an elegant handstand, curving her feet to her forehead, touching her hair with her toes.

'Bet you can't do that,' Isla said, righting herself and wiping the sand from the palms of her hands.

'Yes I can.' The little girl threw down her spade and made a poor attempt at a handstand.

'Want some help?' Isla asked, trying to sound casual, after her third attempt.

'No, I can do it,' she said, breathless with concentration. She tried twice more and failed to keep her feet off the ground for more than a second.

'Your legs aren't straight. You'll never keep your balance until you can straighten them. Here, I can hold you so you don't fall.' Isla stretched out her arm like a ballet barre.

Persuaded, the girl attempted a handstand and Isla caught her. 'Straighten your legs out,' Isla said, 'now bend your knees and tip your head up to meet your feet.' She was so light, Isla was almost carrying her entire weight on her outstretched arm. It was easy to shake out her dress pocket and reclaim the shell. It fell onto the sand and she snatched it back, a satisfying echo of what had gone on before. The girl was upside down and helpless to stop it. She twisted her little body and fell, dress up over her head, on the sand.

'That's mine!' Her anger was impressive. She wasn't intimidated by the age gap and Isla was twice her height. When she righted herself, her face was as red as her hair.

'I found it,' Isla explained patiently. 'I live here. It belongs to me.' Out of the corner of her eye, Isla could see the girl's parents, alerted to the high, whining pitch in their daughter's voice. Isla kept the shell in her hand, feeling the weight of the prize in her palm and knew she would not be parted from it. She turned her back to the child and walked slowly away.

Later, flushed with pleasure, she presented the shell to Astrid, who had admired its perfection and unusual stripe. She told Isla the proper name for the shell was a wentletrap and she'd insisted that as it had made its way to Isla, she was the rightful owner. To Isla's enduring pleasure, Astrid had borrowed it regularly to sketch, recording the intricate, undulating lines in her own, sinister style. It was the only object Isla could think of that linked her to her mother intimately, or happily.

When she arrived back at the house, Penny was in the lane. 'Ah, there you are,' she said. 'I was wondering how you were getting on. Where did you get to? It's not often I call round and you're not here.'

'Just to the islands and back. Come in, will you? I'll make some tea.'

Penny took in Isla's windswept face. 'You're looking perkier. And you've had a tidy up,' Penny nodded towards the bin bags in the hall.

'I've decided to stay. For the time being.' Isla unbuttoned the coat and slung it over the bannister, making a mental note to restore the newel post.

'Well I'm glad you're not going to sell it. Astrid would have approved.'

'I'm going to get the rest of my stuff sent down and live here for a bit. See how it goes.'

'The sea air will do you good. You look better already. Are you going to paint?'

'Paint? I already started painting.' She gestured at the walls in the hallway: a clean, crisp white.

Penny snorted. 'I didn't mean decorate, I meant paint. In the studio. Like Astrid.' She shrugged off her coat and pulled her hat away from her head, raking her hair with her fingers.

'Why would I want to do that?' A swell of unease rose within Isla's chest.

'Because you used to be good at it.' Penny stopped unwinding the scarf at her throat. The surprise on her face was genuine.

Isla frowned. 'I wasn't allowed to touch Astrid's paint.'

'When she moved up to the studio and you were old enough to be left alone, she let you take her leftovers . . . old paints and little bits of canvas. I remember you sitting on the patio and painting there. You did some lovely stuff. You gave me a little picture of the islands for my birthday when you were about nine, I still have it somewhere.'

'I used to be so terrified of her criticism; she extinguished any interest I ever had.' A memory broke the surface of her subconscious. There was once a time when she had tried to please Astrid by copying her technique. She had worked all week on a seascape that she hoped echoed Astrid's hand. But when she showed her, proud of her achievement, Astrid had delivered a lecture. Her style was not to be copied like a maths test at school. She had to find her own way.

'Why can't this be my way too?' Isla had asked, wanting to share something with her.

'Because it's mine.' Astrid's expression had darkened, and her mouth settled into a firm line.

Isla had painted over the canvas with angry strokes of crimson, a colour her mother avoided in her own work. She destroyed the cold blues and greys she had carefully mixed with the heat of her anguish. She had taken the blade of a knife and scratched sweeping lines across the wet paint, revealing parts of the original painting underneath. Then she took it to the door of the studio and left it there like a maimed creature. Astrid removed the painting and didn't remark on her childish behaviour. Isla took care not to share her work with her again.

'So you haven't forgotten, then.' Penny gave her a look.

Isla shrugged. 'No. But it's something I haven't thought about since I was a teenager. I've been trying to remember what it was like, living here. I can't remember having any friends or feeling happy. But I don't remember being *unhappy* either. Everything feels numb. I can't find anything personal or anything that connects me to Astrid.' She thought about the bag of hair in the writing desk and dismissed the image. 'There are no photos of me in this house. It's like I never existed.'

78

Penny followed her into the kitchen. 'Don't take it personally, Isla. Astrid was very . . . complicated. I'm not making excuses, but when they found her sister that day, everything changed. She had a difficult childhood, what with her mother being ill and passing so young. And her father – well, the less said about him the better. Clare was the only thing she had.'

Isla threw her arms in the air as she reached for the cups. 'I'm sick of everyone going on about her difficult childhood! It's in every bloody book that's been written about her. Astrid Jarsdel, the tortured artist with the tragic childhood. What about mine? *I* had a difficult childhood too. Clare was my aunt. Was I *ever* allowed to mention her or ask questions about the accident? No. Her death just . . . hung over us like a curse. If I ever said her name out loud . . .' Isla couldn't keep the whine out of her voice. 'I trod on eggshells for seventeen years in this house.'

Penny spoke gently, in a low voice. 'She did her best. I think she loved you, in her own way, even though she found it hard to talk about her feelings.'

'I never understood how you could tolerate her, Penny. She was such a selfish person. I can't remember her ever saying one nice thing to you.'

Penny smiled sadly. 'She didn't have to. You forget that we knew each other since we were kids. We grew up together. That kind of intimacy, those shared experiences, you can't buy that depth of friendship. You grow into one another. I didn't always like her, but I loved her. I came to rely on her and I know she needed me because she never turned me away from her door.'

'She turned me away,' Isla said quietly. 'She didn't give me a reason to stay.'

'I think she found you hard to look at sometimes . . .' Penny stopped herself. 'What I mean is . . . I think you reminded her of the things she had lost.'

Isla thought about the photograph of Clare she had found. The Jarsdel family resemblance. It made sense, she supposed.

Penny continued, 'She was aware how her moods made your life difficult. It's hard enough bringing up a child alone. She liked to do things properly and I think she knew she failed you and that was difficult for her to acknowledge.' She cocked her head and squeezed Isla's arm. 'She did love you, Isla, in her own way. I think she just thought she was so poisonous sometimes, you were better off without her in her last years.'

'Then why not talk to me? She could have halved the burden. If not with me, then with you.'

Penny shook her head. 'You have to understand that we didn't grow up with all that touchy-feely get-it-off-your-chest stuff. It wasn't the done thing. You didn't pursue a topic if it wasn't welcome. And that went double for Astrid.'

'She never said anything to you about Clare? I find that incredible.' Isla searched Penny's face for the trace of a lie.

The kettle had boiled, but the moment had passed and Penny turned to go. She paused as she picked up her scarf from the back of the chair, frowning. Isla thought she saw her take a breath as if she were going to say something else, but, instead, Penny set her mouth in a firm line, draped the scarf round her neck and gathered her house keys.

'Try not to dwell on it,' she muttered as she saw herself out. 'Poking at the past won't do any good.'

Chapter Fifteen

PENNY

Penny hurried along the path towards home, a familiar feeling gathering in her head; a slow pressure behind her eyes like the massing of swollen clouds, warning of the storm to come. Her headaches had become more frequent recently. She'd gone for years without an episode, and now they were a regular fixture. Like an abusive lover looking for forgiveness, she thought she'd got rid of them but they always returned and she succumbed. Her neck felt stiff and she wanted to lie down. Stumbling on the path, sparks of electricity crackled around the periphery of her right eye. A black hole appeared at the edge of her sight where objects simply didn't register; they fell off a cliff into some kind of oblivion. Not for the first time, she wondered if this was what madness felt like.

She shouldn't have called round. As soon as the words had left her mouth, she had regretted saying them. She had made a promise to herself to keep out of Isla's way, but she was drawn to that house like a tongue seeking a loose tooth.

Her first visit had not been altruistic. The bag of groceries had been an excuse to see how Isla had turned out, whether anything of the quiet child she remembered had clung on. But the more they met, the more she saw that Isla needed help. She had none of Astrid's confidence and all of her insecurity. The urge to smooth things between the living and the dead weighed down on Penny like water, but the responsibility she felt towards both Astrid and Isla was beginning to tilt in Isla's favour, and it left her feeling destabilised. She wanted to help Isla understand why she was loyal to Astrid, but to do that she would need to be more forthcoming and that meant breaking promises. She quickened her pace as she reached her own door. It was getting dark and she cursed herself for not switching any lights on in the house before she left to make it cosy on her return. She unlocked the door, shutting it hard behind her, and groped for the light switch. The house was deathly quiet. Her heartbeat filled her cranium with a low, steady thump; the slow footsteps of an old adversary she knew would be upon her soon. Penny stood in the hallway, listening intently, and waited. The air closed thick around her, stifling her breath. She shut her eyes and tried to make herself calm. The familiar smell of salt water filled her nostrils. But it wasn't the comforting aroma that carried on the sea wind. It was the brackish stink of something on the turn. A small creak came from the top of the stairs and she jumped at the noise, dropping her keys.

'I didn't tell her anything!' she said, as her gaze darted up the stairwell. She tried to persuade herself to go up there, take a bath and pretend everything was alright, but her feet were rooted to the floor. She stood in the hallway for some time, listening to the silence, waiting for the air to slacken.

Eventually, she took a fortifying breath, shrugged off her coat and made her way into the living room. Before she had even opened the door she knew something had happened. In the half-gloom, lying in the middle of the floor, was a shape she couldn't make sense of. Unable to look away, she slowly felt for the light switch, afraid of disturbing whatever was lying on the floor. When she clicked the switch, she breathed a sigh of dismay. Her beautiful parlour palm lay prostrate, separated from its wrought-iron plant stand. Soil scattered in a dirty arc over the cream wool rug. The cup of morning coffee she had left on the side table now lay in pieces amid the chaos, the black liquid binding the soil into a paste and filling the room with its bitter smell. Penny bit her lip and felt the tears come as she bent down, upending the stand and placing it back in its corner. The palm was a huge specimen and had taken her years to grow. As she lifted it tenderly and settled it back into the stand, she saw several stems had been badly bent. On any other day she might have put the broken limbs into a vase to prolong their life, but today she couldn't bear to look at them so she swiftly cut them off and deposited them in the outside bin.

She searched around for the dustpan and brush, unable to remember where she had left them last, her head beginning to pound. She finally retrieved them from the place she liked least, a dark and chaotic cupboard under the stairs she usually avoided using. As she entered the sitting room once more, a soft thump sounded from the room above. Penny dropped the brush onto the floor, a cold swell of fear flooding her chest.

'Please, Astrid. This has to stop. We can't go on like this!'

The force of her voice cut through the atmosphere and suddenly everything seemed lighter. But when she turned to the mess of her beloved palm, the tears came back. She sank to her knees and started sweeping the soil into the dustpan. The filth was ingrained in the fibres and all she did was make it worse. The rug would have to be sent away for cleaning. She would never get the stains out.

Chapter Sixteen

ERIN, MAY

The beach was everything Erin remembered it to be. The only downside had been the weather. May was not a warm month up here and there was a high probability of rain. She had bought Frankie a bright red shiny anorak with a little matching hat. Frankie, delighted, had put it on immediately and had not taken it off since.

It was still early and the beach was deserted. Erin walked along the sand and eventually spotted Mark and Frankie near the end of the bay, peering into rock pools. Frankie stood poised with a fishing net, looking like an overgrown ladybird.

'Have you caught anything?' she enquired, their bent heads turning in unison to greet her.

'Not really.' Mark laughed. 'We need to wait for the shops to open so we can get some bacon. We ran out yesterday, feeding it all to the seagulls, didn't we, Frankie?'

'I can look after her if you want, Mark. You must've been up for ages. You deserve a rest too.' She didn't want him to leave, they had been getting on so well, but she felt compelled to make the offer.

He straightened up. 'Actually, I wanted to visit the islands today. You can't just walk over to them like we planned. There's a leaflet in the hotel that says there's a special route you have to take. Do you remember anything about that when you used to stay here?'

Erin screwed up her eyes. 'Yeah. You have to avoid the gullies or you get caught by the tide, but I can't remember exactly where you cross. I think you can book a guide though, or ask in the coast-guard station further down the beach. When I was little you could ride there on a horse-drawn cart, but I haven't seen any since we arrived. Maybe it's too early in the season.'

'I'll walk down to the coastguard station and ask.'

'Get a tide timetable while you're at it; we have to follow the tide out when we set off. I remember that.'

'Maybe we can pack a picnic and have lunch there if we're quick?'

'Good idea. Go and ask the coastguard and pick up a few things for lunch if the grocery shop is open. I'll take Frankie under the sea-wall and make a sand city with her.' She looked down at her little girl. 'What do you think, Frankie? A sand city?' They both laughed as Frankie turned and ran towards the sea-wall, anorak flapping in the wind.

As Erin found a place to sit and Frankie busied herself making sandcastles, she thought back to that afternoon in March, sitting on a sagging bench with Mark in a filthy playground under a grey sky, planning this week and feeling the surge of anticipation rise like a lifeline. She'd held that memory close, the possibility that things were changing for good. Erin had not gone back to the surgery for medication. The only thing that had kept her going was the thought of coming here, and it had been everything she had anticipated. She'd forgotten how nice it was being looked after for a change.

The curved sandy bay had hardly altered from her childhood memories. Every spring she had come here. They always arrived at her aunt's house in the dead of night, Erin dazed and mute from the journey in and out of sleep. She remembered being carried upstairs by her father, one of the only times he had held her, depositing her limp body into a strange and chilly bed. She remembered being afraid of the seagulls at first, as they would scratch the thin roof of her bedroom when they stirred in the morning. But after the first day her parents seemed to shed their brittle skin and they softened into other people until it was time to leave and resume their former lives. When her aunt died, they had stopped coming and Erin had never known that kind of intimacy with either of her parents again. Whenever she had tried telling them what a difficult time she was having, their reaction had been one of distaste. They saw shame in mental illness and troubled marriages. Feelings were not to be discussed.

She found their usual spot against the sea-wall and put her bag down, feeling tired. Even after a lazy five days, she couldn't shake the deep fatigue, a legacy of six years' sleep deprivation. Frankie had never been a good sleeper. Today, the bottle of wine Erin had consumed the night before compounded the sensation and her temples thumped a dull warning of the headache to come. Thank God Mark had taken Frankie away this morning and let her sleep. She wasn't used to having Mark take over the childcare. This holiday felt like a turning point. Things would be different when they returned home, she was sure of it.

She busied herself with Frankie until they had built a sizeable sand city together. Eventually, Erin straightened her aching back and began to feel her patience waning. Eyeing the cover of her novel peeking out of her bag, she declared the city finished. But Frankie was not to be deterred.

'I want to decorate it, Mummy! It's not done yet!' she scolded when Erin suggested they have a rest.

'Well I suppose we could go and find some shells and seaweed.' The familiar seesaw of guilt that oscillated between wanting to please Frankie and wanting to please herself tipped inevitably in Frankie's favour. 'Come on, we can gather everything together and then you can make your sand city look amazing while I read my book. That sound good to you?'

They searched the sand for shells. It was hard not to think about the incident from her childhood, something that had stayed with her for years and something she still recalled with regret even now. She had watched the older girl digging a channel for some time, wondering how to approach her. As an only child she had yearned for a sister and often sought out other girls her age on holiday to play with, but this girl was older, a local. She walked around the beach as if she owned it. There was something about her that Erin found deeply attractive. Her shorts were cut off from an old pair of jeans, she could tell by the frayed edges. Her T-shirt was short and exposed a tanned midriff. Erin's parents would never allow her to wear clothes like that. They always made such a fuss about appearances. When the girl allowed her to help dig the channel, Erin felt important, useful. When she picked up the shell and saw how much the other girl wanted it, the power she felt was unfamiliar. It filled her with a warmth until she was tricked out of it. She remembered how helpless she had felt, being held upside down on the sand, her dress falling over her head, so she was blind to the betrayal until it was too late. The shame of having it taken from under her nose while her knickers were on display had never left her. She had returned to her parents, hot tears running down her face, and they had not taken the loss seriously.

She had spent the rest of the holiday looking in vain for a replacement, but all the others were smaller, broken and none had that delicate pink stripe running down their backs. It had endured, that memory. Every time she returned to the beach, she sought out the thief who had stolen from her. Erin saw her a few times over the years, walking aimlessly on the sand, or cadging a cone from the ice cream man, but she never acted on the urge to confront her. Even at the tender age of nine, she knew retribution was beyond her reach.

Erin looked at her own daughter, not much younger than she had been when it had happened. An urge to protect her from the world made her throat catch as she watched her hopping from one spot to another, looking for shells, exactly as she had once done. Since Frankie started school, she had felt the painful process of separation. Frankie had never gone to nursery, Erin wanted to look after her until she was obliged to go to school. She remembered the first day she dropped her daughter off at reception class with a horrible clarity. Frankie had spent every day of her life with Erin until then. That morning marked the beginning of Frankie leaving her. She would spend exactly half her waking hours at school, under the influence of others, and already she felt Frankie pulling away. Some days she was still all hers, still the baby looking up to her, hanging on her every word. Other days she saw her growing up; a flash of irritation at something Erin said, a contradiction of opinion; repeating some fact she had gleaned from a book that Erin hadn't read with her. It was a painful process, a succession of splinters under her skin.

'I want to go to the lagoon. I want a crab shell for the top of my big castle!' Frankie shouted.

Erin sighed. She had taken Frankie there at the beginning of the holiday to show her how to catch crabs. There was a slipway at the far side of the lagoon for launching boats. At the end of the day they had released their catch and watched the crabs scurry back down the slope and into the water. It was a favourite place for the seagulls, who picked up the slowest, smashing them against the hard stone. Frankie had been enchanted by the miniature shells. Erin looked at the spot where she had laid out their things. The idea of packing everything up again and carting it up the steps to the wall stiffened her resolve.

'No, Frankie,' Erin said gently, 'we can go to the slipway later. Let's find shells here on the beach.'

'I want to go up there,' she gestured to the top of the wall above their heads. 'I want a crab shell.' Her voice was steady and that should have set an alarm bell ringing. Erin saw the hard line of her lips and a small frown burrow itself into her forehead.

Erin thought quickly. 'If we leave our special spot, someone might come and knock down our beautiful sand city.'

Frankie looked around her. 'There's nobody else on the beach.'

'Let's wait for Daddy to get back, darling. He'll wonder where we are if we leave. I told him we would be here, see?'

'*I* could go. I know where it is.'

'I can't keep an eye on you if you go by yourself, Frankie. Don't be silly.' Frankie's frown deepened and Erin instantly regretted the remark. It was the kind of comment Frankie hated.

'Come on,' Erin said in an effort to distract her, 'let's see if we can find a mermaid's purse.'

They scoured the beach for objects that passed Frankie's exacting standards and eventually the bucket was full enough to mollify her temper. Erin relaxed, her back against the wall of the lagoon, warmed by the early sun and a thick cardigan. She pulled out the book and settled down while Frankie began to sort the shells into sizes. They had come to this spot every day. If the tide was right, the city wouldn't get washed away for several hours.

As she thumbed the pages, Erin looked up, scanning the beach for the runner. Every morning, at about this time, she had seen her sprinting across the sand to one of the beachfront houses and disappear behind a charming red door. Erin could only imagine the kind of parties you could have in a place like that. As her eyes tracked the wide expanse of sand, there was no sign of the woman. She sighed inwardly, remembering her old life as she cracked the spine of the paperback, immersing herself in somebody else's drama.

The words on the page marched past her gaze and it had the effect of hypnosis. Erin closed her eyes, listening to the soporific rhythm of the waves. She didn't see Frankie glance over, pick up her fishing net and walk away. By the time she had found the steps and climbed to the top of the sea-wall, Erin's head had tipped pleasantly back into a recess in the rock. As a bee buzzed slowly past Frankie's gaze and she ran after it, swiping at it with her fishing net, Erin was dozing.

When Frankie lost her footing and fell into the lagoon, Erin was fast asleep.

Chapter Seventeen

ISLA

Further up the beach, beyond the sea-wall, the house with the red door lay empty. Isla had already left in an attempt to keep the demons at bay. She had been making herself leave the house every morning for a walk, but the act of getting out of bed required Herculean effort. The house had become an albatross. Even though she had finished painting the floorboards and the walls, she could feel the weight of it strangling her, wanting her gone. But she couldn't leave until she had discovered more about Astrid and Clare. The photograph under the mattress, the key to the studio; there would be more clues, she felt certain of it. She just had to find out where Astrid had squirrelled them away. She was tied to that house until she got to the bottom of things, and if it took her to the grave, so be it. Unwelcome thoughts of her life aping Astrid's began to press upon her. The need to get out of the house was acute.

The long walks had turned into slow runs. The slow runs had stretched into steady marathons. She had surprised herself: she was good at running. There were landmarks where previously she'd had to rest. Now she sprinted right past them, amazed at the memory of needing to stop. She didn't feel middle-aged. She felt strong and light on her feet. The open water and acres of sand gave her space to think in a way the house could not. She ran through mornings when the frost ghosted her windows and mornings where she felt the sun beginning to gather its strength. There was something oddly comforting about the loneliness of it all.

Penny had observed the change with concern. 'You look too thin, Isla,' she had said. 'Are you eating?'

'Yes. More than ever, actually.' Isla looked down at her arms, stringy but muscular. She had not thought of herself as fit before. A faint swell of pride bloomed as she said it.

'You must take a phone with you. You're gone for hours and I worry when I don't see you.'

'That's kind of the point. To get away.'

Penny gave her a wry look and gestured around them. 'This isn't isolated enough for you?'

'It's the house. I want to get away from the house,' Isla admitted.

Penny narrowed her eyes in concern. 'Why?'

'It sounds silly.'

'No it won't, trust me.'

'I've tried to make it mine. New blinds, everything painted. It still doesn't feel like home. Not really. I thought it was superstition when you said this was a Thin Place, but now I'm not so sure.'

Penny took her seriously. 'Has something happened?'

'No . . . I don't know. It just feels like it still belongs to Astrid. No matter how much I cover it over with paint and fabric.'

'You haven't redecorated the studio, have you?'

'I couldn't do that. The studio will always be hers. I wouldn't want to mess with that.'

'True. God knows what she would do.'

Isla raised an eyebrow in amusement. 'Not much, Penny, she's dead. Remember?'

'Ha.' The laugh was half-hearted and humourless. 'How could I forget?'

Isla had laughed with her, but she had a foreboding sense that Penny was right. Although Astrid was dead, she was still making her presence known. Sometimes Isla felt a kind of charge in the air she couldn't easily explain. A couple of times, she had heard muffled thumps tracking across the floorboards of the studio, too loud to be a rat. Isla had raced upstairs to fling the door open to nothing. She was afraid, but she wanted confrontation. Up to now, she had not been given the satisfaction.

When the spring came, Isla resented the tourists. She left the house early to avoid them, sometimes rising before the sun and running into the dawn. Her route varied. Sometimes she would traverse the length of the beach and cut away into the silent villages, eerie in the half-light; sometimes she would skirt along the lagoon and pick up the cliff path high above the sand, following the headland into the next county.

Today, on her way home, she considered her future. It had only been two months, but the idea of returning to her old life seemed so alien she could hardly imagine how to resume it. Isla wasn't sure she would be able to get her clients back from the agency if she left it much longer. The idea of resurrecting old contacts and finding new ones was exhausting. As she turned a corner and saw the sea rise up from the horizon, a small thread of fear tugged inside her as she wondered what would happen next.

She reached the beach, turned left and jogged, easy and relaxed, down across the bay towards home. A good distance away past the lagoon, she picked out the red door of her mother's house, just above the shoreline. It was still early and she relished the empty expanse before her. As she fell into a steady *slap-slap* of rubber against wet sand, she noted another shape of red, skipping along the sea-wall that curved around the lagoon. It was a child – a girl, in a stiff shiny anorak holding a net, hopping up and down like a little bird. She briefly wondered who would be out crabbing at this time before turning her gaze back to the house. This was the last stretch and she always challenged herself to sprint the final few hundred metres.

Years later, when she reflected on that moment – replayed it in her mind and examined the minutiae of all that went before it – she could never grasp what it was that prompted her to look back once more at the girl. Isla had no enthusiasm for children any more. That door had shut many years ago and she lacked the proprietorial instinct some women adopted towards other people's unattended offspring. The sea-wall was behind her now and there was nothing between her and the house; it was a straight sprint to the door. But as she quickened her pace, something powerful drew her gaze away – she felt it as keenly as someone calling her name. She remembered the prick of annoyance – her focus broken. The feeling of being pulled was so physical, it slowed her feet and demanded she look again. Had there been a noise as the child hit the water? She couldn't say, but the flash of red was unmistakeable as it disappeared behind the sea-wall like a sinister magic trick. She stopped and looked around her. The beach was virtually empty.

They say that truth dawns on people like a light, but it didn't for Isla. It cast a deep shadow. The quick spark of urgency that would have drawn others to intervene did not ignite in her. Suddenly, she resumed her pace with a vigour she couldn't quite control as she ran away from the wall and the frightening scene it obscured.

Time stretched out around her as she ran away and thoughts and images surfaced and sank in her mind. Isla had always believed herself to be inherently good. But living here, sifting through the life of the dead, she had slowly turned into something bad. The photograph she'd found in Astrid's house sprang to her mind violently, in sharp definition. That child in the red anorak hopping along with her fishing net looked about the same age as Clare was when that portrait was taken.

Clarity. That word had been meaningless until now. Suddenly Isla sensed everything around her with such intensity it caused her tangible pain: the beat of blood in her ear, the salted whip of hair on skin. A sharp shaft of sunlight assaulted her retinas and bile rose up in her throat, filling her nostrils with a sharp stench. She sickened herself. She was Astrid's daughter alright: unfeeling, selfish, detached. The shock of who she had become flooded her brain with a brilliance that hurt, but the pain made her lucid. An image of Clare being pulled from the sea by cocklers, something she could not have witnessed first-hand, came to her with such force it could have been her own memory.

She had a choice. Her existence did not have to be coloured by Astrid. It could be something of her own design. Fresh resolve bloomed through tired muscle. She turned around, back to the sea-wall, and ran for her life.

Chapter Eighteen

ERIN

Erin woke up quickly, cleanly. The sickening gravity of a falling dream plunged her into consciousness. She blinked, disoriented, her neck stiff, her arm fizzing unpleasantly. She heard a man's scream split the air and although it was more animal than human, she knew it was coming from her husband and the sound of the scream formed her daughter's name.

It was then that she looked around her, blindly at first and then with focus. She saw the sand city, abandoned, the fishing net gone and she knew something terrible was happening. Erin sprinted, barefoot, around the curve of the wall until she saw the steps. In amongst the panic and fear, she was dimly aware of leaving her old life behind; of entering a different, darker place. The two would never be reconciled.

By the time she reached the top of the wall, her chest heaving painfully with the effort to breathe, she could see the runner with Mark, who was crouched behind Frankie's body, his hands gripping each side of his head as if he were trying to blot out an appalling sound.

Erin was last. She was the last to be there. That dreadful fact would never be expunged. There was no shouting, nor blame, not then. That would all come later.

The runner knelt over her daughter, back towards Erin, her head bent towards the child. She performed her task quietly, reverentially, synchronising beats with breath, whispering a low string of words. A pool of water had spread out, encircling all three, and Erin felt very strongly it formed a line she could not cross. She stood apart from them, paralysed by feelings she couldn't separate. Mark did not look at her. She would always remember that.

It wasn't like the movies. Frankie didn't cough and splutter and wake up. She was still lifeless when the paramedics arrived, pushing the runner firmly aside as they continued the efforts to revive the dying child.

Chapter Nineteen

ERIN

The ambulance screeched through the tranquil roads. Erin sat in the back, numb with fear, holding Frankie's brittle hand. Mark had been shown the front seat, excused from the relentless chatter of the paramedics. Every question directed at her felt like a rebuke.

'How long was she in the water?' asked the driver, over her shoulder.

'I don't know,' Erin's voice answered in monotone.

'Seconds? Minutes?' the driver persisted.

'I don't know,' she mumbled.

'Did she bang her head as she went in?'

'I didn't see.' Her voice faded to a whisper.

She saw the paramedics exchange a look. The enormity of what she had done threatened to engulf her. She tried to think of a life without Frankie and knew it would spell the end of everything. She bit her lip until it bled.

At the hospital, they were shown a place to wait. A small room with a window too high to open or see out. Erin wondered if it was designed like that to stop people throwing themselves out of it in despair. She reminded herself how grateful she had been to Mark for taking Frankie away before she'd woken up this morning. She couldn't believe she'd wished away the last few hours she might have shared with her only, precious child. Dark thoughts full of self-recrimination whirled around her. She shouldn't have had so much wine the night before. If she hadn't been so selfish and tired, she would have had the energy to go with Frankie to find the crab shell she so desperately wanted. Her memory of their time together underneath the sea-wall warped into something ugly. She had been a terrible parent, irritable and impatient.

With a stab of pain, she remembered their argument. *Don't be silly,* she had said to Frankie. A horrible thing to say in a snide, carping voice.

No wonder Mark couldn't look at her. She had failed.

Finally, she broke and the tears came, salty and hot. It was a relief to cry; it was something to do. If Mark wasn't going to comfort her, she would do it herself.

'Erin, please. Give it a rest.' Mark got up from where he was sitting and raked his fingers through his hair.

She stopped crying and looked at him in surprise. In all the years they had been together he had never spoken to her like that.

She gulped, balling a tissue in her lap. 'How do you expect me to be?'

'I know, I know. It's just . . . this room. It's claustrophobic.'

'She could be dead. Why hasn't anyone come to see us?'

'If she were dead, they would have told us. They must be working on her.'

'What does that mean?' Erin wailed.

'I don't know. It's just what I heard the paramedic say.'

'Mark, what are we going to do?'

'We just . . . have to wait.' He seemed disarmed, being asked for advice. She had never consulted him about Frankie before.

'I can't bear it,' she said.

'You have to. There's no choice.' A hardness crept into his voice.

She picked up on his tone. 'You think it's my fault, don't you?' All the things she had been telling herself; she wanted him to confirm them. A perverse desire to be punished, to have an argument in the middle of this awful room, overtook her. Anything to stop the thoughts about what was happening to Frankie crowding in.

'I don't think that,' he said carefully, staring at the floor.

'Yes you do. I can see it in your face. You can't even look at me,' she sniffed.

'I told you. It's this room, it's—'

'You said.'

He looked at her then, unable to hide his resentment. 'OK then, where were you? Where were you, Erin?'

She took a ragged breath before she answered. 'I fell asleep. I don't know how it happened, I was reading a book . . .'

'You fell asleep? I let you sleep in this morning.'

'*You* let me sleep in this morning?' She made a noise of exasperation. 'I'm tired, Mark! A few days away doesn't make up for six years of no sleep.' And then she muttered quietly to herself, 'I've been a single parent practically.'

'Don't go down this road, Erin.'

'Or what?' She had a feeling something was about to be opened that could never again be shut. But she pressed on, unwilling to let it go. 'When I asked you to get ice creams yesterday, you brought her back a vanilla cone. She hates vanilla. It's chocolate, always chocolate.'

'What? I can't believe we're having this conversation.'

She looked at him. 'You don't know anything about her because you're never there. You're always working. It's like we don't exist.'

He sighed, exasperated. 'I'm always working because somebody has to. If I did as little as you, we'd have no business and no roof over our heads.'

'I never wanted the business!' She could barely contain the volume of her voice. 'I was happy in West Kensington! I gave up my home and job because of you. My life! What have you ever given up for me? Nothing. You just do whatever you want to do.'

'You never wanted the business? You could have fooled me. You acted like you already owned the place every time we visited Mum and Dad, swanning around telling them how to run things. Don't pretend it was all my idea.'

She stood up and walked over to him, jabbing her finger, hard, into her own chest. '*I* wasn't even consulted.'

'I don't remember being consulted about anything to do with Frankie. She's my child too, but I'm not allowed to make any decisions about her. No wonder I can't remember which flavour of ice cream she likes; you won't let me near her.'

'You have no idea what I went through to have her!'

'Yes I do, because I was reminded on an hourly basis.'

'You resent her!'

'No, I don't.' He shook his head sadly. 'I could never resent her.' He looked her squarely in the eye. 'It's you I resent. You make yourself out to be so perfect. And you're not.'

The truth fell upon her like fire. It burned, but it was no less than she deserved.

Chapter Twenty

ISLA

Isla pushed the door open, exhausted. She stripped off her running gear and showered for what seemed like an age. The water rained over her as she stood, motionless, wondering what was happening to the girl. She was surely dead. How long had she hesitated before turning back? Seconds? Minutes? She had no idea. She wondered if things might have been different if she had chosen to get to her sooner and those dark thoughts whirled around her head until she pushed them far away. She had reached the lagoon before the child's father. She had not been aware of him until he made a noise as she expelled the last of the seawater from his daughter's lungs. He had shouted something, a name, as she started compressions. She had shushed him, annoyed, she remembered that. She couldn't think with him there. He had got the message and sunk silently to his knees as she got on with it. The woman had arrived later. She could feel her agony behind her back. Isla wondered if they knew she had hesitated. She wondered if they realised she had intended to let their daughter drown.

The startling vision she'd had of Clare surfaced again as the water cooled. She had only heard the story of how the cocklers had found Aunt Clare from the abstract murmurs of the villagers. Never in detail and never from Astrid. Yet she was sure her memory of it was accurate. She still felt that tugging sensation, the irresistible urge to turn back, even now as the cold water poured down her shivering body and spiralled into the black of the drain. Had anybody witnessed Clare struggling in the current, or heard her calling for help that day? She might have been saved.

Isla's face flamed in the freezing torrent as she remembered her instinct to abandon the girl. She had not imagined herself to be capable of such cruelty. But there it was, so near the surface she could almost see its shape.

Frankie. That was what the man had shouted. That was her name.

Isla had been afraid to leave the house the next day, for fear of seeing the couple. She stayed under the duvet, unable to shake off the image of the girl in the water. Oscillating between needing company and wanting to be alone, she willed Penny to stop by so she could gain some small comfort from her chatter. But when there was a knock at the door a few days later, it wasn't Penny, it was someone else.

A woman, uncertain and out of place, hovered at the threshold, hands behind her back. She would have been striking if she hadn't looked so hollowed out. Her red hair was loose and wavy; the wind picked up strands and they flew around her pale face with a life of their own.

'It is you, isn't it?' she began as if they had already been talking together. 'I wasn't sure I got the right house.'

In an unpleasant flash Isla realised she must be the child's mother – how could she have forgotten that hair? – and she cursed herself for opening the door. She looked uneasily over the woman's shoulder for a police car.

'I'm Erin. These are for you.' She proffered a small bunch of flowers that Isla recognised came from the expensive florist in the village. 'Neither of us can do CPR. I can't believe the only other person on the beach could.' She gave a laugh or a sob, it was hard to tell.

'Is she . . .?'

'God, yes, I should have said, sorry.' Erin took a tissue out of her handbag and blew her nose. 'It took a while, but they revived her. The water was pretty cold and that's helpful, apparently. The body shuts down. Something about preserving the blood supply to the brain.'

'The diving reflex.'

'Yes, that's right. And salt water . . .'

'. . . is better than fresh. Yes.' Isla frowned. 'You drown faster in fresh water.'

'Are you a doctor? Is that how you knew what to do?'

'No,' said Isla, 'my aunt drowned. My mother made me learn when I was old enough.'

'Oh.' Erin stood still, suddenly awkward.

'She's lucky. Your daughter, I mean.' Isla wished she could end the conversation politely and then Erin would go away.

'All thanks to you. You saved her life.'

'Right place, right time.' The hypocrisy of her own words crashed over Isla like a wave.

'They've kept her in to make sure everything's OK. Now we're going home. We run a hotel in London and we can't leave it for too long.'

'Oh, I see. You're not locals, then.' Isla felt relieved she wouldn't have to see them again.

'No, we're not. But I used to visit my aunt every year. I've been coming here since I was born.' Erin looked past Isla and into the house. 'Do you mind if I come in for a minute? I just want to talk to you about something. I won't take up too much of your time.'

Isla's stomach flipped over as she wondered what else she was going to say. The blurred edges of a memory began to swim into focus, but no sooner had she begun to see its outline, it disappeared again as Erin stepped past her. Isla forced a smile and stepped aside.

Erin entered the living room and exhaled audibly. 'Wow. I wondered what this place looked like from the inside. I saw you running a couple of times in the morning and I used to watch you race up to your door. It's beautiful, you're really lucky.'

'It's my mother's house. She died a couple of months ago and I'm just sorting through her things.'

'Sorry. I keep putting my foot in it, don't I? Do you mind if I sit down?'

Isla gestured to the sofa, sat herself in the armchair and waited.

'You saved Frankie's life,' Erin began, 'and I've been thinking how I go about thanking you for that.'

'Look, you don't have to . . .' An uneasy feeling rose in Isla and she tried to quell it.

Erin held up her hand for silence. 'I want to do something that will last a lifetime. A life for a life.'

'Honestly, it's no big deal.' Her eyes rested on the wentletrap shell, sitting on the mantlepiece behind Erin's back.

Erin ignored her and carried on. 'We have a small suite in our hotel. Nothing fancy, just a room with a kitchenette and a sofa. But I would like to offer it to you. To express our gratitude. So you can stay in it whenever you want, free of charge.' She paused and smiled. 'As long as you give us notice, of course.'

'Look,' Isla began, 'that's very nice of you. But you don't need to give me anything. Honestly.'

'You never go to London?'

'I lived there most of my life. I'm only here because my mother died.'

She looked crestfallen. 'Oh. You already have a house there.'

'Well, no, actually. I gave it up. To live here.'

She brightened. 'Then you must have plenty of friends and family you want to visit?'

Isla wished once more she hadn't opened the door. She didn't want to explain to this stranger that she didn't have any friends any more. She shrugged and made a neutral face.

'Look,' said Erin, unperturbed, 'hotels are extortionate. Well, nice ones are at any rate.'

'I guess you should know.'

'I know that if it wasn't for you, my daughter would be dead. And I know that if you don't accept my offer, I will feel worse than I do right now.' Her face suddenly darkened as she struggled and failed not to cry.

Isla wondered whether to leave the room to try to find tissues or to stay and say something helpful. But she couldn't think of any words and she had a very definite feeling she didn't want Erin to turn around and see that shell.

Erin swallowed hard and began to explain. 'I fell asleep when I should have been looking after her.' She continued to look down, studying the wet pattern interfering with the print on her skirt. 'It's all my fault, you see.' The confession floated in the air between them.

'It was an accident,' Isla said.

'It's my job,' Erin replied. 'I'm the one who looks after Frankie. If I can't do that properly, I'm afraid . . .' She stopped, lost in thought.

'Afraid of what?'

'Of how it will be from now on.' Erin frowned. 'I don't know if I can be trusted with her again.'

Isla wasn't used to being someone's confessor. It was a role that made her immensely uncomfortable and incredibly flattered at the same time. 'Everybody makes mistakes,' she said quietly. Isla wasn't sure if she was talking about herself or Erin.

'Don't you see? I won't be able to look Frankie in the eye without remembering what I did. I've ruined everything. All that innocence, that trust. It's gone.' She looked up, a miserable expression on her face. 'Vanished.'

'I don't think trust vanishes,' Isla said, 'it diminishes, yes, but it can be built up, lost and rebuilt.' Again, Isla had the sensation of not knowing whether she was directing her thoughts inwardly or to Erin. 'It's not a finite thing that you either have or you don't have. It's like water – it ebbs and flows. You just have to reverse the tide.'

'I don't think I can do that. I don't think I have the *right* to do that.' Erin's voice was flat.

'You told me Frankie's going to be fine. You have a second chance. Take it.' She was talking in sound bites, she knew it, but wanted to offer something of comfort to this wretched-looking woman.

'What about the suite? You have to take it.'

She looked so pathetic, Isla couldn't say no. 'It's very kind,' she conceded.

'Here's my card with the address.' Erin pushed a card across the coffee table between them. 'Call me before you come, OK?'

Her insistence, her absolute certainty that Isla should come to London; the way she had invited herself into the house, it reminded Isla of someone else. An image suddenly became clear in her head. A little girl kneeling in the sand, digging and chatting with an authority beyond her years; a look of triumph on her face as she brushed a tangle of red hair away from her eyes so she could examine the thing Isla had wanted so badly.

It couldn't be, could it?

Isla quickly scrolled through the memory. She couldn't remember much about what they had said to one another, but it was possible she had talked about an aunt and the fact that she came every year. Images came rolling back in pieces; the flotsam and jetsam that swirled in her long-term memory. The little girl's anger, raw and powerful when she saw what Isla had done. The shell tumbling out of her pocket on the sand. Isla wondered what Erin would say if she knew. If, in fact, she even remembered the incident.

Suddenly it became very important to get her out of the house. 'OK, it's a deal,' Isla said. 'I'll call you. Now, if you don't mind, I need to get on with a few things.'

'Oh. Sure. Sorry. Well, you have the card with my details.'

'Yes, I'll keep it somewhere safe.' Isla rose and led Erin to the door.

She watched Erin walk down the lane, her shoulders stooped in misery. Isla felt like a hypocrite for telling Erin to forgive herself, but now she wondered if she shouldn't act on her own advice and take the chance that had been offered to her. She turned back into the house. The door to the dining room was ajar. She was sure she had closed it. You could see the painting. Frowning, she walked over to shut it, making herself look at it. It was not as frightening as it used to be, but she still felt uneasy. It was time to decide what to do with it.

Of course. What was his name? Edward? The man who came to the house with the money. He'd been Astrid's dealer for years. Isla looked down at the card Erin had given her and smoothed her fingertips over the address. He used to come up from London. Perhaps he still lived there. Perhaps he knew what Astrid had done with her diaries, or if they existed at all. Perhaps he knew something about Clare.

She propped the card Erin had given her behind the wentletrap shell on the mantlepiece and went up to the bedroom, suddenly exhausted. For several minutes she lay on top of the covers, motionless, staring out of the window, unable to sink into sleep. It was only when she reached for the photograph on the bedside table and immersed herself in that fleeting moment in time all those years ago that she finally fell into the abyss.

Chapter Twenty-One

ERIN

When Erin arrived at the hospital, Frankie's bed was empty. Mark had already packed her bag and the cupboard that had been filled with little gifts, books and treats had been emptied. They were supposed to be taking her home today, but Erin's heart squeezed painfully when she saw Mark slumped in a chair staring into the space where Frankie should be.

'Where is she?' Erin asked, afraid something bad had happened.

'The nurses wanted to say goodbye to her. They took her off somewhere. She'll be back in a minute,' Mark replied without looking at her.

'What's the matter . . . have they said something to you? Frankie's OK, isn't she?'

'Everyone thinks she's doing great. Apart from me, it seems. If it were up to me . . .' He ran his fingers through his hair. 'If it were up to me, she wouldn't be leaving here. Not yet.'

Erin sat on the empty bed. 'But she's better. They said she was better.'

Mark lifted his face to her. He looked exhausted. 'Open your eyes, Erin. Better? She's nowhere near better. She's completely disengaged. She doesn't talk. Not to me, not to anyone.'

'She's bound to be quiet. It's just a reaction . . .'

'How would you know? You've hardly been here. When you do eventually show up, you can't wait to leave.'

How could she tell him she couldn't bear to be in here? That every time she saw her daughter's face, she was reminded of the terrible thing she had done? The shame of it was almost as painful as the guilt. 'The nurse I spoke to yesterday said she was a model patient,' she said.

'. . . because she doesn't *do* anything. She just sits here looking at her tablet, in a world of her own. Look at the other kids on the ward. You can't keep them in their own beds, the ones that can move around. They joke around with each other, play games . . .'

'Well maybe it's time to take the tablet away.'

'She's not interested in anything else, Erin. She's lost something. Her spark, her drive, I don't know what it is.' He shook his head. 'But it's gone. Don't tell me you haven't noticed?'

'I . . .' Erin thought about the times she had caught Frankie with a vacant expression on her face. She hadn't smiled for a long time. But since their argument in the waiting room, Erin couldn't help feeling that comments like this were directed at her, as some kind of slight. She felt bruised every time Mark spoke to her and wounded every time she saw her daughter.

A doctor appeared at the foot of the bed. 'Frankie's being discharged today, isn't she?' he said. 'You must be pleased to get her back.'

'My husband is worried it's a little too soon to take her home,' said Erin, hoping for a second opinion. 'Frankie's still . . . not herself.'

'She's been through the mill,' said the doctor. 'Some children bounce straight back and some take a little longer. It's normal for kids to withdraw when they're upset. Give her some time.'

The doctor smiled at them both and started to move on, but Mark blocked his way. 'She's not talking,' he tried to explain. 'She doesn't seem interested in anything. She wasn't like this before. You couldn't stop her from asking questions all the time.'

The doctor replied, 'I'm sure when she goes home and is surrounded by her familiar things, you'll see an improvement.' He could see Mark wasn't convinced. 'Look, Mr Baker, I wasn't present when Frankie was admitted, but from what I gather she was in the water less than ten minutes, which is a tipping point in terms of recovery. The temperature of the water was less than ten degrees: that's a good thing. I understand she received CPR at the scene. There are a lot of positives. She hasn't had any seizures. Her coordination is unaffected. We're really pleased with her recovery.' He gave Mark a look of sympathy. 'You've been through an ordeal too. It's normal to feel anxious. Give it time.' The doctor nodded his goodbye and turned to walk down the ward.

But Mark hurried after him, unable to let go. 'Can you give her a CAT scan, or an MRI? Just to check?'

'We don't scan children lightly, it's not a pleasant experience. An MRI would only traumatise Frankie more and children should only undergo CAT scans when medically necessary. Simply put, we don't feel Frankie needs one.'

'You don't understand,' Mark persisted. 'Frankie is really intelligent. Any test you've given her – you should be judging her against a nine or ten year old, not a six year old. She should be outperforming all your expectations, not scoring a "fine".'

Erin watched, unable to contribute or intervene. Some kind of transformation had overtaken Mark. He was now the one who was fighting for Frankie's interests while she shrank away into the background. Was he doing this to prove a point? To punish her?

A look of annoyance crossed the doctor's face. 'She's being discharged today. We wouldn't discharge a child unless we thought they were well enough. Take her home. Look after her in her own environment. I think the best thing for you all is to let her get over this in her own time, in her own way.'

Mark watched the doctor leave the ward and finally turned back to Erin. She could see by the look on his face that he wasn't convinced.

'Where did you get to, anyway?' Mark asked her, sinking back down into the chair. 'I thought you were coming to pick us up ages ago.'

She considered for a moment whether to tell him. 'I went to see the woman who saved Frankie.'

He looked surprised. 'How on earth did you find her?'

'I've seen her before, on other days, running. She always disappeared into one of the houses on the beach, so I went over there and knocked on the door.

'And?'

'And . . . She's nice. She's glad that Frankie is going to be OK.'

'Did she say anything about what she saw? How it happened?'

'Not really.'

'What did you talk about, then?'

'I offered her the suite. As a thank you.'

'You did what?' said Mark, taken aback.

Erin was defiant. 'I thought we should give her something, so I offered her the suite. It's not booked out all that often.'

'It's worth a lot of money when it is, though.'

'She saved Frankie's life!'

'We don't know anything about her,' he said in a tired voice.

'We don't know anything about all the other people that stay under our roof,' Erin replied tartly.

'That's different,' he muttered. 'Come on, let's find Frankie and get out of here.'

The drive home was a bitter parallel to the previous week. They spent most of the journey in silence. Erin tried not to remember how they had sung songs together, full of anticipation. They had played I Spy for hours. Frankie had spent most of the journey with her nose pressed against the window, charmed by the fields of sheep, cows and horses. Now she was mute, as if she had been emptied out. Erin saw the sign for the service station they had stopped at on the way up. They had treated Frankie to a mug of hot chocolate with a huge whirl of cream on top and she had clapped her hands in delight. Erin averted her gaze, pressed her foot on the accelerator and drove another sixty miles before she allowed herself a break.

Chapter Twenty-Two

Isla

Isla had watched the Baker family leave. She hadn't meant to, but she had been on the High Street and saw Erin packing suitcases into the car outside the only hotel the village had. She instinctively shrank into a doorway and waited for her to drive away.

So that was it then. Life could go back to normal. She wondered why she didn't feel relieved. It had surprised her to admit it, but she had liked talking to Erin. It was flattering to be drawn into someone else's confidence like that. There was something touching about her honesty, how open she had been about her mistakes. Isla wondered what she would say if she found out she had been the girl who had taken the shell. That Frankie hadn't been rescued in the way she had imagined. The shame of that morning was still fresh, but it had been soothed somewhat by the news that Frankie was going to be fine. Did that make everything right again? Was she absolved?

Since Erin had left her house, Isla had spent a lot of time thinking. She had been in her own company too long. The corners knocked off by client contact had been shored up by solitude. Maybe the presence of others blunted one's less-appealing traits.

Perhaps that was why Astrid had been so difficult. All those years living alone in a house at the edge of the sea. Even her job kept her away from others. What kind of a mother would she have turned into if she'd been surrounded by a proper family, if her parents or Clare hadn't died so young? Maybe Astrid was to be pitied, after all.

Isla looked up at the sky and smelled the popcorn machine from Hettie's sweet shop. It was finally beginning to warm up. The desire for a fresh start rose up in her chest like a cresting wave. It was a sensation she didn't want to lose. Not wanting to go back to the house, she wandered along the cliff path in the hope of spotting a lone seal she had recently seen bottling off the coast. But when the light began to fail, she turned around. She'd made the mistake of walking back in the dark without a torch once before and didn't want to repeat the experience. When she eventually entered the rutted lane that ran behind the houses, she stopped.

There was a light on in the studio, illuminating the skylights in the roof. It wasn't the spotlights in the apex; she could see those were off. This must be the desk lamp on the table below. It gave out a yellow glow. Slowly, the light flickered as if something had moved past it. Could Penny be up there? Isla remembered locking the house before she left and Penny was the only one with a spare key. She hurried down the lane, but as she passed Penny's house, it was in darkness. Isla remembered her saying something about going to Jacob's for a few days. She must have left the lamp on herself, Isla reasoned, but when? She hadn't been up there for days. How could she be so careless? The lamp was old, it could cause a fire. But instead of rushing forwards, she hesitated in the half-light, suddenly uneasy, her eyes glued to the windows in the roof.

She stood there for some time, the child in her afraid of shadows, the adult urging her into the house. There it was again – a movement – a black shape crossing the room. The adult took charge and she willed herself forwards, holding her keys in front of

116

her like a weapon. Through the stippled glass of the door, she could see the hallway was in darkness. The thick silence that had settled in her absence was broken by the hinges giving out their customary shriek as she opened up the house. She snapped on the light and, galvanised by the noise and a forty-watt bulb, marched up the stairs. The studio was locked, the key sticking out of the door. If anyone was up there, they had locked themselves in from the outside, which was impossible. With a shaking hand, Isla turned the key, heart pumping, and took the stairs two at a time.

The lamp was on, the casing was hot. The light flickered weakly; the bulb was clearly failing. She stretched over the table to the wall socket to switch it off, but as she did so, she saw a shadow in the corner where the table met the wall.

It was a small nest of hair. Isla picked it up and examined it under the lamplight. The hair wasn't hers. It was long, silvered grey. She thought about the bag of Astrid's hair in the writing desk. An uncomfortable scenario passed through her mind. If she took this now and added it to that bag, might more of these offerings appear in the house? Is that what this was, an offering?

She straightened up, berating herself. She'd had a difficult few days. That child had nearly drowned. She needed to take her mind off everything, not start with this. Whatever this was.

Nevertheless, something stopped her from throwing the hair in the bin. She put it back where she found it, switched off the lamp and pulled out the plug. The room fell into darkness. The same sense of childish fear overtook her and, for a few seconds, she couldn't move, sure there was something else in the room, observing her. She listened, holding her breath. Even the rhythm of the sea below her seemed to pause and she had the uncomfortable sensation that whatever it was was holding its breath, too.

Very slowly, she crept towards the stairs and descended them with as much dignity as she could muster. When she closed the door behind her, she removed the key and when she reached the foot of the stairs on the ground floor, she switched on every light she could find and called Penny.

'Isla?' Penny answered. 'Everything OK?'

'How long are you staying at Jacob's?'

'Until the end of the month,' she answered. 'You sound a bit wound up, Isla, are you sure everything's alright?'

'I'm fine. I just wanted to talk to someone, that's all.'

'Has something happened?' Penny sounded worried.

'No,' Isla said firmly. 'Nothing's happened. But I'd like you and Jacob to come over for dinner when you're back. I think I need some company.'

Chapter Twenty-Three

PENNY, JUNE

'Do you think we should dress up?' Penny pulled out clothes from her wardrobe while Jacob, who had been ready for some time, lay semi-recumbent on the bed, watching her in amusement.

'What's gotten into you, Pen? You're not going on a date, it's dinner. With a neighbour. Relax.' As if to demonstrate, he settled his back against a bank of pillows and put his hands behind his head.

'We've never been invited over before. Not for dinner.'

'So?'

'I don't know. It feels a bit . . .'

'What?'

'Where the bloody hell did I put that nice skirt? I'm sure it was in here . . .' She rummaged through a forest of wire hangers.

'Dry-cleaner?'

'Yes. I forgot. This will have to do.' She untangled a long velvety dress and threw on a fringed shawl she favoured. Even though it was June, Astrid's house could be cold.

'Lovely,' said Jacob. 'Shall we go?'

Penny touched her forehead and squeezed her eyes shut. Her neck felt stiff. 'I think I can feel a headache coming on. Maybe we shouldn't go.'

'Penny,' Jacob sat up, swinging his feet to the floor, 'is there something the matter? Why the big fuss over dinner with Isla? You've been antsy all afternoon.'

Penny sat on the bed next to him and smoothed the duvet cover with her hand. The flower pattern depicted a little bee on one of the anemones; she hadn't noticed that before. Or maybe it was a wasp? 'It's hard to explain,' she said, covering the insect with her fingertip, blotting it out.

'Try.'

'I don't want to rake over the past, Jacob. But I've a feeling she does.'

'This isn't the first time you've said something like this about Isla. Why are you afraid of talking with her? It's natural she wants to know a little more about her mother. I'd tell her myself if I knew anything, but you two always kept yourselves very much to yourselves, as I recall. I'm amazed I was able to steal you away to the harvest dance before I left for medical school. Plenty of us joked Astrid would be taking you instead.'

Penny looked amused. 'You thought we were . . .?'

'Well, not me, I knew differently. Remember Nancy Ballantyne's birthday? When we came down to the beach and swore we would keep a fire going all night? I seem to remember there was something else warming me that night.' He raised a bristly eyebrow and gave her a coquettish look.

'Oh! I had forgotten all about that!' Penny clapped her hands to her cheeks and laughed.

'Now that's something I haven't seen for a long while,' Jacob said, 'a laugh coming out of you.'

'It's been . . . difficult.' Penny's voice dropped, the laughter gone.

'It's not just Astrid's death, is it? There's something else you're not telling me. Whatever the secret is, it might make you feel better to share it.' He nudged her and they swayed together momentarily, the springs of the mattress singing under their weight.

Penny looked ahead at the closed bedroom door. There was a narrow strip of light that shone in from the hallway, a slim rectangle of yellow where the door hovered above the threshold. Very slowly, a shadow rolled across it and then disappeared. Her eyes felt swollen, like they had too much fluid in them. She blinked slowly, imagining the delicate skin of her lids stretching over eyeballs that were too big. It was coming on slowly but she knew, eventually, it would come. She imagined it tightly budded, like a fist, ready to open and bloom in the side of her head.

'Secrets aren't meant for sharing,' Penny muttered, locating a bottle of pills on the bedside table.

'Come on.' Jacob took her hand and kissed it. 'I'll pour you a glass of water.'

'No,' Penny replied, swallowing them dry. 'We should go. She's waiting.'

Chapter Twenty-Four

Isla

Isla had worked hard cooking a meal she thought Penny and Jacob would appreciate. Soup from Jacob's allotment vegetables, locally caught plaice with a cockle sauce made with garlic and cream. Samphire, harvested near the salt marshes, still in season and not yet bitter or woody. She had prepared the food all afternoon methodically, her hands remembering how to clean and shell the cockles; a job she recalled was hers from childhood.

'You've done wonders with this place, Isla,' Jacob said when he and Penny arrived, stroking the fresh paintwork in the hallway. 'It looks very Scandinavian. Does this mean you've decided to stay for ever? Penny would hate it if you sold up.'

'I don't know. It still doesn't feel like my house somehow. Even though the only thing that remotely resembles Astrid's taste is the studio.'

'You've kept it intact, then?' Jacob asked.

Isla nodded. 'I wondered about trying to contact her old dealer to ask about the paintings on the walls up there. I'm not sure if they should be preserved in some way.' She walked them through to the patio. She had already laid the table and placed a smooth grey stone at each corner of the white tablecloth to stop it being blown about. A bottle of white wine stood in a chiller, making a damp patch in the centre. Isla picked it up, wiped the condensation from the glass with a linen tea towel and unscrewed the cap. 'Do you remember her dealer, Penny?' she asked.

'Hmm.' Penny squinted into the past. 'He stopped coming when she didn't need the money any more. Haven't seen him for years and I don't think Astrid kept in touch with him.'

'I think he was called Edward, I met him once. He was nice to me.' Isla still remembered that day, his kind words and the custard creams dipped in milk.

'He was the only person who had the patience to deal with her,' snorted Penny. 'Astrid rarely set foot in London, you know. He always had to come here to pick up the work and pay her. She used to instruct him to bring cash, but when the value of her work shot up he would bring her a cheque and drive her to the bank to cash it.'

'I only remember meeting him once,' Isla said. 'I've been trying to track him down. Have you any idea where he lived?'

Penny shook her head.

Isla sighed. 'I don't know his second name and the internet connection here is non-existent. I've been going to the library in town, but can't find anything on him; it's all about her.'

'He can't be that hard to find,' Jacob said. 'If you phoned around or went to London. Penny, what's the name of that street where all the galleries are?'

'Cork Street, I think,' Penny replied.

'Yes. Cork Street. Or Bond Street, even. Someone there may be able to help. She's still fairly well known, isn't she?'

'Yeah. Partly because there's not much of her work on the market. She always knew how to keep the mystique.' Isla had a wry look on her face. 'Maybe I should go to London. Knock on a few doors. I could do with a change of scenery. I don't think you were here when all the drama happened last month.'

'What drama?' Penny asked, looking surprised.

'A little girl fell into the lagoon.'

'No! Is she alright?'

'Yes. I happened to be there. I pulled her out. She was in hospital for a few days, though.'

'I read about that in the local paper,' said Jacob. 'Don't you remember me telling you about it, Penny?'

'I think I would have remembered a thing like that,' said Penny, upset.

'She's going to be alright, though? The little girl?' asked Jacob, attempting to smooth things over.

'Yes,' said Isla. 'Her mother came here the other day to tell me she was going to be OK.'

'What a terrible thing. And right here, in front of the house. She could have died. Another young death,' Penny said sadly.

'I know. It was only because of Astrid that I knew how to do CPR.' The familiar anxiety crept over her and she shivered. It would take a long time for the shame to fade when she thought about that moment.

'Of course. Poor Clare. It wouldn't have helped her though, she was beyond help when they found her,' Penny said, her forehead creased. She touched her temple gently with her fingertips.

'Do you know much about what happened, Penny?' asked Isla. 'Astrid never told me.'

Penny shook herself. 'Family history is best served on a full stomach,' she said grimly. 'We should eat before we pick over that particular carcass.'

The shadows grew long, and Isla lit the storm lanterns. When the sun finally slipped away, they could hear the sea but no longer see it and it sounded to Isla like a melancholy thing, sighing in the darkness.

Eventually, Jacob cleared the plates and poured more wine. 'Well, that was delicious,' he said.

Isla smiled. 'I used to do most of the cooking when Astrid trusted me to do it properly – it's funny, she was so laissez-faire about bringing me up but when she wasn't painting, she insisted on cooking properly and eating what was growing around us.'

'Probably a hangover from childhood. I think social services would have taken Clare and Astrid in if they weren't seen to be eating properly,' Jacob replied.

'Was it really that bad? She never mentioned it,' Isla said, hoping to pick up the thread of family history. To her relief, Jacob stepped into the growing silence.

'Well, Penny knows more than anyone,' said Jacob. 'Astrid and Clare virtually moved in with you, didn't they? Didn't your parents look after them when Nell died?'

'Well, on paper they did. They tried to.' Penny nodded at Isla. 'But the girls were pretty self-sufficient before Nell – your grandmother – died and although they liked knowing we were there, they didn't seem to need us that much. I think Alf was a fairly errant father. I don't remember him being around that much, and, when he was, he was usually in a temper. Nell was different, though. She was as sweet as Alf was sour.' Penny smiled to herself, briefly, before her face fell into sadness. 'I think she always knew she didn't have long on this earth. She was very sickly, always getting chesty in the winter. The girls looked after her from when they were quite young. I remember Nell teaching Clare and Astrid how to fish, how to cook. In that very kitchen, in fact.' She pointed through the open doors to the kitchen beyond. 'Clare was tall enough, but Astrid always stood on a little milking stool so she could reach the countertop.'

Isla tried to imagine a little girl, balancing on a milking stool, learning how to cook with her sister because her mother feared she would no longer be there to look after them. She pictured them as teenagers, orphaned, trying to replicate what they had been taught, trying to be a family with their parents dead within a year of one another. Did they still sleep in their own bedroom after Nell had died? Or did they shrink into her room, sharing her bed at night, smelling traces of her on the pillow, whispering words of comfort to one another in the dark as the sea and the wind howled through the islands and onto the shore? And when recovery became a reachable goal, a final blow: the drowning of Clare. To lose the only person who had navigated Astrid through those terrible times must have been unbearable. To be the last in that house, with a newborn. Alone. A child herself. She hadn't really thought about Astrid as a child before – she was the kind of person you assumed had sprung from the sea fully formed, parentless. To think of her as vulnerable, afraid, desperately sad and isolated, the depression and, later, the rages – it all made sense. What didn't make sense was her reticence around Clare's death. There was something conspicuous about it.

The evening had lost its warmth and they wrapped up in blankets, looking down at the stretch of beach. The murmur of the tide had receded and the moon had finally emerged from cloud cover, illuminating the bay below them. The sand was cut through by fine rivulets of water that looked like long strands of snaking hair, silvered in the moonlight.

'What was Clare like?' asked Isla, returning her gaze to Penny.

Penny paused for a long time, considering the question. Isla was afraid she might not want to answer it. But she did eventually, slowly, remembering. 'Wilful,' she began, 'strong, fun. She was exciting to be with. Popular in the bakery, where she worked. Liked by everybody. I remember her coming home with all sorts of food parcels her boss had given her. I think they would have done that anyway, even if her circumstances had been easier. People wanted to please her. Astrid adored her. She would sometimes go off for the day with a friend, a bakery girl or boyfriend perhaps, and Astrid would sit on the sea-wall and wait for her to come home. She would always get back before the sun set. That was the arrangement. Astrid was never left alone after nightfall.'

'Were you there when she drowned? Did you see what happened?'

'No. Not me. But Astrid was. She saw them pull her out of the water further down the bay. The men who found her . . . They all knew her, the cocklers. Some had known her since she was a toddler. Most of the men drank with Alf and they tolerated him well enough. But they all loved Clare. She was their bonny baby. They could see it was too late, even before they pulled her out. Some of them never got over it.'

'But she knew the bay so well! I don't understand how she could have been caught by the tide like that,' said Isla. 'Astrid was always going on about how knowledgeable they both were about the area. Did they do a post-mortem? Maybe she'd been drinking?'

'Clare never drank,' said Penny sharply. 'She saw what it did to Alf and she wouldn't touch it.'

'Then what? You must admit, Penny, it seems odd.'

Penny sighed in irritation. 'Why does your generation always seem to think there's a conspiracy theory around every corner? Sometimes accidents happen – tragedies like this – and there isn't some sinister explanation. It's just . . . bad judgement.'

'I didn't mean . . .' Isla sensed the atmosphere had changed. She had stepped over a line, but, for the life of her, couldn't see where it was.

'No. Well. I think it's time to call it a night.' Penny stood up, shook her blanket off and folded it up.

'I was going to make coffee.' Isla couldn't keep the disappointment out of her voice.

'I'm getting one of my headaches. We've an early start tomorrow. Thanks for dinner, it was delicious. My turn to have you next time.' She kissed Isla quickly on the cheek. Jacob shrugged, put his wine glass down, still half full, and followed her out of the house.

Chapter Twenty-Five

PENNY

Penny marched down the lane in silence. Jacob, usually tolerant of her reticence, stumbled behind her getting more and more annoyed as she strode on with the torch. He waited until the door was shut behind him before he spoke. 'Well, do you want to tell me what that was all about? You don't have an early start tomorrow any more than I do.'

'I just thought it was time to go, that's all. It's late.' Penny's voice was sulky. She unwound her shawl from her shoulders and hung it on the bannister. Her head throbbed quietly, a precursor of what would come. She wanted to lie down and take another pill.

'Penny, you couldn't get out of there fast enough. She cooked us a delicious meal and all she wanted in return was a bit of information about Astrid and Clare, but you couldn't do it, could you?'

'I gave her lots of information! And I'm getting a headache. I told you.'

But there was no sympathy from Jacob. 'You talked in general terms, Penny. You were as thick as thieves with those two, yet you tell Isla they were pretty self-sufficient and didn't seem to need you that much. From what I remember, you were in each other's pockets when you were teenagers.'

'Astrid wouldn't want me to drag all that stuff up. If she wanted to talk to Isla about it, she would have done it by now.'

'That's the point though, isn't it? She died so suddenly, who knows what she really intended? Astrid doesn't deserve your protection, Penny, she's dead. Isla is very much alive and needs you right now. It was only a short while ago that you were wringing your hands about how you weren't there for her when she was little. Well, now you can be. Stop chasing after ghosts and start helping the living.' He threw down his jacket, crossed the hallway into the sitting room and got the whisky bottle from the drinks cabinet.

'Alright. Pour me one of those,' Penny said suddenly, feeling reckless.

Jacob sat down in one of the armchairs. It was cold in the house despite the fact it was mid-summer. Penny knelt by the fireplace and laid a firelighter in the grate. She balled up several sheets of newspaper and unceremoniously scattered several dried bits of driftwood on top. She lit the firelighter, rested on her heels and felt the heat escape into the room.

'I'm going to tell you something I swore I never would. I kept it a secret because Astrid wanted it that way. Now she's dead. Well . . . I just don't know what to think.' She shook her head slowly and stared into the fire. 'I can't even be sure Astrid didn't kill herself. Nothing seems certain any more.'

'Go on,' Jacob said quietly.

'My parents used to say that Alfred and Nell Jarsdel came to parenthood late in life and exited early. They were both dead before Clare was seventeen. You know this already, of course.'

'True,' replied Jacob. 'Alf was looked after by my dad as I recall, though he was always tight-lipped about his patients. The soul of discretion. I don't think it was a huge surprise when his time came. But it was all over town when Nell died.'

'Yeah. Alf wasn't missed much: he had a temper, he was a drinker. But when Nell died,' Penny sighed, 'you can't imagine the effect Nell's death had on everybody. It went deep with my parents, especially my father. I think he was besotted with Nell. He placed himself between her and Alf when he was in a rage and I think he fell in love with her cheerful stoicism.'

'Did they have an affair?'

'No, I don't think it ever came to that. If they had, it would have run its course in all likelihood. But unspoken love . . .' Here, Penny paused and looked into the fire. '. . . unspoken love has a potency that's hard to dispel. When Nell died, my father was distraught; more than he ought to have been. It confirmed everything my mother suspected and she became very bitter about it. When my father suggested that Clare and Astrid should move in with us, my mother was dead against it. She wanted a fresh start without the Jarsdel sisters underfoot.'

'Were there no other relatives to take them in then?'

'No. No relatives. I think my father tried hard to find someone else. But they didn't really need anyone in the end. Clare got a job in the local bakery. Astrid was already selling watercolours to tourists. They got by.' Penny turned to Jacob and looked him in the eye. 'I told Isla the truth about Clare and Astrid being self-sufficient. What they didn't know about the beach and what it could give them, nobody did. They knew more about the dangers of the water than most of the fishermen, they could cook as well as any housewife in the village.'

'But they were still teenagers. What were they? Sixteen and fourteen years old? Too young to be left,' Jacob said sadly.

'Yes. But a teenager back then was looked upon as an adult. Only my father saw that they needed a parent. I remember one night hearing them arguing about it. My mother wanted to hand them over to the authorities, but my father persuaded her to agree to guardianship – on condition that they didn't live with us once it was official.'

'And did it work?'

'The arrangement was they kept to themselves and had contact with my parents only through me. My mother wanted nothing to do with them and my father agreed to this because he wanted to save his marriage.'

'That was a lot of responsibility on your shoulders, Penny.'

'It wasn't put to me like that. It was done casually. I remember my father used to come to my room at night and he would sit by my bed and question me about them. He took great pleasure in hearing about Astrid's painting and I enjoyed telling him stories about what we were getting up to.' She turned from the fire and looked at him. 'You were right, Jacob. We were as thick as thieves, the three of us. We used to roam for miles around the islands. We would spend the day on them, cut off by the tide, and set out for home when the sand was safe to walk on. It was all very innocent. Until . . .'

'Until?'

'Until one day, Clare told us she was pregnant.'

'What?'

'Yeah. We knew she was friendly with a couple of the boys from the factory in the town and we all hung around with the younger cockle pickers. We didn't really think beyond that. She had an internal life we weren't privy to. I was closer in age to Astrid and I suppose the age gap feels wider for the eldest child. Anyway, as you can imagine, the news wasn't welcome, but there was no question of an abortion in Clare's mind. I don't think she would have known how to get one, in any case.'

'Who was the father? Did she tell you?'

Penny closed her eyes. 'A mistake. A fairground worker, here for the summer season. It would never have worked; they were so different. The biggest problem was trying to keep it a secret; she was adamant about that. Didn't want any help. The isolation she lived in meant that she had more privacy than most and wouldn't have to bring a baby up single-handed under the usual public scrutiny. My parents avoided her, so Clare figured she could keep things quiet. She planned to work until the baby was born.'

'And how did the bakery react to that?'

'They didn't know, or they chose not to notice at any rate. I told you, everyone loved Clare.'

'But surely somebody saw her and wondered what was going on? How the hell did she get away with it?'

'Bakery work is early work, don't forget. Clare walked there before most of the village were up and about. She was bundled up in her mother's coat or wrapped in baker's whites, stationed behind the tables that fed the ovens. You don't see what you don't look for. I don't remember her showing that much, anyway.'

'Towards the end she would have done.'

'That was where Astrid came in. The idea was that she would take Clare's place at the bakery.'

'I can't see Astrid working at the bakery, somehow.'

'That was the problem. Neither could she. Clare had always promised her that she could paint. She had just won a place in a pretty decent art college and was preparing to start her course. When Clare explained she would have to pack it in, Astrid was furious – but she could see there was no alternative. They couldn't afford to lose the wage at the bakery. I think there was also a certain amount of jealousy that Clare had carved out a life of her own that didn't include Astrid. It became clear to me that Clare had never confided in Astrid that she was even dating anyone.'

'That must have stung.'

Penny nodded. 'It was a tipping point for them both. Astrid felt betrayed and excluded. Clare felt unsupported. Looking back, that summer was the beginning of the end for them. Astrid painted in isolation, as if she was still going to college. Clare went to work and didn't mention the baby. When September rolled around, Astrid started college, against Clare's wishes. She still had a few months to go before the baby was due, but she felt that if Astrid started her course it would be even more difficult to leave it when the time came. They had terrible rows about it. But it saved them both in the end. No one could deny Astrid's capability and she was picked up by a dealer in London when her tutor referred her. I think he knew she needed money and was not going to complete the course, so he facilitated the relationship before she left. The dealer arranged for her to show some paintings in a group exhibition in London and she sold the lot in one night. The rest, as they say, is history.'

'What happened next?'

'The baby was born the following February. My mother helped with the birth. It was straightforward enough. But something happened to Clare. Clare . . . she'd always gone through highs and lows. I think that's why she was so popular. When she was on a high she was so much fun to be with you felt lost when she left. When she was low, she kept herself to herself so I don't think people really picked up on it. But this was different. The highs just didn't come any more. She didn't bond with the baby. She didn't sleep, but felt tired all the time. She stopped eating properly and refused to leave her bed. I think that the events of the past few years finally caught up with her.'

'Sounds like she had postnatal depression, amongst other things,' Jacob said, frowning.

'It was like she just gave up. And Astrid . . . she felt let down by Clare. She was bitter. I feel so bad about it. I wasn't really there. I . . . wasn't interested in the baby and Astrid was terrible company.

She didn't come out any more so we sort of lost touch for a bit. All my fault.' Penny hauled herself off the floor and onto the armchair opposite Jacob. She threw another stick of wood onto the fire and it caught immediately. Still she would not look at him.

Jacob shifted in his seat. He looked uncomfortable. 'Penny,' he said softly, 'what happened to the baby?'

'Astrid . . . she looked after the baby as much as she could, but she had to get on with her painting. It was the only thing keeping their heads above the water. After a few months, Clare got a bit better. She put on some weight, she seemed happier, she even went out every now and again. They had an arrangement. Clare would leave in the afternoon when the baby was sleeping. She always returned before sunset. Except . . . that day, she didn't.'

'Penny . . .' said Jacob.

Penny watched the flames catch. It was remarkable how fire was so similar to water. 'You know, Isla was right. Clare knew the sea better than anyone. It was a spring tide. No one in their right mind would have gone out in that.'

'Penny . . .' he repeated.

Penny remained in the past, trying to catch hold of thoughts that swam away from her, just out of reach.

'What happened to the baby, Penny?'

Finally she raised her gaze and looked at him. 'Isn't it obvious?'

'Jesus.' Jacob sat back in the chair, running his hand through his hair, rubbing his beard as if he was trying to wipe the idea away from him.

'I didn't realise at the time, but now I wonder if it was an act of revenge that Astrid brought Isla up and never told her about Clare. She didn't see why Clare should get immortalised when Astrid had done all the parenting. She obliterated Clare from Isla's life like an unwanted character in one of her paintings and put herself in her place. By the time I saw what had happened, it was too late.'

Penny searched Jacob's face. He didn't return her gaze. 'You have to understand, Jacob, I was a child too.'

'You just said teenagers were like adults back then.'

'I didn't think about the consequences, I just wanted to help. Astrid was a force to be reckoned with even then. She convinced us all it would be better for Isla not to know about Clare being her mother. The whole village thought she was Astrid's anyway because Astrid never went back to college. The story went round that she'd been sent home in disgrace with a baby on the way, and nobody contradicted it. They assumed Clare gave up work to look after her sister. Like I said, people don't see what they're not looking for.'

'I've known you since we were children, Penny. How on earth did you keep this from me? I could have helped.'

'You'd already gone to medical school and I wasn't sure I would ever see you again. There didn't seem any point telling you. In any case, they swore me to secrecy.'

'What on earth did your parents have to say about it?'

'Not much, actually. They were the ones who were supposed to be keeping an eye out for them. They could hardly take the moral high ground, could they? They were as drawn into the conspiracy as I was.'

Jacob stood and paced the room. 'You are the only person in this sorry mess who can put it right, can't you see that?' He gestured to the house along the lane. 'There's a middle-aged woman who hasn't begun to have a life yet because she's too busy trying to unpick a fabrication conceived by someone she believes to be her mother. Don't you see how heartbreaking that is? She's been living a monstrous lie that you could have resolved. What are you waiting for? Don't you think she deserves the truth?'

Penny, disarmed, defended herself. 'It seemed wrong to tell Isla everything when she was trying to deal with losing Astrid so suddenly. I didn't think it was my place.'

'I thought we knew each other, Penny, told each other our secrets?'

'Please don't be like that, Jacob. It wasn't my secret to tell.'

'That's where you're wrong. This is very much your secret to tell. There is no one left to tell it. And what about Isla's father? Is he dead or is that a lie too?'

'He's dead,' Penny said evenly. 'The fair used to come back once a year so we got to know some of the regular lads. They said he dropped dead on a site in Northumberland. Heart trouble, I think it was. Clare never told him about the baby. About . . . Isla.' A streak of pain originating from above her right ear snaked its way behind her eyes and across her cheekbone. She winced, closing her eyes momentarily. 'Can you fetch me some painkillers, please? There should be something in the kitchen cupboard.'

Jacob didn't move. He seemed to make up his mind about something. 'If you don't tell her the truth . . .' The threat lay heavy in the air between them. He stopped pacing. 'Until then, I'm sorry, Penny, but I don't want to see you.'

Penny watched, stunned, as he put his empty glass on the table, took his coat from the back of the chair and walked away.

'Come and find me when it's done.'

She heard the front door open, heard the soft click of the latch as it closed behind him and listened in vain for his footsteps to return to her. When it was certain he was not coming back, she looked around the room, alive with shadows cast by the firelight, and felt very afraid.

Chapter Twenty-Six

Erin, July

It was a quiet Sunday even though it was July, one of their busiest months. The weekend guests had left the hotel and there was a golden bubble of time, only a few hours, that occupied the space between departures and arrivals. Before the accident, Erin used this time to pretend that she didn't share her house with strangers, that she had the whole place to herself. Now she had other things to think about.

After she'd made sure Mark was out, she instructed Faisal, who was filing paperwork, to steer clear of the guest sitting room. On the ceiling above the lobby, she could hear the muffled din of the vacuum cleaner wheeling across carpet. But as she opened the door to the lounge and it closed quietly behind her, she was enveloped, as she knew she would be, with a blessed hush. Faisal had already been in here to change the flowers. The tables were polished, the Sunday papers ordered into tidy piles. The contrast to their own squalid flat in the basement was something Erin tried not to dwell on. Neither she nor Mark had made an effort for weeks. Erin drew a line between the work the cleaners did in the hotel and their own living quarters, but now she wondered if it wasn't time to throw herself at their mercy. No, the guest sitting room was the most comfortable place to test Frankie.

It had been two months since they'd returned from their disastrous holiday and Frankie still wasn't talking. It was remarkable how little she needed words to communicate. Erin couldn't help but feel a grudging respect for the artful way in which her daughter could say what she wanted with a pointing finger, a shrug of a shoulder, a nod or a shake of the head. But two months was long enough. The doctor who had been treating her in London called it selective mutism. When he explained to Erin her daughter had nothing physically preventing her from talking, Erin stopped him right there.

'So you're telling me she can speak if she chooses to? She just doesn't *want* to?'

He'd smiled kindly at her, well acquainted with her frustration. 'It's not that simple. Frankie doesn't feel able to speak. There is a difference between wanting to do something and not feeling able. Try and imagine someone who is scared of heights being made to take a bungee jump. It's perfectly easy to step off the platform and let yourself fall, but some people physically cannot do it. Their body stops them. The anxiety is too great.'

'So how long does it take for the anxiety to go away? How long before she starts talking again?'

'I don't have a definitive answer for you. Frankie will start talking when she feels comfortable enough to do it. It might begin very gradually. For example, she may choose to talk only in certain situations, or to certain people. Many children are able to speak at home, but are non-verbal at school, where the atmosphere may be more overwhelming.'

'But she's not speaking at home. She's not speaking to anyone.'

'Not yet. Give it time. She might begin with one or two words only, or she may begin to speak in a whisper. Frankie has experienced trauma, and her body is reacting to that. She needs to process what has happened to her and this is one way of doing that. When she feels more relaxed, secure, the language will come back.'

Erin couldn't help it: she felt slighted. They were supposed to have a special bond. If there was anyone Frankie felt safe with, it should be her. The guilt of falling asleep on the beach that day sliced through her once more as she wondered if, like Mark, Frankie held her responsible for the accident and this selective mutism was a way of punishing her. But Frankie wasn't talking to Mark either.

Erin had a tray in her hands, and she put it down on the long, low table that ran parallel to the sofa. On it were several things that were dear to Frankie's heart. Her precious tablet, a packet of her favourite sweets and the toy she took to bed with her every night. She sat the rabbit up and arranged the sweets in its lap. Then she propped the tablet up in front of the rabbit and waited. She knew Frankie would come looking for her screen. Sure enough, less than ten minutes later, her puzzled face appeared around the door and Erin had a moment where her resolve faltered and she wondered if what she was about to do was very wrong.

She put on her brightest voice. 'Mr Rabbit was just asking me if I knew where you were. He's got something he would like to say.'

Frankie's face lit up as she saw what was on the tray and she reached her hands towards it as she crossed the room. But Erin leaned over and slid the tray out of her reach.

'Frankie, can you sit down for me? I need to talk to you.'

Frankie sat obediently on the sofa next to Erin, looking across her, eyeing the tray. Erin shifted away from her daughter. She picked up the rabbit and put him on her knee, very gently, arranging his ears nicely.

'Mr Rabbit has been very worried about you. He's been very sad that you haven't been talking. He misses your voice.'

A shadow crossed Frankie's face. She looked up at her mother, uncertain.

Erin ignored the pulse jumping in her neck and pressed ahead. 'We thought that it would be really special if you could try and say a few words today. Just to me and Mr Rabbit. There's no one else here, Frankie. It's only us. If you can say a few words to me, then you can have Mr Rabbit back.'

Frankie shifted her hands underneath her legs and rocked forwards, looking at the floor.

Erin swallowed and said softly, 'How about I give you a sentence to say? Would that be easier?'

Frankie nodded slowly.

'OK. Why don't you say, *Can I have Mr Rabbit, please, Mummy?*'

Frankie said nothing and stared at the floor.

'It's just one sentence, Frankie. For me. And for Mr Rabbit.' She lowered the rabbit to the floor and waggled his velvet head so he was in line with Frankie's vision. Frankie rocked slowly forwards, as if she was about to get up, and then she leaned back again into the sofa, head lowered.

'OK, how about this,' Erin said, beginning to feel the situation sliding out of her control. She imagined someone coming into the sitting room and seeing her holding a stuffed rabbit to ransom. 'Why don't you have Mr Rabbit for the moment and see if you can talk with him on your lap?' She nudged Frankie's knee with the toy and Frankie snatched it quickly, folding it against her stomach, crossing her arms as if it might escape. Her nail caught Erin's wrist and grazed the skin.

Erin felt a small dart of hurt. 'Frankie, you scratched me.' She tried to keep the edge out of her voice. 'OK, now I've given you Mr Rabbit but I can't give you your tablet or these sweets until you say something to me. You have to ask for them before I give them to you, OK? It's really easy, darling. You just have to talk.'

Frankie looked at Erin and she looked at the tray. Erin felt a spark of hope.

'You can have the sweets right now, even though it's nearly lunchtime. I'll even let you eat the whole pack in one go.'

Frankie reached for them.

Erin moved the tray away, feeling the blood rise to her face. 'Not until you ask nicely, Frankie. It's not hard.'

Frankie met her gaze and something subtle happened that Erin would never be able to explain. Erin saw a change behind her daughter's eyes. There was a hardening: some kind of crystallisation of thought. When Frankie eventually stood up, it felt as if she was the adult in the room. Erin remained seated on a naughty step of her own making. When her daughter walked away, Erin fought the urge to fling herself on the carpet and kick her heels in frustration.

Chapter Twenty-Seven

ISLA

Isla was beginning to worry. She hadn't seen Penny since the meal they'd had together almost a month ago. It was not like her to steer clear. There were times, Isla felt, she was never away from the house. Every few days, there seemed to be a knock at the door, an arm extended holding a bag of allotment extras, a small jar of honey from the beekeeper who kept hives over the bluff. But not any more. Isla wondered how much she had offended Penny by insisting she talk about Clare that night, insinuating her aunt had been drinking, speculating whether she was suicidal. The more she pondered, the more she began to think she'd been insensitive. She thought about going over there and apologising, but wondered if that would just make it a bigger deal than it actually was. After much thought, she decided to do nothing. Penny would come back when she felt better. Isla wouldn't go knocking at her door, she would give her some space and let the dust settle.

Isla collected an old canvas tote bag, put her purse in the bottom and headed for the village. The tide was out, so she marched over the sand, avoiding Penny's back door. The beach was getting busy now and the seasonal stalls selling inflatables and plastic toys were already established in their usual spots. She left the beach, picking her way through sandy towels and toddlers covered in sun cream. When she reached the road, she walked up the hill away from the bay towards the narrow high street. The grocery store had hardly changed since she was a girl and it was still run by the same family. Wide wooden shelves, tilted at an angle, lined the lower walls of the shop displaying fresh fruit and vegetables in their original crates. Above, there were colourful rows of tinned goods. Isla helped herself to a punnet of strawberries, the air heavy with the scent of a fresh delivery. Above the asparagus bundles, bunched like kindling and tied with string, a fluorescent handwritten label in the shape of a star announced *last of the season*, scribbled in unique grocer's script. The sun came through the window momentarily and bathed everything in a soft warmth, burnishing the skins of apricots and gooseberries, showing up the smears on the window that the cleaner had missed.

The door opened and the coil on the mechanical bell stretched and rang the mechanism. Isla hardly registered who had entered the shop, but the southern accent asking for raspberries, the sharp *clip clop* of a nice pair of sandals made her turn.

'Isla! Am I glad to see you!' She looked different, more put together than the last time they'd met, but the smile seemed superficial and the delicate purple stain that ringed her eyes told her things weren't right.

'Erin?' Isla was stunned. 'What are you doing here?'

Erin looked shifty. She cast her eye around the shop. Mrs Arbles waited patiently behind the counter, openly listening in. 'Can we talk outside?' she said, 'I only came in here for these.' She lifted up her punnet, paid in cash and, to Isla's dismay, waited outside the shop.

What did she want? Why had she come back so soon? Isla scanned the street and couldn't see any sign of the rest of her family. She dreaded seeing the child.

'Friend of yours, is she?' Mrs Arbles asked pleasantly as she packed Isla's groceries into her canvas bag.

Isla pretended to look for her purse.

The bell cheerfully announced Isla's departure and Erin spun around. 'Which direction are you going in?' She talked as if they were old friends.

'Home.' Isla nodded down the hill.

'Do you mind if I walk with you for a bit? It's such a nice day.'

How could she refuse? 'Yeah, sure,' Isla said. 'Are you back in the hotel?' She set off at a brisk pace.

Erin kept up. 'No. We rented a house. For the rest of the summer.'

'Really?' Isla tried to keep the disappointment out of her voice.

Erin laughed, a hollow sound. 'I know how it looks. But we wanted to bring Frankie back. Doctor's orders.'

Isla's stomach dropped. 'Doctor's orders?' she echoed. 'Why?'

'I think we left too quickly. Before she could process everything. And being back home, at the hotel . . . it's difficult. There are so many people coming in and out. It's not very relaxing. She needs to rest. The doctor she's been seeing suggested she came back.'

'Oh, I see.'

'I also want her to meet you, and I'm sure Mark would like to meet you properly too,' Erin added.

Isla felt as if she was in a bad dream. This family lived hundreds of miles away and she had nothing in common with them. Yet here they were, on her doorstep for the foreseeable future, demanding friendship.

'Why don't you come over? To the house we're renting?'

'I'm not sure . . .'

'How about a walk, then? Along the cliff path?'

Isla hesitated.

'Look,' said Erin seriously. 'I wouldn't ask if I didn't think it was important. It might help Frankie if she sees you. Please. I promise I'll stay out of your way afterwards. Just this one meeting. An hour.'

Isla nodded, slowly. What harm would it do? She could say hello to the child and leave after a decent interval. It might exorcise the shame that still pricked her conscience.

Isla stopped walking and looked at Erin. She seemed desperate. A memory of that long-ago afternoon came back: Erin, as a child, fruitlessly trying to retrieve the shell she believed was hers. How quickly her desperation had turned to anger. Isla considered her own part in Frankie's recovery. She hadn't behaved like a model citizen. She owed this family. She owed this child.

'OK, sure. I'll come. Just for an hour.'

Erin's face broke into a smile. 'Fantastic. Come tomorrow. And you'll never have to see us again. I promise.'

Isla nodded her head once more in confirmation and felt an echo of what had gone on before. Erin didn't know it, but their history stretched back further than she supposed. That afternoon, all those years ago, before she had found the wentletrap shell, Erin had stuck herself to Isla like a burr. The same was happening now, she could feel it. And, for all her promises, she felt certain Erin had no intention of leaving her alone.

Chapter Twenty-Eight

Erin

Erin watched Isla walk across the sand for some time before she turned and trudged back up the hill. She didn't know why, but she wanted to cling to this woman. She was so calm, carefree. Owning that beautiful house, living life simply. Nobody relying on her. Erin thought about how complex her own life had become and felt an urge to shed it like an unwanted skin.

The advice Isla had given her that day she came knocking, Erin had remembered every word. She arrived in London after that dreadful car journey home, determined to build up Frankie's trust again, to make her better. Since then, their lives had been filled with medical tests and assessments, some of them as part of an aftercare package set up by Frankie's GP and some of them privately organised by Erin. She hoped Frankie would snap out of the mutism, begin talking after a few weeks, but when she didn't the same thoughts circled in Erin's head, like birds over carrion. Did Frankie blame her for the accident? Was she being punished by her silence? Whatever was going on, it was as if an essential part of her had drained away in that lagoon and Erin had no idea how to get it back.

Erin had sent Frankie back to school, wanting to establish a routine, but after a few days it became obvious she couldn't cope in the classes she had been promoted to. The staff were sympathetic, but they needed to move her back down into her own age group. Several of the parents had come over to commiserate with Erin. But as they spoke to her, she could see that they looked at her with pity and – was she imagining it? Some of them looked a little bit pleased. She was no longer the mum of the high-achiever. She was one of them now. Ordinary, unremarkable.

The various meetings at hospitals and clinics were frustratingly oblique. All the tests performed on her were *within normal limits* or *inconclusive*. Erin wanted to see something, be able to point a finger at an X-ray or a scan and be able to look at the thing that was ruining her daughter's life, but there was nothing there.

Dr Lim, a familiar player in their family drama, tried to explain. 'The neurophysiological examination is inconclusive. It is possible she has suffered some short- or long-term memory loss, from which she may or may not recover. This is perhaps one of the reasons she feels anxious and cannot speak,' he tilted his head slightly, 'although that's not to say she doesn't *want* to speak.' His elucidations were frustratingly oblique.

'How will she ever get back on track at school?' Erin interrupted, trying to get her point across.

'Which brings me to my second point,' Dr Lim continued, steepling his long fingers, sharp elbows on his desk, 'psychologically, she has clearly suffered trauma and while some children are able to experience traumatic events without apparent ill-effects, that cannot be said for everybody. Trauma can disrupt physical as well as emotional development. I think Francesca is already undergoing some form of therapy?'

'Yes,' Erin replied, 'she has a cognitive behavioural therapist once a week.'

'Then I suggest if we cannot pin down anything physically *here*,' he stabbed a slender brown finger at the bundle of documents that had amassed over the past few weeks, 'we must give her emotional state of mind a chance to heal and that can take time and patience.'

'But . . .' Erin protested, desperate for clarity.

'Sometimes it is easy to focus on what patients cannot do. But I would encourage you to laud your daughter's capabilities. Focus on what she *can* do. Maybe she needs a break from all of this.' Once more, he indicated the files in front of him. 'It's not my specialty, but sometimes it can be helpful to go back to the source of trauma. You left pretty quickly after she was discharged from hospital, yes?'

'Of course,' Erin said. 'We wanted her home, among her familiar things. That's what the doctors said to do. Surround her with something familiar.'

'But you live in a hotel, yes? There must be many strangers coming and going?'

'I suppose,' Erin conceded, feeling another pinch of guilt for not giving Frankie a proper home.

'It's just a suggestion. But you could go back to the site of the accident. You said she was having a good holiday before she fell? It might be beneficial for her to return, to understand that it's not as scary as she remembers.'

'Maybe. She was having a lovely time there before it all happened,' Erin conceded.

'It might help her to complete those happy memories, if she isn't making progress at home. You can always come back to London if she deteriorates.'

Erin wasn't sure. She felt she was doing something by hiring a speech therapist and a cognitive behavioural therapist, but when she got back to the hotel and relayed the conversation to Mark, he agreed with Dr Lim.

'I think it's a good idea,' he said as they stood in their cramped kitchen. 'We should go back.'

'You can't afford to leave now. It's coming up to our busiest time.'

'What's Frankie going to think if I stay here? It needs to feel like a holiday, just like before. She'll get anxious if I don't come up. She'll think there's something wrong.'

'I don't think Faisal will be able to deal with everything by himself.'

'I'll get a temp to help him. It shouldn't be difficult.'

'We've only just started making a profit, Mark.'

'Then we'll have to use it, won't we?'

'I don't think stopping all her therapy is going to be helpful. She needs to get over this. She's so behind compared to all the other kids in her class.'

'That's what this is really about, isn't it?'

Erin said, sulkily, 'I don't think taking her out of school is going to help her catch up, no.'

'It's virtually the summer holidays. She'd only be out of school for a few weeks longer than everyone else.'

'She needs all the time she can get. She's lost so much, Mark. Even if she's not speaking, she can listen. I can organise some extra tuition for her in the holidays, get her back on track. I know I can.'

'What are you afraid of? That she'll grow up to be average instead of a genius?'

The silence that followed shocked them both.

'My God, that's it, isn't it?' Mark said, incredulous. 'Your kid is turning out to be just the same as everyone else's and you can't stand it.'

'No . . .'

'Erin, why can't we just aim for happiness? Frankie's happiness? What's wrong with that?'

150

'She needs help, Mark.' Erin winced. He had put his finger on the truth and it hurt. She stood before him, paralysed. His grasp of the situation made her feel the deepest, blackest shame.

She had spent the last six years pushing all her aspirations onto her daughter and it had generated the kind of satisfaction she had not imagined she could experience again.

Frankie was the proof she needed to show the world she was a good mother. With every achievement, Frankie had exonerated Erin. The awful feeling of guilt just after her birth had all but gone, only for it to return tenfold for falling asleep on the beach. It was up to Erin to make it up to her once more. There was a unique bond between her and her daughter. They understood one another. Until now.

She had lost the argument with Mark. Out of spite, she had rented the most expensive house she could find in the village. This experiment would end soon if they couldn't afford it, but she was determined to live somewhere decent while it failed.

Chapter Twenty-Nine

Isla

Isla knew the house. It was one of the nicest in the village. A perfectly proportioned Georgian cottage with its own front garden, symmetrical and neat. It was high on the hill with a view of the bay below. The lagoon was obscured by the church tower, but the sandy shore could be seen as a long, gentle curve, the islands beyond breaking the surface of the water.

Isla walked up the path leading to the front door, which was freshly painted the colour of cornflowers. The owners had edged the path with lavender. It grew happily enough during the summer months, but quickly became woody and thin. Penny had told her once that the owners, who lived somewhere in Manchester, ripped out the plants every year and replaced them with new ones. The waste infuriated the village, who had a low tolerance for incomers.

She rang the bell, feeling sick. She felt an uncomfortable anticipation about being around the child. There might be a presumption about some kind of bond between them, something she didn't wish to foster. She reminded herself she need be there for only sixty minutes and then she could escape and avoid them for the rest of the summer.

Erin opened the door, beaming. She was smartly dressed, hair knotted, face made up. Isla hadn't thought about dressing up and immediately felt at a disadvantage.

'I made lunch,' Erin said smoothly as she led Isla into the back of the house.

'Lunch?' Isla echoed. 'I didn't think . . .'

'We owe you so much. It's the least we can do.'

Isla felt outmanoeuvred.

'Come and meet Frankie. She's in the garden. I'm not sure where Mark's got to.' Erin swept through a cavernous gap at the back of the house. The owners had removed the original windows, knocked out most of the back wall and installed glass-panelled doors which folded back like a concertina. Isla made a mental note to tell Penny, who would be scandalised.

'Frankie, this is Isla, the lady who saved your life.' Erin gently took hold of Frankie's shoulders and spun her round so they were standing face to face.

Isla was uncomfortable, but not as uncomfortable as the girl, who looked as if she would prefer to be anywhere but here.

'Hi.' Isla smiled. 'I don't suppose you remember me very much.'

Frankie stood resolutely at Erin's feet, grabbing on to her mother's dress. The fabric bunched up in her fist and she shook her head, hiding her face in the folds of fabric.

'Frankie, don't do that, my love, you're creasing my skirt.' Erin tried to smooth the fabric down unsuccessfully. 'What do you have to say to Isla? Can you say thank you?' Once more, she turned Frankie gently by her shoulders to face forwards.

Isla, embarrassed, waited for a thank you she did not want nor deserve. 'It's fine, honestly. Let's just forget about it, shall we?'

'Come on, Frankie. We talked about this, remember?' Erin stroked the child's curls as if she was trying to smooth them out too.

'Leave it, Erin.' A low voice broke the moment. Isla jumped and turned round. Mark was leaning against the brickwork of the house. Isla had no idea if he'd only just arrived or been there all along, watching.

'It's just common courtesy, Mark,' said Erin. 'It's not hard to say thank you. We can't let her get away with not talking at all.' Erin dropped her gaze to her daughter and squeezed her shoulders. 'Two words, Frankie, can you say them to Isla?' Her voice was brittle and artificially bright.

Frankie's fist wound the fabric tighter round her knuckles and Isla was reminded of a boxer getting ready for a fight. She suddenly felt an urge to sweep the child up in her arms, run through the door and set her free.

'Why don't we have a drink?' said Mark, ducking into the house.

'Good idea,' agreed Erin, who seemed relieved at the change in conversation. She indicated Isla should follow. 'Shall we? What would you like?'

'Water's fine,' Isla answered.

'Oh I think we can do better than that,' said Erin.

Mark was already opening a bottle of wine. Isla looked at her watch. It was barely past midday. An image of Penny with her hip flask bobbed up in her mind. Is this what people did at lunchtime?

'So you're our knight in shining armour. I'm Mark, by the way.' He extended his hand across the table. 'Red or white?' His words were welcoming, but his gaze made her feel uncomfortable. There was something unfriendly about him.

'Just water, please,' Isla said faintly.

Mark and Erin consumed the bottle of wine remarkably quickly. From the way they both moved around the kitchen, avoiding contact with one another, and the lack of affection in their conversation, Isla guessed their marriage was in trouble before Erin served out the meal. By the time they finished lunch and a second bottle was emptied, it was clear Mark was drunk. Erin put a movie on in the next room and deposited Frankie, who had remained silent throughout the meal, on the sofa with a brown velvet rabbit in her lap. Isla looked at her watch. She had been here for more than ninety minutes.

'How is she doing?' Isla asked, when Erin returned.

'Not very well, actually,' Mark replied, his words uneven.

'Mark,' Erin pleaded a warning that he didn't heed.

'But . . . I thought you said that she was fine?' She turned to Erin, who was staring down at a stain Isla had made on the table-cloth earlier. 'You said yesterday that she needed a break, that's all.' Her stomach descended at sickening speed.

'Erin's wonderful at putting a gloss on things. She used to work in PR, you know,' said Mark.

'I worked in event management, not PR,' said Erin under her breath before she turned to Isla. 'What I said is true. She needs a break. But Frankie isn't quite herself yet. Psychologically, she's struggling and we're trying to figure out how to help her.'

'So it's not permanent?' Isla asked hopefully. She could feel heat gathering inside her body and willed it not to reach her face.

'She has selective mutism. Due to cerebral hypoxia. How long is a piece of string?' Mark said darkly.

Isla looked to Erin for clarification.

'It's hard to explain,' Erin said. 'There's some research on how adults are affected when they have a near-drowning experience, but not much on children. Frankie's been quite withdrawn since the accident and she doesn't want to talk. So we have to wait and see if she gets worse – or better.'

'It would help if we knew exactly how long she'd been in the water before you found her, Isla,' Mark interrupted, 'do you know?'

'I – I didn't see her go in. I just saw her and then – I didn't.' She felt so hot she thought she was going to pass out.

'That's what you said to the paramedics, wasn't it?'

'Mark, what the hell is wrong with you?' Erin scolded. 'You can see it's upsetting Isla to talk about it.' She patted Isla's arm. 'It must have been awful for you, too. I'm sorry.'

Erin stood up and cleared the rest of the table. 'I'm going to see if I can persuade Frankie to have a nap. She's been up since five. Isla, please stay and have a coffee with me when I get back.' She turned to her husband before she left the room. 'Mark, I think you should have a nap too.'

Mark didn't go. He stayed at the table, stroking his wine glass. Isla willed Erin to return. She heard her talking to Frankie in the sitting room, trying to wrestle the remote control out of her grip, reasoning with her in gentle tones.

Mark broke the silence in the kitchen. 'I was there, you know. I saw you.' His fingers brushed the stem of his glass, up and down.

'Sorry?' Isla watched his face take on an unpleasant expression, as if he could smell something bad.

'I was coming back from the coastguard station. Too far away from the lagoon to be of any use to Frankie, but I had a good view of the bay. I saw you running. I watched you run right across the beach. You're quite fast, aren't you?'

Isla didn't answer. She heard Erin carry Frankie up the stairs and into one of the bedrooms above. Their voices muffled and then there was silence as she shut the door.

Mark tapped the tablecloth with his index finger. It was wet and left a damp spot on the fabric. 'And then, quite suddenly, you stopped. I thought maybe you'd hurt yourself, pulled a hamstring. But you were looking at the lagoon wall. Like you'd seen some-thing. So I followed your line of sight, tried to see what had put you off your stride. I couldn't see anything apart from a buoy, floating in the water. And I knew it couldn't be that. You could only see the wall from where you stood, not the water. You were too low down.'

Isla couldn't take her eyes off his tapping finger. It was like he was working everything out in morse code.

'And then, quite suddenly, you shot off. I thought: *that's weird.* But not as weird as when you did a U-turn, straight back to the lagoon. Like a bat out of hell. And when you scrambled up the steps and onto the wall . . . that's when I realised that buoy wasn't a buoy at all. It was Frankie's anorak.'

Mark had a faraway look, as if he was seeing it all again. 'I only started thinking about it properly when we came back here.' His finger began beating out the truth once more on the tablecloth. 'The only way you knew she was in the water was if you'd seen her on the wall first. And if you'd seen her on the wall, you must have known she'd fallen in. That red anorak. It was hard to miss.'

Isla made to speak, but nothing came out. She could barely breathe.

'You have no idea,' he said softly. 'You have no idea what that does to me. Knowing you could have been there faster. Knowing that you *chose* not to help her straight away.'

Isla took a breath. Finally, the words came. 'I went over as fast as I could. As fast as I could. I promise.'

'I don't believe you.'

'I don't know what you want me to say.'

'I want you to say that you didn't hesitate before you went to her. I want you to say that you saw her fall and you didn't wait, because she needed you.' He was pleading with her.

Isla shook her head. 'One minute she was there and the next she was gone. I . . . didn't know what was going on.'

'You were already pumping Frankie's chest when I got there. You shouted at me to give you space.'

'I couldn't think with you there.'

'After a while, you forgot all about me. I could see your lips moving and I thought you were counting, because that's what you're supposed to do, isn't it? You count the compressions. But when I listened, I knew it wasn't that; it was Frankie you were talking to. It was so quiet I could hardly make it out. The same two words, over and over. I didn't understand until now what you meant.'

It was then she remembered the whispered words that fell on Frankie's still face as she tried to save her life. She had forgotten until now. They had tumbled from her lips like an enchantment.

Isla looked at her hands and said, 'I'd better go.'

Suddenly he looked exhausted. 'No, don't do that,' he said. 'We need you. It might actually help Frankie to see you, I don't know. And I suppose . . . she'd be dead if you hadn't got to her first. I need an explanation, that's all. I am . . . grateful . . .' the word was hard for him to say, '. . . for what you did. I just don't understand why you waited.' He rose slowly from the table, swaying slightly.

Isla heard him, feet heavy on the stairs, terrified he was going to tell Erin. She quickly gathered her things and let herself out of the house.

Chapter Thirty

ISLA

She should have known Erin would seek her out, but when the knock at the door finally came two days later, Isla assumed it was Penny and so she opened it, unthinking, with a smile. Her heart sank when she saw who it was. Erin with Frankie, their hair dishevelled by the wind. Frankie was clutching a slim metal contraption that hung around her neck from a ribbon.

'Do you mind if we come in? Just for a minute?' Erin's smile was fixed. Isla wondered what on earth lay behind it. She didn't want Erin in her house again, so she ushered them both onto the patio. 'It's a nice day,' she commented, even though the wind had a bite to it and there were dark clouds rolling in from the west. 'Let's sit outside.' Isla grabbed an old towel that hung on a rusty hook by the door and gave the chairs a wipe. There was a pause when she felt sure Erin was hoping to be offered a drink, but she resisted. She didn't want them hanging around.

'Frankie, why don't you go and play on the sand?' Erin nodded to the beach below. 'While Isla and I have a chat?'

Frankie hesitated, looking at her mother for reassurance. Erin nodded briefly, and Frankie wordlessly took the patio steps to the beach. Erin turned to Isla. 'I'm sorry about the other day. Mark had too much to drink and Frankie didn't want me to leave her. I can't believe you had to let yourself out. You must think I'm a terrible person. I'm so embarrassed.'

Mark hasn't told her, Isla thought to herself. *I can't believe Mark didn't tell her.*

Erin continued, 'I wanted it to be a nice afternoon and it just got ruined somehow.'

'It was fine. You have a lot of stuff to deal with right now. I still got to meet Frankie and Mark. Objective achieved.' *So why have you come to my house?* she wanted to say.

They both lapsed into silence and looked at Frankie, who was carving shapes in the sand with her fingertips. Her hair was tied up and exposed the gentle curve of her neck, the slim ribbon digging in. Even though she was being observed by two adults, she looked alone. For the second time, Isla felt a surprising jolt of tenderness towards her. She remembered doing the same thing at that age, in practically the same spot. She wondered what was going through her young mind.

'It's a Dictaphone,' said Erin, nodding at her daughter.

'What?'

'The thing round her neck. It's a recording device. I thought she could maybe . . . talk into it, if she didn't want to talk to us.'

'Huh. That's a good idea.'

'Borne of desperation,' said Erin, mirthlessly. 'You press a button and it records your voice. Even a whisper. I listen to it at the end of the day when she's sleeping.'

Isla pressed her lips together. 'Look, do you want a drink or something?'

Erin's face broke into another wide smile, but this time it looked genuine, grateful. 'That would be so nice. Frankie! Are you thirsty, darling?'

Frankie looked up, nodded.

'Do you have any juice? Apple or orange? Something like that?' Erin asked.

'Er, yes, I think so.'

'Perfect. Lovely.'

Isla moved into the kitchen and got the drinks. It wasn't so bad, having company. She tipped the rest of the strawberries she'd bought from the greengrocer into a bowl and brought everything out onto the patio.

'So, has the Dictaphone worked yet?' Isla asked.

'No. I'm trying to be patient. But it's hard. Everybody keeps telling me these things take time, but I want my daughter back. I miss her. Honestly, Isla, you should have seen her before . . . She was so inquisitive and clever. Did I tell you she was premature? I was so frightened she was going to . . . anyway, she wasn't, just the opposite in fact, after a few years. They had to move her up several classes at school because she was so ahead.'

Isla could hear the pride in her voice. It made the guilt cut more deeply.

'We were more than just mother and daughter. We were really good friends, you know?'

Erin stopped talking when Frankie approached the patio to drink her juice. After several swift gulps she went back onto the beach, her hand full of strawberries, head low, looking for something on the sand.

'If she doesn't improve soon . . . I just . . .'

'Nobody's said she won't ever talk again, have they?'

'No, but.'

'So you know it's going to happen at some point. Maybe if you stop looking for it all the time. A watched pot never boils. Is that the saying?'

'It's not just that. Frankie's the only good thing in my life. Since the accident, the atmosphere at home's been . . . difficult.'

Isla didn't know what to say.

'Sorry,' said Erin quickly, 'I shouldn't bother you with my problems. It's just . . . We've never understood one another, Mark and I. Not really. Mark thought I wanted to run the hotel with him. I thought we were happy as we were. We seem to have lost the ability to talk to one another.' She smiled sadly. 'That's not a good recipe for marital bliss.'

'And Frankie? Where does she fit into all of this?'

'Part of me thinks she will recover and we will all go back to normal, like waking from a bad dream.'

'And what about the other part?'

'That part of me doesn't want to imagine what will happen if she doesn't. Without Frankie, I don't have an ally any more.'

'Do you need one? An ally?'

'Doesn't everyone?' Erin looked surprised.

Isla shrugged. 'I don't think I've ever had an ally in my life.'

'Not even your mother?'

'Especially not her.'

'I'm sorry to hear that. But what about when you were an adult?'

Isla suppressed a smile. 'Since I came back, my neighbour Penny has been rehabilitating me. She thinks I should get out more.'

'Are you saying that you haven't ever had a relationship? Not even a romantic one?'

If they had known each other for longer, Isla might have told her then something she had never shared with anyone. That she'd been in love with someone once, who seemed to love her back. He was her tutor, though the age gap didn't matter to either of them. She could easily have described to Erin how there was a time

162

in her life she thought a future without him was impossible. She had felt soft, like clay, with him. She had adopted his preferences, moulded to his ideas. Concave to convex. She could have explained right there on the patio about the time she'd thought she was pregnant; that when she told him, his reaction had been unkind. She had been altered by the experience. She'd thought, like him, she hadn't wanted a child, but when the possibility of one had taken shape, when she could imagine the weight of it in her arms, she had changed her mind. In the end, she hadn't needed to go to the clinic he had mentioned. She hadn't even miscarried. Her body had simply made a mistake. When he finally left, all the soft parts inside her hardened until she could never be moulded to anyone else. She got over him, eventually, but the ghost of a child she never had continued to haunt her for years.

All this information – she felt it rise in her throat, struggling for air. She knew Erin would be sympathetic and say the right things. But the habit of not sharing secrets was a hard one to break. 'I always thought that blood ties didn't matter. That when I left here I'd make new friends, make a family of my own. But you can't escape your roots. I even came back to mine.' She gestured at the house behind them. 'My mother and I had a difficult relationship, but here I am, living in her house, trying to unpick a past that wasn't kind. I should be running a mile.'

'What was she like? Your mother?'

'Complicated. She was an artist and spent a lot of time in the roof of the house painting. I didn't see her very much. She was incredibly hands off as a parent.'

'She was a painter? How exciting. My parents are as boring as can be.'

'I think I'd take boring over Astrid.'

'Is that what you do, too? Creative genes often run in families, don't they?'

'Well I used to, when I was little. Penny, the neighbour I mentioned? She told me I was quite good at it, but when your mother is as successful as Astrid was, I never got anywhere. She squashed any ambition I ever had in that direction.'

'But she's not here now to do that, is she?'

'It's a bit late, I think.'

'Wow. For someone who lives in the most beautiful spot on the planet in the most gorgeous house, you're a real pessimist. You should get some revenge. Pick up a paintbrush and do your own thing.'

At that moment, Frankie ran over to Erin, looking anxious. Some kind of silent code passed between them that Isla didn't understand.

'Do you want the loo, my love?' said Erin.

Frankie nodded.

'It's upstairs, Frankie, straight ahead.' Isla pointed through the open door.

'Do you want Mummy to come?' Erin called, but Frankie shook her head and ran into the house.

'We should get going, I suppose,' Erin said eventually. Isla could hear the reluctance in her voice.

They walked onto the beach to wait for Frankie. She had made a pattern with shells and stones, framing it with slim pieces of driftwood and seaweed.

'So this is what she's been up to.' Erin bent down to look at the picture.

'It's pretty.' Isla felt sorry it would be washed away. Again, she felt a nudge of emotion for Frankie. She was touched by what the little girl had done while she and Erin talked. There was something about the way in which way she, too, was an only child, the way she was content to entertain herself on the beach. Even her urge to do something creative like this; it threw her back to her younger self.

Erin straightened up. 'Do you think we have time to cross back over the sand? Or do we have to go on the road?'

Isla looked at the sea and read the waves. 'The tide's beginning to turn. But there's plenty of time. Just don't stray out too far onto the sand or you might get caught on a sandbar. It's easy to do. Walk a direct line from here to the church steeple and you'll be fine.'

Erin touched her arm. 'It's been so nice talking to you. I wasn't sure about coming back here, but I'm changing my mind. It's been a pretty lonely few months.'

Isla felt her cheeks heat up.

'Sorry. I've embarrassed you, haven't I?'

'No. Not at all.' How could she tell her that every time Erin complimented her, she felt doubly awful for those few minutes she hesitated? She looked at Frankie's picture and felt an impulse to make everything right. 'Listen, here's an idea. My mother used to say she could bury all her troubles in the canvas. Maybe Frankie would get something out of it? Painting, I mean.'

Erin shook her head. 'The house we're renting, I don't think they'd be very happy if Frankie set up a paint shop in there. Kids are clumsy at that age. And painting's such a messy business isn't it?'

'What about the garden?'

'I wouldn't want to chance it. We can barely afford the house as it is. We'd lose our deposit.'

'OK. Just a thought.'

Frankie came out of the house.

'You took your time, madam.' Erin reached for her hand and kissed it. 'Say thank you to Isla for having us.'

Frankie looked at Isla. She smiled shyly and gave a small wave.

Isla was charmed. She smiled too and gave a little wave back. They set off and Isla turned back into the house. Erin was so sure of herself, coming here and knocking on the door. She had the same feeling as last time, when Erin first came to the house. That resistance to being in her company, that feeling of being worn down, and, finally, when she'd gone, a surprise that it had all turned out to be fine.

As soon as she closed the back door behind her, she felt something was different. The light in the house was brighter, somehow. Frowning, she walked into the hallway and realised the light was pouring down from above. The studio door must be open. She was sure she had locked it. She walked up the stairs, wondering when she'd last been up there. Sure enough, the door was wide open; light from the roof windows filled the stairwell. Frankie must have opened the door thinking it was the toilet. Isla was about to close it again to lock it up, when she heard a noise, a scraping sound, like fingernails on a blackboard. She stopped, her heart a wild animal scrambling desperately in her chest. A slow smell of something brackish and sour enveloped her, something dirty and dead. For a moment, she lost her balance, and she clutched the bannister, swaying with the effort to stay upright. Then she steadied herself and tried to rationalise what was happening. Was there something on the roof outside? It could be a couple of gulls sliding on the slate, their claws unable to grasp the stone. She waited, hoping to hear their squabbling cry. Because if the noise didn't come from the roof, then it must have come from inside the house.

She forced herself to walk up the stairs even though her heart begged her not to. The air in here had been disturbed; she couldn't say why or how. Something had left a trace of itself, unsettling the atmosphere like ripples on a lake. Halfway up the stairs, her head came level with the floor. It was as empty as it always had been. Nothing seemed amiss. But when she came to the top of the stairs, there was something on the long wooden table under the window. A picture. A sketch in charcoal and pencil. An angry face scowling out of yellowed paper, smudged and scratched with lead. It was a powerful drawing, almost a caricature, and Isla knew it could only have come from Astrid's hand. She picked it up and examined the face. It was a woman, her dark hair rising up like snakes. She looked almost witch-like. With her heart beating furiously, Isla flipped over the picture, wanting her suspicions confirmed. Sure enough, in Astrid's writing, there was a message inscribed on the reverse.

Chapter Thirty-One

Erin

By the time they got home, the sky had turned to winter. The weather here was unpredictable and it looked like rain. Shivering, Erin heated up a pizza for Frankie, ran her a bath, read her a story and put her to bed. There was no sign of Mark. She looked in the fridge and the only thing she felt like having in there was a bottle of wine. She pulled it out and reached, without looking, for a glass in the cupboard above her head.

Throughout their university years and into their work life, Mark and Erin had always celebrated and greased the wheels of disappointment with alcohol. Running a hotel meant supplies were plentiful. Mark was always the first to suggest they open a bottle. He was the first to finish his glass, the first to pour another. She hadn't worried about it; had assumed they would deal with it together if it became a bigger problem. But there was always a reason to pull the cork: grief at losing his parents, money worries, difficult guests, celebrating Frankie's various milestones. Now this: a persistent feeling of hostility that permeated their relationship. A deep sorrow dividing them in the shape of a daughter they couldn't heal. Erin had noticed that his reliance on a bottle of wine to solve his problems was beginning to contaminate her as well.

'I'll have one of those,' said Mark ungraciously when he returned.

'Where have you been?'

'Trying to make phone calls. There's no reception here. You have to walk right over the other side of the hill.' His words were slow and too carefully spoken.

'Let me guess,' said Erin, 'you popped into the pub on the way back.'

'You can talk.' He indicated the bottle on the table.

'Whatever.'

They sat opposite one another and drank. Nobody made dinner because nobody could be bothered. So they drank some more and they argued and they wept for their daughter and for themselves. Even through the fog of booze, Erin knew it was the beginning of the end.

She left the table first, feeling sick. The bedroom window had been left open and she closed it, shivering in the cold. It was close to midnight and the view over the bay was briefly, sharply etched in silver before the clouds diffused the moonlight. She pulled the curtains together, the view bringing her no joy. When had she started disliking her life so much? Brief memories surfaced of late nights in London, coming home in black cabs, buzzing with the happy energy of an event well planned and well executed. She missed working in a team. There was no camaraderie in her life. She felt so alone. A horrible thought wormed through her. Frankie wasn't going to get better. Her marriage wasn't going to get better. Her talent was to plan events, create contingencies. But she hadn't planned for any of this; it had all crept up on her like a nightmarish game of grandmother's footsteps.

She stumbled to the bathroom and cleaned her teeth, washed her make-up off and brushed her hair. She looked at herself in the mirror. She was past forty, but still beautiful. There was time, but it was closing in. Hard decisions needed to be made soon.

On the floor below, she heard Mark snoring on the sofa and knew she would, at least, have the bed to herself tonight. Erin went into Frankie's room and watched her sleep, wondering if she was mute in her dreams. *Why won't you talk to me?* she thought sadly as she watched her daughter's eyelids flutter in the darkness. *Don't you love me any more?*

She crouched down to pick up the clothes Frankie had discarded on the floor, folding them up neatly and stacking them on a chair. A small oblong of reflected light exposed something she'd missed, and Erin caught the ribbon in her fingertips and retrieved the Dictaphone. She crawled into bed, pulling the duvet up to her chin, and then she pressed *'Play'*, holding the machine up to her ear like a shell. She was used to the disappointment of not hearing Frankie's voice, but she had recently taken to recording the sounds of the village and Erin liked to hear her audio diary of their day. She listened to the seagulls; the rattle of stones as the waves drew back from the beach; she heard her own voice, muffled, talking to Isla on the patio and smiled to herself, wondering if Frankie was trying to eavesdrop. Erin closed her eyes and counted her blessings. Her daughter was alive and well, she had found a friend in Isla. It had been a good day.

There was a shuffling sound on the Dictaphone, directions from Isla as to where the toilet was. Little footsteps running into the house, mounting the stairs. A pause and then a silence. Then, very faintly, the turn of a key in a lock and the slow tread of feet on another set of stairs. A small exhalation. Then a voice.

Chapter Thirty-Two

PENNY

Penny had been avoiding Isla successfully for weeks. Several times, she'd put her cardigan on and reached for the door, determined that this would be the day she told Isla everything. But something always stopped her. Her headaches were getting worse. She would sense the heavy feeling behind her eyes and the pain would be upon her more quickly than before. Retreating to the sofa with a couple of pills was the only thing she could do. The pain was tangible, something she could ease with medication. The other thing stopping her was more tricky. A feeling she was being prevented. A pressure exerted from an external force, something beyond her control. No sooner had she thought to herself *today's the day* than she felt a coiled energy unfurl, pressing her back into the house. It frightened her. She couldn't call Jacob. He'd sent her to Coventry and she was dammed if she would break it first. She knew it would be over if she didn't do as he said and he was the only thing in her life that was keeping her sane.

She didn't expect Isla to come to her. She didn't expect that at all. But Isla came with an apology and a drawing she hadn't seen for years.

'Penny, I know you think I overstepped the mark when you and Jacob came for dinner and I'm sorry about that. I don't want to upset you, asking about Clare, but I've found this and you're the only person who can shed any light on it.'

Penny had been asleep on the sofa and her defences were down. She was sure her cheek had crease marks from the seam of the cushion. She touched her chin, hoped she hadn't been drooling. But when she saw the picture she forgot about her own dignity.

'Oh dear,' she said. 'Yes, I remember that.'

'What does it mean?'

'I don't think Astrid was talking to Clare at that point, so she drew pictures instead. It was the only way she could communicate.'

Isla turned the picture over. There was an inscription:

Clare,

Look in the mirror and bring me my sister back.

'It's a horrible, horrible picture, with a nasty message,' said Isla. 'I thought Astrid loved Clare, why would she do something like this? It doesn't make sense.'

'You and I don't have siblings, Isla, but sisters don't always get on.'

'You told me Clare was loved by everybody. That Astrid adored her.'

'Astrid would have done anything for Clare. Anything. But sometimes Clare could be . . .'

'What?'

'Careless with other people's feelings. She was very used to getting her own way. Astrid was younger than Clare and I guess when they were little she toed the line. But after Nell died, I think she resented being told what to do by her big sister.'

'Astrid told me she always uncovered the truth in her paintings. Always the truth.'

'Yes,' said Penny quietly. 'I know.'

'So what does this mean? Is this the real Clare?' Isla waggled the paper in front of Penny's face.

'It means that people aren't perfect, Isla.' Penny made a noise of frustration. 'This is why I get irritated. There's never any room for subtlety with you, is there? Life isn't black and white, good and evil. People are complex, contradictory beings, and sometimes we do things that don't make sense. For your information, Clare could be beastly and, yes, Astrid gave as good as she got.'

Isla looked crushed. 'What do you mean, she could be beastly? The whole village loved her. They said she was kind.'

'She was manipulative. And she sometimes went back on a promise. But she could also be a wonderful human being, just like Astrid was. I sometimes think you want to see all the good in Clare and all of the bad in Astrid. They weren't one or the other, Isla, they were both.'

'But that's my point. I don't remember any of the good. I only remember the bad things, the missed opportunities, the things that didn't happen. Can you blame me for wanting to find out about the good people in my family? I'm sick of thinking about the bad stuff all the time. I want to make a life here. I want to start building something positive for myself. The memories that Astrid left me with . . . they can't be my legacy. I won't let them.'

'Then perhaps you should stop looking at the past. What good is it doing you?'

'Because I want to know the truth, Penny. There's a reason Astrid never spoke about Clare. They both died bizarre deaths.

Sure, that might be a coincidence but something feels wrong about all of this. Astrid hid her life away and now it's coming back to haunt me, bit by bit.'

The conversation didn't go the way Penny wanted. She should have told Isla everything then, but the moment slithered away from her grasp like an eel. When she heard herself telling Isla she should stop looking at the past, she could have kicked herself, because Penny needed the opposite to happen. The truth had to be aired. But when Isla said she was sick of thinking about the bad things, Penny didn't want to add to her burden. It seemed wrong. It all seemed so wrong. Penny was caught between a rock and a hard place, between Astrid and Clare, between Isla and Jacob. No wonder her head hurt.

She walked through the house and sat on the steps leading down to the sea. The tide was in and the water looked grey and miserable. What was she going to do? She drew her cardigan around her middle and stared into the water, hearing it slap against the steps, feeling the throb of a headache emerging in her temple. She couldn't carry on like this, that was certain. Something needed to give.

Despite her age, there was something about Isla that was very childlike. She had stopped looking up to Penny, unquestioning and full of trust. She had begun to push back. She imagined how the conversation would go if she told her the truth about Astrid and Clare. She imagined the look on Isla's face as her faith in Penny disintegrated and she knew she couldn't do it. This was a lonely place. She couldn't afford to lose another friend. There had to be another way of telling Isla the truth. Penny watched the clouds rolling in from the west. Fat, warm raindrops fell into the sea. The gulls scattered and left the sky. She didn't blame Astrid for making that picture. It was better than having a row. She recalled that when

Clare saw it, tacked to her bedroom door, it had actually been a force for good. Penny remembered the relief in Astrid's voice when she relayed that she was going to college after all.

Penny nodded to herself and stood up. She would take a leaf out of Astrid's book. She would commit the truth to paper and hope that Isla would understand.

Chapter Thirty-Three

ISLA

The little village had transformed from when she was a girl. Now, beside the shops where you could buy the staples, there was a smart cafe, several gift shops, and the small gallery that Astrid despised. Isla walked halfway up the hill to the high street, thinking about the conversation she'd had with Penny. It had felt like an argument at the time, but now she'd had a few days to mull it over, she began to wonder if she wasn't looking at Astrid through an unforgiving lens. Penny had a point. People weren't black and white. She certainly wasn't. She shouldn't expect Clare to be squeaky clean. And maybe, just maybe, she had to start reframing the way she remembered Astrid. Isla tried to imagine what it must have been like to put your ambitions in the hands of a sibling. But she had no siblings, so it was impossible.

She put the charcoal picture away in a drawer; she couldn't bear to look at it again. She also couldn't stop thinking about how it had suddenly appeared. Isla had torn that house apart and put it back together with her bare hands. There was no corner she hadn't peered into. Frankie must have gone up into the studio and found it, or she'd found it elsewhere and taken it up. But where had she discovered it? And how do you get a mute girl to talk? If she could get Frankie alone, gain her trust, she felt sure she could get to the bottom of the mystery.

Isla turned down a side street, hoping the shop she was looking for was still there. When she came to the right place, she was taken aback to see it had tripled in size. It was a tiny, dark place when she was little; cluttered shelves tightly packed in an order only the owner understood. It looked like they had bought the shop space either side of the original and knocked everything through. Now it had an enormous window with a huge display of art supplies. The door was propped open by a giant fake tube of paint and spotlights illuminated display cases containing brushes and tools. She stepped in, trying to square this vision of modernity with the Aladdin's cave of her youth.

'If you need any help, just let me know, OK?' A middle-aged man refilling a paint display with new tubes of gouache called to her from the back of the shop.

'I do need some help, actually. I'm looking for a painting set. For a beginner.'

'Watercolours, oils or acrylic?' The man clambered to his feet and joined her in the middle of the shop.

'Probably watercolours? They're easiest, aren't they?'

'Yeah. Cheaper, too. Let's have a look. Follow me.'

He led her to the side of the shop where the watercolour sets were laid out in size, from tiny portable tins that could fit in a pocket to huge wooden boxes holding hundreds of colours.

'Is it a gift?' he asked.

'Good question,' she answered. 'I haven't quite worked that out yet.'

'Hang on,' he said, looking at her, 'you're not . . . Isla, are you? Isla Jarsdel?'

She turned to look at him. He had an intense, amused expression on his face. 'Yes, I am. Who's asking?'

'Don't you remember me? We were at school together. My parents used to run this place.'

'Of course . . .'

'Daniel.'

'Daniel. Danny. I remember now.'

'I heard you were staying in Astrid's place. My condolences, by the way. If that's appropriate.'

'Ha. Right, thanks. You remember what she was like then.'

'I do. A force to be reckoned with. But we owe her. She's responsible for bringing this shop into the twenty-first century.'

'Really?' Isla looked around, unable to square the clean modernity with Astrid's aesthetic.

'She used to order her supplies through us and criticised our stock all the time when she came to pick them up. When the shop passed to me, I started listening. She told me what we needed to stock for the serious artists who come here to paint as well as the tourists and locals. We have a loyal customer base. A lot of mail order now, thanks to her.'

'I had no idea she was so helpful,' said Isla, puzzled.

Danny laughed, 'Oh don't run away with that impression. She was still rude and impatient. But we got on very well in the end. I heard she stopped painting, but she started coming in again for oils and canvas a couple of years ago, so I guess she couldn't keep away.'

Isla was intrigued. 'Did she? Are you sure they were for her own use?'

'Yeah. Who else would it be for? She wasn't big on buying gifts.'

Isla was confused. 'It's just, I can't find any of her recent work. The house is empty. Do you know what she did with her work once she'd finished?'

178

Danny dug his hands into the back pockets of his jeans. 'I have absolutely no idea. She never took me into her confidence. I wouldn't put it past her to pile it on a bonfire and burn the whole lot, though. She was never one for sharing. The gallery here would have given their eye teeth for an exhibition of her work.'

Isla suppressed a giggle. 'Apparently she never liked that place.'

'I can see why. It's a bit twee. But she could have changed that, you see. She never wanted to get involved, though. Always kept herself to herself. A shame really.'

'Yeah.'

'You were quiet, too, as I recall. But you aren't the same as her.'

Isla looked at him in surprise. 'Aren't I?'

'Nope.' He shook his head. 'I'm sorry she won't be darkening my door again, but I'm glad you're back.' He looked at her in mock suspicion. 'Or are you selling up? I heard you've renovated her place single-handed. Impressive, by the way.'

Isla felt an unexpected jolt of happiness at the compliment. 'I'm not selling up. I'm going to stay.'

'Well that's good news.'

Danny brought out some watercolour sets for Isla to look at and talked about the quality of the paint. 'There's still a few of us around, from school I mean,' he said after a while. 'Some left and came back, some never went away at all. We're usually in the White Lion on a Friday evening, if you fancy company. It's not exactly disco central where you are.'

Isla chose sable brushes, mindful Astrid would not approve of nylon. She bought two watercolour pads, one large, one small, the paper creamy and thick. She chose a set of paints that looked as inviting as a box of chocolates, and, after promising Danny she wouldn't be a stranger, she marched the whole lot to the top of the hill where she knew she would find Frankie.

Chapter Thirty-Four

ERIN

Erin hadn't spoken about the voice on the Dictaphone. She couldn't make out the words. She couldn't even tell if it was Frankie, but as Isla lived alone it had to have been her. Erin played it over and over again. It was just a few whispers, but they formed words; she was certain. The knowledge felt so fragile that when she pictured telling Mark, confronting Frankie, she knew the progress Frankie had made would collapse. So she kept the news to herself and, every evening, played the Dictaphone when Frankie was asleep and listened for more.

But nothing more happened. They went for walks and Frankie recorded the high winds on the cliff and the call of the gulls as they surfed the thermals. They got caught in a downpour and Frankie recorded the low growl of thunder and the rain racing in the gutters down the high street. She recorded the bees harvesting pollen from the gorse over the bluff. But at the end of every day, the thing that Erin wanted to hear most was missing.

Perhaps now was the time to think about leaving for London. Contrary to his promises, Mark was spending most of the day not with them but on the phone to Faisal. Maybe he would be glad to get back if she suggested it. She assumed she wouldn't see Isla again, so when she rolled up to the house with a bag of art supplies, inviting Frankie to come to her house to paint, Erin's first reaction was pleasure. Isla wanted to be friends after all. But it became clear the offer was for Frankie only, not her as well. Erin experienced a twinge of annoyance. She had already explained to Isla that she didn't want Frankie to get into all of that, but when Isla had opened the box of watercolours she'd seen Frankie's face light up. It was the first time she'd looked so enthusiastic for weeks. She'd been outmanoeuvred by both of them. It pained her to think it, but she wondered if Frankie went back to Isla's house, if perhaps she was away from her mother's gaze, she might find her voice again.

So Erin agreed to bring Frankie over and leave her there for the afternoon. Isla had set up a table with paints, water, a roll of kitchen paper and a set of paintbrushes.

'This looks very professional,' Erin said as they walked up the steps from the sand and onto the patio.

'Buy cheap, buy twice. That's the saying, isn't it?' said Isla. She looked unusually animated.

'I thought you didn't paint any more.'

'I don't. But I remember some of the things about technique that Astrid taught me. I can pass that on to Frankie. She'll have a good time, even if she doesn't want to learn anything. We can just make a mess, can't we?'

Frankie didn't reply, but Erin felt her pull away from her hand; her daughter straining to inspect the table laden with colours. And did she imagine it? Straining to get away from her. Erin had the feeling she was being exposed somehow. Next to Isla, she felt dull and unimaginative.

'Well, I'll leave you to it, I suppose,' Erin said. 'Bye, Frankie.'

Frankie turned her head, only slightly, to acknowledge her mother, but her eyes stayed on the table.

Erin turned to walk back over the sand. She couldn't help it, but a part of her hoped that Frankie wouldn't like painting after all; that she would want to stay with her. She ran her eyes over the horizon, the beach, the cliffs, the village, the lagoon, and she knew where she was headed. Frankie hadn't wanted to go near the lagoon when they returned and Erin hadn't wanted to make her. But that afternoon, with Frankie out of her hair for a few hours, Erin couldn't help herself. She had felt its dark pull ever since they'd returned, like a shadow under a bed.

It wasn't a long walk, a few hundred metres at most, but each step wrought a weight upon her. The sea-wall was curved. It wasn't possible to see where she'd fallen asleep from here, but she could see the length of the journey Frankie had taken to the place on the sea-wall where she had mounted the steps. She remembered waking up: that horrible, sickening feeling. The split second of clarity; the realisation she was about to become a different person when she mounted those steps to find Frankie. As she reached the top of the wall and saw how far Frankie had walked by herself, the audacity of her daughter's journey filled her with a melancholy pride. Frankie's sense of independence had always been strong. Erin walked along the wall to the spot she was sure Frankie had fallen and stared at the black surface of the water for a long time, wishing for the past to change.

Erin's mother and father had insisted on Frankie being baptised. Mark and Erin weren't religious, but it mattered to her parents and there was a history of churchgoing in both families so they relented. Erin saw in her mind's eye the perfect form of Frankie, three months old, held aloft over the font, anointed with water.

Thank you, Father, for the water of baptism.
In it we are buried with Christ in his death.
By it we share his resurrection.
Through it we are reborn by the Holy Spirit.

If she believed in God, she might have thought that Frankie had been taken from her as punishment for her vanity. For she believed that she'd been robbed. She'd been vain, she admitted that. Did God punish you for loving your child too much? Was it more pious to affect a level of detachment? She wondered if the world had conspired to teach her a lesson. She wondered if she had learned that lesson, and what would happen next.

Moving slowly, she completed the length of the sea-wall and descended near to the place where she'd sat down on that crisp and sunny morning with her book. She wondered where the paperback had gone. Her bag and shoes had been gathered up and returned to the village hotel by a thoughtful local, but the book was absent. It must have been left behind in the panic. It was a stupid story, something frivolous. She couldn't believe she had wanted to read that more than she had wanted to play with her daughter.

It was low tide, just as it had been that day, and she found the spot where they'd made that beautiful sand city together. How long had it lasted, with the delicate shells and tracery of seaweed carefully laid around each base by little fingers? She imagined it being dismantled by lapping waves, drawing Frankie's treasures back into the water as she lay on a hospital gurney being resuscitated by a team of medics.

Erin made herself sit in the same spot, her back against the same stone, and she wept for what might have been. Not many people noticed her huddled in the shadow of the lagoon. Those who did swiftly averted their eyes.

Almost every day, she dropped Frankie off at Isla's to paint. At first, Erin didn't know what to do with the spare time. But, gradually, she reacquainted herself with the idea that she could choose how to fill her afternoon. Mark used the time to work, setting up his laptop on the kitchen table, the lack of phone mast and temperamental Wi-Fi forcing him to make phone calls on the other side of the hill. She walked the cliff path, alive with insects and wildflowers, and thought about her future. She found the local library and resurrected her CV. She emailed some old contacts who would be prepared to take her on again. She felt excited, for the first time in ages, about her future.

But the excitement gradually turned to something else when she saw what was going on between Frankie and Isla. She had hoped Frankie would record the lessons so she could hear them at night. But when she listened the first couple of times, there was silence. Frankie had switched the device off. When Erin asked her about it, she just shrugged. At the end of the day, Frankie presented her with pictures, not words, and this wasn't what Erin had hoped for. So she took charge. She dropped Frankie off, she took the Dictaphone from her neck and placed it on the table. As she said goodbye, she quietly pressed the 'Record' button, covered it with a sheet of paper and left them to it.

The first few times, when she settled down in bed to listen, it was all Isla, telling Frankie what to do. But she didn't talk like a teacher. She explained that painting was personal; there were no rules. There was no right nor wrong. She heard her making encouraging noises, explaining what the paint would do if you added more water, rubbed it with a tissue, used a finer brush. She talked about how the colour of the sea was never flat, how it changed where the sea met the sky into a more intense blue on a sunny day, but faded to nothing when the mist came in. They disappeared to collect stones and shells, the Dictaphone automatically switching off when there was no sound to record, but it came back on again when they both returned with treasures from the beach. The two of them observed the shadows that fell across their forms. Erin heard Isla explain that shadows are never black, they were always filled with colour, you just had to look harder to find it. Isla described how mistakes were sometimes gifts, that unexpected things happened when you gave up control. Erin could hear them splashing water across the paper, seeing how it would draw the colours together. She heard them tear off wads of tissue from the roll to mop up the mess. Yet again, she had the feeling of being shown up. The hours she had spent reading to Frankie, teaching her numbers, it all seemed so feeble next to this riot of imagination.

And then she heard Frankie giggle.

Erin sat up in bed and rewound the device, playing that giggle over and over. She gasped in delight at the sound of it, but the feeling was quickly extinguished by a wave of melancholy that she hadn't been the one to make her daughter laugh, Isla had.

A few days later, words followed. A *yes* and a *no*. An *uh-oh*. But what Erin couldn't get over was the fact that Isla ignored the progress Frankie was making. She carried on talking as if Frankie was still mute. And it seemed to work. Frankie began to say more; just a few words, here and there, in a low whisper at first, and then in louder, longer sentences. Every time she came back from Isla's, she could hardly wait to get her daughter to sleep so she could listen to the recording she had made. She sat in bed, Mark snoring on the sofa below, eavesdropping on the intimate moments of Frankie's day, feeling more and more left out. It wasn't just that Frankie had chosen to talk to Isla, it was that Isla was also behaving differently when Erin wasn't around.

Erin wasn't stupid. She knew Isla hadn't been enthusiastic about them coming back – she could read it all over her face in the grocery store. Erin had tried hard to bring Isla into her confidence. She always made a point of having a chat when she came to pick Frankie up. But Isla was guarded whenever Erin tried to be intimate. There was always the feeling that Isla was holding something back, keeping secrets from her. But whenever Erin listened in to the recordings, this didn't happen with Frankie. Isla was spontaneous, funny even. She gossiped about Penny, her neighbour, she talked about when she was a little girl. Her conversation had a lightness that Erin never experienced. It was clear that whenever Erin had a chat with Isla, she got the edited version. When she spoke to Frankie, there was an intimacy between them that made her afraid.

She thought back to her own, clumsy attempts at getting Frankie to talk and felt ashamed. Isla made it sound so easy. A small seed of spite planted itself in Erin's heart and she tried not to nurture it, but it couldn't be helped. Why did Frankie want to talk to this woman, someone who seemed so broken? What was she giving Frankie that she, Erin, couldn't provide?

Suddenly, the label *selective mutism* seemed very cruel. Frankie had selected a stranger to talk to, not the person who loved her the most. The pleasure of hearing her daughter speak was poisoned with the pain of knowing it wasn't meant for her ears. Was Frankie somehow transferring her affection onto this woman? She'd seemed so grown up since she stopped talking, it was as if Frankie had started travelling on a different path away from her, one that Isla understood how to navigate but Erin couldn't follow.

The feeling she'd had of fragility, of everything hanging by a thread, persisted. Erin felt certain if she let Frankie or Isla know she was listening in to their conversations at the end of the day, they would become stilted, artificial. The gratification came from hearing something unself-conscious.

So Erin didn't ask. Instead, she waited for Isla to tell her what was happening. She waited for several days, then several more. Nothing was said. Erin acknowledged the betrayal and pushed it to one side. She would deal with it in her own way, in her own time.

Chapter Thirty-Five

ISLA

Isla had told Erin she bought Frankie that watercolour set on a whim. But, really, it was a small act of defiance. Although Astrid and Erin were different on the surface, Isla could see there was something that drew them together. An attitude that it was only their opinion that mattered. That things should be done according to their rules. She could see Erin loved Frankie to distraction, but there was flint at the heart of her, the same thing that Isla had seen in Astrid, something that wouldn't bend. There was a kinship between her and Frankie, she felt it running through them both: the same, sad faultline. The same kind of loneliness.

As she showed Frankie how to use the paints, the watercolour lessons Astrid had given her when she was a child broke the surface of her memory. It surprised Isla to recall that it hadn't always been a catalogue of derision from Astrid – she had taught her skills that Isla hadn't forgotten. Maybe Astrid had been softer with her when she was young and eager to please and it was when she began to paint in her own way, get her own ideas, that Astrid had resented this departure. The image of the painting she ruined and left at the door of the studio came back to her. Is that what being a mother felt like? To have absolute control over someone's life and then to have to learn to relinquish it? Isla remembered the anger she'd provoked in Astrid and she saw the same brand of fire behind Erin's eyes. Frankie, she thought, must be shown there was another way. When it became obvious that Frankie loved to paint, she felt a point had been made and a small surge of satisfaction rose up in her. When Frankie began to speak, it was like watching something miraculous unfold and that surge turned into a fierce swell of pride. She was proud of herself for being the catalyst and proud of Frankie for having the courage to speak. She knew instinctively it was something that shouldn't be mentioned, not least to Frankie. She knew she had to pretend nothing of significance had occurred. Even so, every time the girl said a little more, Isla had to stop herself from leaping on the table and doing a little dance.

Several times, Isla tried to ask her about the drawing of Clare she had found in the studio. But each time the words formed in her mouth, they sounded like an accusation. Frankie would have known the studio was private because the door was locked. If Isla wanted to know where the picture had come from, she would have to tell Frankie she knew she'd been snooping up there. However she phrased it, it felt like the kind of allegation Erin would make. So the question remained unspoken, and the time they spent together felt like a restorative process. It wasn't solely that she was giving something to Frankie, teaching her to paint; she was getting something in return. She would never have children; she had come to terms with that many years ago. But being with Frankie felt like she was getting a second chance. Her past with Astrid would never be reconciled. It hadn't occurred to her she could be healed by someone else, someone completely unconnected.

When Erin picked Frankie up at the end of the day, it always felt as if the spell was broken. Isla could tell she wanted some kind of a report, another exchange of intimacies. But Isla couldn't do it.

She saw the words that Frankie formed as tender objects that would break if handled badly. If Frankie wanted to show her mother she could talk, that was her decision and hers alone. So she remained quiet, with the knowledge that she now kept two secrets from Erin, the first concerning the wentletrap and the second concerning her daughter. Isla hoped she was doing the right thing. Secrets only stacked up so high until they toppled and spilled. But something was happening between her and Frankie and all her instincts told her she had to preserve it. When Frankie left at the end of the day, Isla could close her eyes and still conjure up the weight and shape of her. She saw her in snatches, burned on her retina; the curve of her fingers around a brush, the tip of her tongue escaping from lips, pursed in concentration. The images brought about an ache that made Isla wonder if she was mourning her own childhood or the child she never had. All she knew for sure was that it wouldn't fully go away until the little girl came back to her.

They would begin with the same routine. They both waited for Erin to leave and then Isla opened the paintbox, cleaning any colours off that needed it with a damp tissue. The smell of the paint filled her with nostalgia for a childhood she couldn't quite recall, but it was beginning to come back, in small pieces, after every lesson she gave. Mindful of the way Erin smothered Frankie with attention, Isla deliberately left Frankie to it, choosing instead to emphasise the idea that rules were made to be broken. Frankie had begun with hesitation, worried about doing the wrong thing. But after they'd spent the day making deliberate mistakes, seeing how the paint ran across paper with a spill of water, dropping blobs of colour on the page, Frankie had begun to anticipate how the paint would behave, and some unschooled instinct in her understood how to control it just enough.

After a few lessons, Isla had begun to watch Frankie paint with growing interest. For a girl who had lost her attention span, it was curious how long she could focus on this activity. It was also a puzzle that she didn't make the usual mistakes that beginners did. Her colours never muddied, she covered the paper with confident strokes. After a few suggestions of what to paint that day, Frankie began to shake her head, deciding what she wanted to do with a clarity that was older than her years. At first, the shapes she made began typically – a house, her family, a collection of animals. But recently these shapes had grown into something less obvious, something that drew uncomfortable parallels. Isla began to watch the process of Frankie translating what was going on in her head onto paper.

Today, Frankie's arm moved with assured, steady strokes. She had been working on the same painting for half an hour and hadn't once stopped to fidget. She hadn't even paused to admire her own work, which was shaping up into something both beautiful and sinister.

'Are you painting the sea, Frankie?' Isla asked.

Frankie nodded, not looking up. Her face had no expression. It was as if she were in a trance.

Isla looked at the picture and saw it wasn't the view of what lay in front of them, it was an alternative vision of something that lodged in Frankie's head. Layers of blue and green reached down the paper into an inky, bottomless black. In the corner, a stray hair had fallen onto the wet paint, trapped in a dark tangle. It gave Isla the creeps. 'I can take this off for you if you like,' she said, reaching over. But Frankie's hand shot out and grabbed her wrist in an unusual act of intimacy. Her grip was vice-like and stronger than Isla could have imagined.

'Leave it,' said Frankie darkly. 'It belongs there.'

The shock of her words chilling the atmosphere, the strength of Frankie's grip sent Isla away. She ran to the bathroom, closed the lid of the toilet and sat there for some time.

It was too ridiculous. There was no connection between Frankie and Astrid. Isla must have imagined the tone of voice, and a hair falling onto a table was hardly unusual. She chided herself for being superstitious, and rubbed her wrist where Frankie had gripped it. There was a faint red mark, nothing much to speak of, but as Isla drew her arm up to inspect it, the unmistakeable smell of roses filled the air.

Chapter Thirty-Six

Isla, September

Isla could feel Erin's resentment growing by the day, and she struggled to keep the bond she and Frankie had formed away from her penetrating gaze. Under Erin's observation, the instinct to distance herself from the Baker family gathered strength. The only thing stopping her was Frankie. The summer would draw to an end, eventually, and Erin would take her back. After spending years without any family to speak of, Isla had found herself in the middle of one and the idea of Frankie leaving was beginning to cause her an unfamiliar anxiety. She blamed herself. It was no good, getting close to people. They couldn't be relied upon.

Her thoughts turned to London once more and the possibility that Astrid's old art dealer, Edward, might know something about the rumours of her missing work. He might know something about Clare. He may even have met her. If she couldn't ask Frankie just yet, she could ask him instead. There had been no sign of Penny, so Isla scribbled a note, telling her she was going to London and would be back in a few days. She posted the note through Penny's door and set off down the road. The tide was high and the sea flooded over the edge of the lagoon, obscuring the stone wall. The angle of the sun gave the water a flat metallic sheen, the edges lapping mercury against the path to the village. The tide wouldn't be out for a couple of hours. Getting to Erin's house would take longer, but Frankie deserved to know what her plans were, first-hand. It didn't seem right just to leave without a word. When she reached the house and knocked on the door, it was Mark that answered – not Erin.

'They aren't here,' he said. 'They've gone to the churchyard to pay their respects to Erin's auntie.'

'Oh.' Isla was crestfallen.

'You can go and catch them up, but she said something about bringing back some fish and chips and I'm not sure which fish bar they were planning on going to.'

'I wanted to tell them I'm leaving tomorrow. For London. I won't be able to have Frankie for the next few days.'

'Where are you staying?' Mark asked.

Isla hadn't thought that far ahead.

'Erin offered you the use of our hotel, didn't she?'

'Yes. But it seems a bit odd to stay there when you're both here.'

'Well, that's not actually going to be the case. I have to go back for a few days myself. There's some trouble with the temporary manager and I need to sort it out. I was going to leave this evening to avoid the traffic. I'll give you a lift? And you can have the room, it's fine.'

'Um . . . I'm not sure.'

'Look. Forget about what I said that time. I got a bit carried away. Erin tells me you and Frankie get on like a house on fire. Frankie seems much happier since she met you.'

Isla smiled, she couldn't help it. 'She's great. I love having her.'

'Well, if you don't mind sharing a car with me, you can get a free ride and a free bed for a few nights.'

It was tempting. It would take her ages on the train and a last-minute ticket would be expensive. She would have the whole day tomorrow to find Edward. For the sake of a few hours in a car with Mark. She nodded. 'OK, it's a deal.'

Mark picked her up after Frankie had gone to bed. It was still light. The drive took several hours and the sun began to set when they reached the motorway. It was awkward at first, but, when darkness enveloped the car, it became easier to talk. She had expected Mark to be just like Erin, but there was something easy about him that made the silences between them seem less significant. He was a completely different person to the man she had met several weeks before.

'I guess you and Erin are thick as thieves by now.'

'Not really,' Isla answered truthfully.

'She didn't want to come back, you know. She had Frankie visiting any doctor that would give her the time of day. No wonder the poor kid won't talk.'

She was caught in a lie and the weight of it suddenly became apparent. Unless Frankie started speaking to her own parents, Isla would have to tell them she was talking to her before they left. She crossed her fingers in the dark, hoping it wouldn't come to that.

The motorway was empty, but Mark drove carefully, keeping to the speed limit and signalling when he changed lanes. The steady sweep of streetlights above was soporific and Isla relaxed.

'Do you mind if I ask you a question?' Mark said quietly. 'I'm not asking to start an argument. I'm asking because I want to understand, that's all. I promise I'll just listen.'

'Go on,' she said.

'What made you hesitate? It's not like you didn't want to save her. You didn't have to do all the CPR and you don't have to have anything to do with us now. But you do. You're with her almost every day. I just want to know what went through your mind, that's all.'

Isla looked out of the window. They were passing an exit and a string of cat's eyes in the road changed from red to green. It was hard to explain. 'I guess we all want to think we'd act quickly in an emergency. But for every person that runs into a burning building, there's someone who runs away. We don't know who we are until it happens. I froze. I didn't know what to do.'

'So you were scared?'

Isla nodded. 'My aunt drowned on that beach.' She turned to him. 'I'm not using that as an excuse, by the way. But my family never talked about it. I was too small to remember, but there's this huge silence around it. I guess I just freaked out. I would have got there quicker if I could have. But my body wouldn't let me.'

Mark nodded. True to his word, he didn't argue. They drove in silence until the petrol gauge ran down. Mark filled up and came back with coffee. He parked before the motorway slip road and they got out into the cool night air to watch the traffic speeding below them, sipping their drinks, their elbows almost touching.

She wanted to tell him then, about his daughter being able to speak. She wanted to give him something back. But using her relationship with Frankie to do that felt wrong. The time she spent with her was private. Not something to be shared and analysed by others. Besides, Mark's forgiveness was not yet set between them and she couldn't bring herself to unsettle it.

Chapter Thirty-Seven

PENNY

Penny didn't often look at herself critically in the mirror. She had long stopped being disappointed by what she saw and had learned to accept the lines that time had etched into her skin. She had minded turning fifty. Sixty had felt manageable, but seventy was going to be a struggle. It was true what they said about odd decades; they were harder to hurdle. She first noticed a definite step towards old age in her face when she was forty-eight. She had matured gracefully, a genetic gift from her father who had always kept his boyish good looks. As she approached her forty-ninth birthday, she noticed it around her eyes. A slackening of her left upper eyelid, slowly beginning its sliding descent. Creases emerging either side of the bridge of her nose, tracing the curve of her eye socket, leaving her looking permanently tired. She had been with Jacob for so long now it hadn't occurred to her what it would be like to be single again. She hadn't quite believed that she wouldn't see him again, but as the days passed into weeks her doubts began to crystallise and take shape. She looked at her reflection now and saw it as others would: a grey-haired pensioner, no longer a useful contributor to society. She had never felt so old. Between them,

Astrid and Jacob had kept her feeling young. Now they had both gone, something else had gone with them and the absence left her feeling dried up.

Penny hadn't seen Jacob since the night she told him about Clare. That was in June. Now it was September. She kept expecting to bump into him in the village, but after several trips she stopped looking. She knew he was avoiding her. His fixed ideas of right and wrong were one of the things that attracted her to him. Principles were in short supply these days and she admired a man who stuck to them. But now she was the object of his displeasure she found she disliked his principles very much. All these years she had been perfectly content to live without him. Now she was left alone, she craved his company. As she studied her face in the mirror, she saw a shadow move across the room behind her. She resisted the temptation to turn around. She knew she wouldn't see anything when she did.

'You can read my mind, can't you?' Penny said this quietly into her reflection, waiting for the shadow to reappear. She shook her head. 'I'm not going to live out my days alone like you. I'm going to do as Jacob asked and tell Isla about Clare, that's all. There's no need for this.'

A familiar breath of air curled and sighed around her neck.

The gooseflesh rose up and Penny slapped it down with the flat of her hand. 'Stop it. I mean it, Astrid. I've decided.'

How could she possibly tell Isla about Clare and Astrid? She had thought about it briefly that day when she first went knocking at the door with the bag of groceries she had scraped together as an excuse to pop round and see what Isla's plans were. Astrid had deliberately kept her distance from Isla in later life and that included not mentioning her to Penny. The upshot was Penny knew very little about her and had stopped being curious years ago.

When Astrid died, she assumed Isla would sweep in from London in a very large car and sell the place immediately to developers. What she was confronted with dismayed her. She was just so – unhappy. Penny hadn't stopped to think that Isla had lost her mother and might have minded that. She had assumed the silence between her and Astrid was mutual. She remembered Isla descending the stairs that day, a slight woman in scruffy trainers and an old pair of jeans that hung off her bony hips. It was striking how childlike she was, even in middle age. At the time, it seemed too big a burden to unload her own dreadful knowledge onto such fragile shoulders.

What had really surprised her as they sipped tea together in Astrid's kitchen was how this vulnerability had been underscored by a deep anger directed at Astrid. She hadn't considered her best friend from Isla's perspective. The damage Astrid had inflicted was evident and Penny felt very sorry for Isla as she watched her search through the house for answers. She remembered how upsetting she had found it all, how she didn't want Astrid's things touched. But now she understood that there were gains to be had from holding the truth up to the light. She had grown to like Isla. She hadn't figured on that. It was a problem that was going to make truth telling harder. But if she was going to salvage her own relationship with Jacob, then tell the truth she must. She wasn't going to lose another friend if she could help it.

She had tried to imagine telling Isla face to face about Clare, but she was afraid the conversation would slide into recriminations. A letter was best. Isla could keep it, re-read it, burn it, whatever. It was also easier to deliver now she had gone. Penny could let herself in, leave it on the kitchen table and allow events to run their course. She wasn't sure when Isla was coming back, her note wasn't clear, but she felt she could say she had done her best and start repairing her relationship with Jacob. When Isla returned with inevitable questions, he would be by her side to help defend her actions.

The letter she wrote to Isla was as factual as she could make it, but it was hard to trace the line between the truth and defending her best friend. She understood perfectly how Astrid struggled to make things right, but her good motives were difficult to convey when they were recorded so starkly in ink. Penny felt the occasion demanded the use of a proper fountain pen on laid paper, a labour that took all afternoon and some of the evening. When she was finished, she wrote Isla's name in cursive script on the envelope. The atmosphere thickened once more as she licked the flap and sealed it shut.

'It's done.' Penny announced this to the quiet of the room. 'I told her no more than I had to. Which is more than I can say for you.' She twisted round in her chair. 'I don't think you told me everything about Clare, did you? She was a good swimmer but she never would have gone out when it was spring tide. And why did you have that necklace on all the time? How bad had things got between you two? You were different these past two years, Astrid. Something was going on with you. I know I didn't imagine it.'

She returned to the letter and studied it. 'I can't keep your secrets any more. They need to be told to protect the living. Do you understand?'

The fronds of the parlour palm waved imperceptibly as something in the atmosphere unsettled them. Penny held her breath to see if it would fall.

By now it was dark and she felt like a thief as she picked her way down the lane, slipping into the house and dropping the letter softly on the kitchen table. As she left, she paused at the foot of the stairs, listening to the silence, unwilling to leave. This was probably the last time she would be able to stand in her friend's house like this. After the letter was opened, she might never be allowed back.

This house meant almost as much to her as her own did. It, too, was a survivor on the same piece of rock, surrounded by elements that constantly conspired to bring it down. From her birth, the door had always been open, first as a child reaching up for the handle, then as an adult reaching down. Now she felt a closing. She absorbed the quiet and reflected on a life full of drama and an equally theatrical death right where she stood. She hoped Astrid hadn't suffered in those last moments. She hoped it had been quick.

Chapter Thirty-Eight

ISLA

Coming back to London was like showing up late to a house party that was already in full swing. Her feet, once so swift at skirting around people and traffic, became clumsy and stumbling as she picked her way through tourists and foreign exchange students at South Kensington tube station. She had lost something of herself by leaving. Some kind of urban instinct, a sharpness that had been blunted by time and distance.

They had arrived late last night. The hotel appeared grander than Mark had led her to believe, but she could tell he was proud of what he'd achieved. Dark wrought-iron railings and white stone pillars flanked the wide door, glossy and black with a huge brass doorknob that mirrored his hand as he reached to push it open for her. It was what magazines would describe as a boutique hotel. Small in size but successfully stylish, homely and superior all at once. A couple of comfy-looking armchairs sat next to tables laid with magazines and elegant reading lamps in the foyer. She could see a further sitting room through a door to the left of the reception desk in front of her, a generous sofa and more armchairs set around a long low table, scattered with newspapers and centred by a huge vase filled with graceful blooms. The carpet was thick underfoot and absorbed interior noise. As the door closed softly behind them, muffling the street noise, they were cocooned.

'I don't have to stay in a suite, you know. A single room is fine. I don't need anything fancy.'

'We're full,' Mark said. 'It's the only room available. Besides, a promise is a promise. It's not fancy, anyway. So don't get your hopes up. Follow me.'

The suite was right at the top of the building, along a door-lined corridor. Isla read the signs on each one as they passed: 'Linen', 'Housekeeping', 'Storage'. There would be no other guests on this floor to bother her. Her room lay at the end of the corridor and read simply 'Suite'. The door opened into an L-shaped space with windows in its crook overlooking a jumble of London roofs, illuminated by streetlights. It was difficult to see beyond the shadowy scramble of TV aerials and chimney pots, but she could make out the spires of the Natural History Museum illuminated in the distance. It couldn't have been more different from the beach house.

'I'd offer to have breakfast with you tomorrow, but I have a ton of paperwork to look at and a new temporary manager to find or Faisal's going to quit. Are you OK looking after yourself?'

'Sure. I'll probably go for a run anyway. The galleries don't open until late morning.'

'Which exhibition are you wanting to see? We can sometimes get discounts on entry price.'

'Not that kind of gallery. I'm trying to track down the dealer who represented my mother's work. There's a place on Cork Street in Piccadilly she used to sell through, so I'm hoping they know something.'

'Well OK, come and find me when you get back. I'll be ready for a drink by then.'

'Sure.'

'Well. Night, then. Sleep well.' He turned to leave the room and gave her a small salute.

'Good night. And thanks for this.' Isla gestured around the room. 'It's lovely.'

He looked at her sincerely before shutting the door behind him. 'It's the least we can do.'

Put off by the crowds at the tube station, Isla consulted a map and figured it would probably take the best part of an hour to walk, so she moved away from the tube station and headed off to central London on foot. As she entered Piccadilly and turned in to the Burlington Arcade, she slowed and almost went back. She had not realised the area would be full of very well-dressed people. She looked at her own attire and felt irritated. Why hadn't she worn something smarter? She took off her anorak and rolled it into a ball, stuffing it into her backpack. The T-shirt she had on underneath wasn't so bad, but she wished she'd worn trousers instead of jeans, and certainly not her running shoes. She stopped outside a pewter shop, staring at a multitude of silver figurines and drinking vessels. The price tags were astronomical. Who on earth needed this stuff? And why? Suddenly she felt sympathy for Astrid not wanting to come here. It was a million miles away from the beach house and it felt so fake in comparison. Isla felt a small pang of – what? Homesickness? Bereavement? Kinship? Whatever it was, it spurred her on to finish what she had come to do. She did a dog-leg out of the top of the arcade and found herself at one end of Cork Street.

The gallery looked as if it had been there for years; the door had old glass panels in it, flecked with tiny bubbles, leaded and gilt against the black gloss paint. She pushed the door and it remained shut. There was a round brass bell for customers to gain entry. Someone sat at a desk at the back, reading an art catalogue. When they buzzed Isla in and rose to greet her, she saw it was a short-haired woman in men's brogues and a pinstripe suit.

'Can I help?' she asked politely, lacing her fingers behind her back.

'Sorry to bother you. I'm looking for someone who knows about Astrid Jarsdel's work,' Isla said.

'I'm afraid we don't handle her work any more. It's all sold privately now through auction. Are you a collector?'

'No, actually. I'm her daughter.'

'Astrid Jarsdel's daughter?' The woman appraised her like she was a piece of artwork herself.

'Yes,' replied Isla.

'Goodness. In that case, please take a seat. Can I get you a drink? Water? Coffee?' She indicated a beautifully upholstered chair next to the desk.

'Actually, water would be great.' Suddenly Isla felt a great thirst that had nothing to do with the walk over here and everything to do with feeling like an imposter. Her mouth was dry and she hadn't thought exactly what to say. She didn't belong here. She was struck by a deep sympathy for Astrid. This was her world, but Isla felt sure she, too, must have felt like an outsider. Is that why she stayed where she was and didn't take part in the melee that surrounded her work? As the woman left to get water, Isla looked around the gallery and took in the work. She didn't recognise the artists, but guessed that the house style was mid-century and figurative.

'Here.' The woman returned with a heavy-bottomed cut-glass tumbler and a silver jug of water. As she poured the water out, Isla was reminded of the pewter shop in the arcade and wondered if the jug had come from there and how much it had cost. 'So. How can I help you, Ms Jarsdel?'

'Call me Isla.' She drank deeply and began to gain some courage.

'I'm Kate.'

'Are you the owner?'

Kate laughed, showing two rows of strong white teeth. 'No. My dad is actually, I'm learning the trade.'

'That's nice.'

'It's been in our family for almost a century, so I didn't really get much choice.' She laughed again. 'Luckily, I love it.'

'Wow.' Isla couldn't imagine having a job that was predestined and shackled you to the same people year after year.

Kate's face clouded. 'Astrid Jarsdel died this year. March, was it? I'm so sorry. She was such a powerful painter.' She nodded thoughtfully.

'Yes. She was. Thank you.'

'So.' Kate cocked her head to one side, waiting for Isla to begin.

Disarmed, Isla began. 'Well, my mother had a dealer. Edward. I don't know his second name. I'm trying to get in touch with him and your place came up as somewhere that used to regularly sell her work, so I'm hoping you may be able to help. He'll be in his seventies or eighties now, I think. So it might be too late, but I thought I'd try.'

Kate frowned. 'The name doesn't ring a bell. Seascapes aren't my area, you see. My dad would know, though.'

'Is he here?'

'Ah, no. He doesn't come in every day.' Kate looked apologetic.

'Oh.' Suddenly Isla realised what a stupid idea this was; turning up with no warning, expecting the people she wanted to see to be there, waiting, ready to provide her with the information on request.

'Look, um. Why don't you leave me your details and I'll see what I can dig up? I can't promise you his number, but, if we find him, we could provide him with yours? And he could contact you?'

Isla fished in her bag and pulled out a card with the hotel address on it, scribbling the details of the beach house on the reverse.

'This is where I'm staying in London, but only for the next day or two. I'm living in the same house my mother did, so he can always reach me there if I've gone back.'

'You know,' Kate held the card by the edges and flexed it slowly, 'you can just come directly to us if it's a question of getting your mother's work valued. There were rumours after her death about a number of paintings she kept back. Paintings that were never circulated for sale?'

Isla almost laughed out loud. Kate thought she was trying to find Edward to facilitate the sale of her mother's estate. If only she knew there was virtually nothing left of it. 'Oh, it's nothing like that,' she said as she rose to leave. 'It's a personal matter.' She wondered if Kate would pass the information on to her father or put it in the bin, now she knew there were no Jarsdels for sale.

Chapter Thirty-Nine

PENNY

Jacob could be stubborn, but Penny could not believe he would let so many weeks slide by without contact. She thought his curiosity might have driven him to pick up the phone by now, even though she knew, deep down, that once he had made up his mind he never went back on a decision. *Come and find me when it's done.* That's what he'd said. It was up to her to break the silence, then. Her mood oscillated between sulky defiance and self-pity. Today, she was defiant.

The only positive that Penny could take from Jacob's disappearance was that she could smoke pot in the house, unchallenged. She took her tin from the mantlepiece, poured herself a whisky and sat at her kitchen table, pulling out the contents and laying them in an orderly line like surgical instruments in an operating theatre. Rolling papers, tobacco, lighter, ashtray and a flattened chunk of dark-brown resin wrapped up in clingfilm. The overhead lamp threw a yellow circle of light onto the centre of the table and the rest of the kitchen receded into darkness.

Her supplier, a lad from the village called Oscar, had tried to persuade her to buy skunk. 'That's what everyone wants these days,

Ms Walton. That and nitrous. Coke if you're over forty.' He was a polite boy. Penny never invited him to use her first name. It didn't do to become too friendly with one's dealer.

'You know I don't like skunk,' she said. 'It's horrible stuff. Can you get my usual again for me or not?'

'Whoa.' He held his hands out as if she were a startled foal. 'Anything for you, Ms Walton. You're my most reliable customer. Hash it is.'

She handed him the money and he fished in his jeans pocket and pulled out a small clear plastic wallet. 'Keep it sealed. It'll dry out otherwise.'

'I know. I'm not a complete idiot. See you next month.'

'I'm off to uni soon. Got a place at Edinburgh.'

Penny narrowed her eyes. 'Well that's lovely for you, but who's going to keep me topped up while you're gone?'

'My brother will take over most of the rounds.'

'Hmmm.' Penny growled in disapproval.

He held his hands up again and laughed. 'I can stop by in the holidays. You might have to buy more but less often, yeah?'

'Alright. Don't forget about me, though.'

'I couldn't forget you if I tried, Ms Walton. You're a legend.' He sauntered up the lane, stuffing her money into his back pocket. He would do well in Edinburgh, a bright boy like him. She wasn't so keen on his brother, though, who had the emotional intelligence of a turnip.

Penny warmed the resin over the flame of her lighter, crumbling it into the line of rolling tobacco that lay in the crease of the Rizla. Carefully, she cradled the parcel in her fingers, licked the edge of the rolling paper with the very tip of her tongue and rolled a joint with expert precision, twisting the end paper tightly shut. She poked around in the tin for a small strip of cardboard she could use for a roach and rolled it up into a tight tube, stuffing it neatly into the open end and putting it to her lips. She lit the twist and inhaled, blowing out the flaming paper with her exhalation.

It had been several weeks since she last saw Jacob, and, although she had written that letter, she knew Isla had not been back to read it yet. As she felt the effects of Oscar's wares snake into her limbs, she wondered if she had done enough. Did the letter mean that technically she had done her duty or had she only completed her end of the bargain when it had been read? It was as if she were back in school, uncertain what to do where boys were concerned, trying to navigate a set of rules that weren't written down. With elbows on the table, joint in one hand, she gazed, mesmerised, at the thin trail of blue smoke making its way in a perfectly straight line up to the ceiling. She had always loved the smell. Something sweet underlined by something earthy, almost incense-like. Her eyes travelled down to the backs of her hands. She had developed a few liver spots over the summer, but she minded these less than the monstrous proportions her veins had taken on. Great knots of green and grey swelled and twisted across her knuckles. Disgusting. She had once made the mistake of pressing one down and had been horrified to see it slowly fill again, like a greedy leech.

Suddenly the smoke smudged horizontally, as if an invisible hand had cut through it, disturbing the atmosphere. She resisted the urge to sit back and snatch her arm away. She stayed where she was and took another drag, feeling the air close in.

'We used to do this a lot, didn't we?' Penny said in a low voice. 'I remember the first time you made me smoke a joint. I was sick in the lane on the way home and swore I'd never do it again. But you persuaded me otherwise. I don't know why I still do it, I never liked it as much as you.'

The line of smoke righted itself and it travelled once more in a vertical line towards the heavens.

Penny reminisced into the darkness beyond. 'We had so much fun together, it's hard to believe it won't happen again. You could be very funny when you put your mind to it.' She exhaled. 'The only other person I have fun with isn't speaking to me. I'm sure you don't care tuppence about that, but I do.'

Penny swirled the liquid in her glass, drained it, and continued. 'I'm going to find Jacob as soon as Isla returns. And when she does, things will be different. For starters, you need to leave her house. It's been long enough. What do you need with it, anyway?'

Somewhere nearby, Penny could hear a faint ticking sound, but it wasn't mechanical.

'Secondly, you need to leave me alone. I have to start making a life of my own. I can't be mooning around all day missing you. It's been six months.'

She looked around. The ticking sound persisted. It couldn't be the heating coming on; it was still too warm for that. She sat for some time, head tilted to one side, listening. The tide was low and the birds were already roosting. The silence in the house expanded and seemed to take on a noise of its own.

Penny tapped the ash into the ashtray and rose to refill her glass. As she turned to make her way towards the drinks cabinet in the next room, she stopped and saw a small, perfectly circular puddle of water in the middle of the linoleum. The ticking had not been a ticking at all. It had been a steady *drip drip drip*. She looked up and saw no sign of a leak in the ceiling. She crouched down and touched the water. It was cold and clear. Something, she did not know what, made her bring her fingers to her face. As she touched the tips of her fingers to her tongue, she tasted salt.

Chapter Forty

ISLA

Isla returned to the hotel feeling that everything would be left to fate. There was nothing else she could do. Either Kate would give Edward her number, or she wouldn't. She got her laptop out and, once again, Googled his name, but there was no information apart from the gallery in Cork Street that gave a clue as to where he lived.

She showered and, as instructed by Mark, went downstairs to the lobby. She located the reception desk and found the little sign that said 'Private' above the staircase leading down to the family quarters.

'Hello?' she called, descending them with trepidation.

'In here.' Mark was in a small kitchen, sitting at a round table with a pile of paperwork and a bottle of red wine. 'I'm just finishing up. This pile needs signatures. Help yourself to a glass over there in the cupboard. There's some olives in the fridge and cheese. It's the only food in there that won't poison you. Have you eaten?'

'Yeah. I had a very late lunch.'

'Just as well,' he said cheerfully.

He asked about her day as he scribbled signatures and told her about his. It was odd. The contrast between him and Erin was stark. Isla imagined her fussing around, embarrassed about the lack of food.

'What are you smiling at?'

'I'm just thinking about Erin. She would be appalled you only had olives and cheese for dinner.'

He gave her a look, not sure if she was serious, then he laughed and nodded sagely. 'She would indeed. But Erin is easily appalled. You might have noticed that. It's actually quite a useful personality trait when you're running a business together. But the last few years, not so much.'

'What do you mean?'

'She's spent the last six years pushing Frankie through life at breakneck speed and the past few months dragging her like a deadweight.'

Isla winced at the simile.

'I think she's running out of steam. She's planning something,' Mark said, reaching for an olive.

'Like what?'

'You don't need to be Miss Marple to see that things aren't great between us. I saw you watching us when you came over to the house that day.'

'Uh . . .'

Mark waved his fingers dismissively. 'Frankie's accident has put a strain on us all.'

'I'm sorry.'

'So am I. Did you know we met when were eighteen? We were students. I don't know what to do to keep her, that's the truth. Any advice gratefully received. I mean it.'

'This probably doesn't help.' Isla indicated the empty wine bottle. 'I get the feeling she wants everything to be under control.'

Mark sat back in his chair and ran his fingers through his hair. 'You don't pull your punches, do you?'

Isla shrugged. 'You just asked me for advice.'

Mark gave a wry smile. 'You're probably right.'

'Do you think it would help if Frankie got better and started speaking?' She held her breath after she said it. A part of her didn't want Frankie to start speaking to anyone else. It was a selfish and unreasonable wish, but she couldn't help it.

'Honestly? No, I don't. I think things haven't been working for a while for Erin and Frankie is the latest on a long list.'

It wasn't like talking to Erin, who had some kind of an agenda. It wasn't like talking to Penny, who kept things back. Mark chatted to her as if they had known each other for years. It felt disloyal, speaking like this, but they continued to talk well into the night.

Chapter Forty-One

Erin

She'd torn the house apart, looking for it. Erin stripped back the bedsheets and shook out the pillowcases, knowing she wouldn't find it there. It wasn't under the bed and it wasn't in any of Frankie's pockets.

'Where is it, Frankie?' she said to herself, her head inside the wardrobe as Frankie stood mute, watching from the doorway to her bedroom. Erin hadn't realised the Dictaphone was missing until Mark had left. It had taken her by surprise, him leaving suddenly, and she'd had a row with him about it. She hadn't noticed the recording device was lost until the next morning and Frankie wasn't being any help at all.

'When was the last time you had it, darling?'

Frankie said nothing.

Erin closed the wardrobe door and looked at her. 'Did you have it with you in the churchyard yesterday?'

Frankie shook her head slowly.

'The fish and chip shop?'

Frankie shook her head.

'What about the day before? You had it for your painting lesson, didn't you?'

Frankie nodded.

'Did you leave it at Isla's house?'

Frankie shrugged.

Erin needed that device: Frankie's voice was on it. If she never spoke again, Erin would at least be able to listen to her talking to Isla. Mark said they would only be away for a few days, but she didn't want to wait that long.

'Come with me,' she said to Frankie, grabbing her hand, 'I have an idea.'

As Erin marched over the sand with her child in tow, she argued with herself about her motives. Frankie needed that Dictaphone to help her recovery. Now that Mark was gone, she needed it even more to keep herself busy. But there was something else. Erin was tired of being shut out. This was an opportunity to get inside Isla's head without being given the cold shoulder. Isla only had one neighbour. If she came calling round, Erin could explain what she was looking for. Easy.

Isla had tarted the place up, but she hadn't replaced the windows. There was a small window next to the front door on the side of the house away from the beach. It had been slightly ajar when she first knocked and it had been slightly ajar ever since. Maybe the wood was swollen or maybe she liked the breeze. Nobody would see them; the road was deserted. She explained to Frankie what she should do and gave her a leg up. Frankie just fit. She looked like a little worm wriggling into a hole. But she couldn't open the door, it was too stiff. Erin ran round the building. Sure enough, Isla had left her keys in the back door and Erin gave thanks for the lax security of the countryside. Frankie opened the door without much difficulty and Erin stepped through, a small thrill of excitement at the thought of having this house to herself for the afternoon. Isla always handed Frankie over on the patio at the back, she never invited Erin in. The interior was as beautiful as she remembered. White painted floorboards throughout the ground floor reflected any light that came into the house and she was immediately bathed in a lucent energy when the sun emerged. The effect was Nordic and rather chic, if a little rough around the edges. Frankie found the Dictaphone almost immediately and looked puzzled when Erin made no move to go.

'I'm just going to check the house is locked up properly for Isla. Let's make sure there aren't any other windows open, shall we? Do you want a drink or something?' Erin went into the kitchen. She noticed the letter immediately. It was propped up between the pepper and the salt cellar on the kitchen table. The rich cream envelope was expensive looking and embossed with a rather beautiful old-fashioned texture. It looked too thick to be a birthday card, and Isla's name was written on the front in proper ink and underlined in a way that lent it gravitas. Perhaps it was an invitation or something to do with her late mother. Whatever it was, it demanded attention. She traced the penmanship and restored the envelope to its original place. It had not been opened. Pity.

She looked at the strange painting in the dining room and went up the stairs. There was a window at the end of the landing, and the view was incredible. Not for the first time, she imagined herself hosting parties here, coming up for weekends and holidays. She couldn't help feeling that if she'd renovated this house, she would have asked professionals to do it. The finish wasn't good enough.

The rooms on this floor were bedrooms, their doors slightly ajar. A small bathroom overlooked the road behind the house. The only door that wasn't open had a key in it, and Erin didn't think twice before turning it and mounting the stairs. The wood creaked slightly as it took her weight. She felt the light fall onto her head from the roof light high above. She had the strangest feeling of being baptised, of rising into a different dimension. But when she blinked and saw what was painted on the walls, she became afraid. She was surrounded by the sea. Not the nice kind of beach you went to for holidays, but an angry force that crashed over her head, crushing the air from her lungs. She wanted to turn around and leave, but something propelled her forwards to one of the walls. She needed to get a closer look, even though a voice inside her warned her not to. She saw shadows under the waves, things she couldn't quite make out and something told her they weren't human. There was a smell, like something was festering under the paint, something salty and wrong. She saw dirt and human hair embedded in the artwork and it made her want to retch.

Suddenly, she had the feeling of being observed. There were figures and faces watching her from the walls; their eyes seemed to follow her as she walked around the room. She could make out words scratched into the paintwork, spells perhaps. There was something malevolent about this place, she could feel it. And she had let her daughter come here for whole afternoons. No wonder the door was locked. Had Frankie been up here? Had she seen what Erin was seeing? It was enough to give a small child nightmares. Afraid she had left Frankie alone two floors below, she fled down the stairs, calling her name. Frankie was in the sitting room, cross-legged on the floor, a collection of beach finds in the dip of her dress.

'Frankie, we need to leave. Put those things back where you found them.'

Frankie held the hem of her dress, using it as a hammock for the shells and stones. She scrambled to her feet awkwardly.

'Here, let me help. Where did you find them?'

Frankie looked up to the mantlepiece which was now bare.

'OK, let's put everything back.' She held out her hand and Frankie deposited one thing at a time: a stone as smooth as skin with a perfectly round hole, a collection of mussel shells, blue-black and white, a small piece of twisted driftwood, lighter than it looked.

'Is that everything?' Erin asked, holding her hand out for more. Frankie pulled the last thing from her dress, letting the skirt drop, holding it out carefully. A familiar, conical shape. Something Erin had thought about many times over the years. Frowning, she took it from Frankie's fingers, holding her breath at the familiarity. It was just like the ladder shell she had lost that day. She turned it over and nearly dropped it when she saw the pink stripe running down its back. Could it be the same one? It was as big as she'd remembered, and it was perfect. She couldn't close her fist around it back then, but she could now. It sat in her palm as if it belonged there. The hours she had spent looking for a replacement – she had even gone to the local shops to see if she could buy one, but all the shopkeepers told her that ladder shells didn't get that big and didn't have stripes. But this one certainly did.

The girl who had stolen it from her was local, but Isla had told her she'd lived in London for most of her life. She couldn't have been more than thirteen, so it might have been her. Erin thought back to that afternoon. The girl had the same colouring as Isla, the same reticence. Erin remembered wanting to befriend her, but it was hard because she didn't give much away. A nasty thought entered her head. Did Isla know who she was? Was this the reason Erin wasn't allowed into her house? Was Isla laughing at her, the child she had duped all those years ago? The shame of being fooled like that came back, still fresh and hot. She had looked up to Isla. She had taken her into her confidence. She had even entrusted her with Frankie. But she'd been repaid by lies and deceit. The relationship that was developing between that woman and her daughter, that horrible room upstairs and now the shell. Erin couldn't think what it all meant, but she knew it must be something bad, and something must be done.

Chapter Forty-Two

ISLA

Isla left Kensington Gardens behind her and jogged back to the hotel, pining for Frankie. She could conjure up the shape of her, like a missing puzzle piece, and it hurt. It had only been a couple of days, but she thought about her all the time. She had looked for a gift to take back, but everything seemed so plastic and temporary here. So Isla decided to give her the box of watercolours and the brushes instead, to bring back to London. She wouldn't want to use them anyway, after Frankie had gone. She would go back to Danny's shop in the village and ask him if there was a way he could put Frankie's name on it, or a message so she would remember who Isla was. She couldn't imagine Frankie living here, in a hotel surrounded by traffic fumes and tourists. She wondered if Mark and Erin would allow Frankie to come and stay with her in the school holidays. They could spend whole summers together, just the two of them. Didn't Mark say how the hotel was always busy when Frankie had school holidays? She could come for Easter and Christmas, and, when Frankie was older, she could get the train by herself. Isla imagined meeting her on the platform, grabbing her hand and racing down to the beach to paddle barefoot in the waves.

Frankie had not absorbed Mark's dark features, but she did have his corkscrew hair and a cleft on her right cheek that appeared only when she smiled widely. It was a joy for Isla to see this dimple emerge and it was beginning to appear more and more often these days. The only time it disappeared completely was when Frankie painted. When she sat at the table with the paper in front of her, her face set itself into an expression of deep thought. Any interruption was frowned upon and Isla didn't want a repetition of being spoken to in that chilling tone of voice. Isla had learned to keep away, observing her from a distance in silence, watching the stack of paintings Frankie produced grow taller. Isla had suggested that they put them all up on a wall in the house, but, once she had finished, Frankie seemed to lose interest, as if she couldn't remember making them in the first place. Once Frankie had settled on painting the sea, she never deviated from the subject. It was as if she were compelled. And sometimes . . . sometimes, when Isla stood quietly behind Frankie to see her put onto paper something she couldn't articulate any other way, she thought she caught the scent of roses. It never lasted, and Isla couldn't be sure she wasn't imagining it.

She rounded the corner and came to the top of the street where the hotel lay, halfway down. She stopped on the steps, enjoying the sunshine, stretching out her calf muscles. When she entered the lobby, Mark was behind the reception desk.

'There's a guy waiting for you in the sitting room.' He jerked his thumb towards the room behind him.

It had to be Edward. Isla suddenly felt nauseous. She needed to eat and she knew she smelled. 'How long's he been here for?' she asked, panicking.

'Just a few minutes, that's all. He's the man you were looking for, I assume.'

'I think so. Is he in his seventies, eighties?'

'Reckon so. He's pretty well turned out too. Refined.' Mark raised his eyebrows and looked amused.

'Look at me, I'm a mess. I need a shower.'

'I'll ply him with tea and biscuits. Go and get showered and I'll keep him company so he doesn't escape.'

'Thanks, Mark. You're a lifesaver.'

She ran upstairs to her room. Legs weak, Isla stepped into the shower. So he had come looking for her. She felt afraid. Now he was actually here, the longing to meet him turned into apprehension. What if he told her things she didn't want to know?

As she descended the steps into the lobby, her heart began to race. Mark was there, sitting on the sofa opposite a man in an arm-chair, legs crossed, elegant. She recognised him instantly.

'Good grief! Isla Jarsdel.' He rose from his seat in a slow and graceful manner, a colourful cravat knotted at his throat. He extended his arms towards her and took her hands gently into his. His skin was soft and warm. 'The last time we met, we shared a packet of custard creams, if memory serves me right.'

Chapter Forty-Three

ERIN

'Erin?' Mark's voice floated across the living room from the answer machine in the house. He could have been standing next to her and it made her jump. 'Erin, I think we need to talk. I can't get hold of you on the mobile. Can you call me tonight? I just want to . . . Well, just call me, OK?'

She looked at her watch. It was already getting late. She had spent the whole day brooding and had put Frankie to bed early so she could brood some more. She went to the kitchen in search of wine. She would need some before she talked to Mark. She poured herself a glass and walked into the garden. It had rained in the afternoon and the grass soaked her canvas shoes. Knowing she couldn't put it off forever, she eventually went back inside and settled herself on the sofa, reaching for the landline.

'Mark?' She braced herself for slurred accusations. Mark would be into his second bottle by now. She pictured him sitting at their little kitchen table, glass in hand. He would be especially incoherent if he hadn't eaten.

'Hi. Glad you called. How are you?' Mark's voice was calm and clear. She was on her second glass and suddenly felt wrong-footed.

'I'm OK. Frankie's already asleep if you wanted to talk to her. She was tired.'

'Don't worry. We're coming back tomorrow,' said Mark. 'I thought you should know. I'll stay here for a couple of hours to see the temp settle in and then I'll get off.'

'Is Isla coming too?'

'Yeah. She's seeing her mother's old art dealer tonight. They're having dinner. But she wants to come back. She's missing Frankie, I think.' She heard the smile in his voice. 'She doesn't stop talking about her.'

Erin felt a prick of annoyance, the familiar feeling of being excluded. 'It's not like they've known each other for long.'

'Listen. I've been thinking. I want things to be different when we come back. I've decided to stop drinking.'

Erin was genuinely surprised because she believed him. His voice was full of conviction. But she couldn't help herself take a dig. 'And how long do you think that will last?'

'I don't know. But I want to try and make things better between us. I think it will help Frankie, to know we're OK. She can feel that we're not, I'm sure of it.'

'Frankie has no idea.'

'She must. Isla knows. And if she can tell, so can Frankie.'

The annoyance turned to anger. 'Since when have you two been having cosy chats together about our marriage?'

'Oh, come on. It's not like that. I'm allowed to talk with her, aren't I?'

'Not about the state of our relationship.'

'We don't sit around discussing you all evening, don't worry.'

Erin pictured them both talking conspiratorially together about her and it smarted. 'She's my friend, Mark. You haven't made any kind of effort towards her before. Just because you spend a couple of days together . . .'

Mark changed the subject. 'Do you remember when Dr Lim said we should stop focussing on what Frankie couldn't do?' he said gently.

'*I would encourage you to laud your daughter's capabilities,*' mimicked Erin unkindly.

Mark ignored her. 'It's the same with us. I've spent the past few months feeling so angry: with you for falling asleep, with myself for being too far away to save her. I couldn't get past it. It coloured everything. And then, when I met Isla that evening at the house, all I could think about was how she could have helped more, I hated her for it. But we have to get beyond our mistakes. We need to put the past behind us.'

'What?' Erin shook her head in confusion, her thoughts muddied by the wine. 'You hated Isla for . . . what? Not helping? I don't get it.'

'Oh.' His voice faltered and she could picture him raking his free hand through his hair.

'Well?' she asked.

'It's complicated.'

'What's she told you?'

'When Frankie . . . fell.' There was a beat while they both absorbed the inadequacy of those words.

'Keep going,' Erin said in a monotone.

'Isla was out running that morning. She saw what happened, but she didn't go over. She ran away because she was scared. But she came back. And the upshot is, Frankie is going to be fine. We are all going to be fine, Erin, if we want to be.' He let this information travel hundreds of miles into Erin's ear.

'Hang on a minute.' Erin started to shake as her mind unravelled the words and made sense of them. 'You're telling me that when Frankie was drowning, Isla saw her and ran away?' Her knees bounced up and down as she sat, teeth chattering, staring at the carpet. 'How do you know this? Where's your evidence?'

'I saw her do it as I was coming back from the coastguard's office,' Mark admitted. 'I was too far away to get to them, but I saw everything.'

Erin felt as if she were being compelled to complete a monstrous jigsaw puzzle. 'You mean you're in on this too? You've known about this all along?'

'I didn't know for sure until I spoke to her that night at the house. But we cleared everything up when we drove down together. She's upset about it too. I think she's had a pretty screwed-up life, actually. Did you know her aunt drowned?'

Erin had an image of them without her, discussing Frankie's progress and exchanging intimacies.

'Are you sleeping with her?' she blurted out.

'God, no. Of course not.'

'Why are you on her side then? You should be on *my* side. Your wife's side.'

'There aren't sides, Erin. It's a mess. All we have to do is clear it up as best we can and put a lid on it.'

Erin's head was spinning. Why wasn't Mark as angry as she was? 'What you're saying, I can't believe it, Mark. How can you be so sure?'

'When I got there, Frankie was already having her chest pumped. Isla was whispering to her. I don't think she realised I could hear.'

'What was she saying?'

Mark swallowed. 'She kept saying *forgive me, forgive me.* She was apologising for not coming sooner. Over and over.'

Erin felt sick. Her heart beat angrily. 'I'll kill her,' she breathed.

'That's not why I told you. God, this has all come out wrong.' Mark's anguish meant nothing to Erin.

'She let Frankie drown! How can you be so . . . matter of fact about it? She's a *monster*.'

'Erin, she saved her life. If she hadn't been there, Frankie would have died.'

'But she might have been alright if she'd run over straight away!' Erin wailed.

'Frankie *is* alright.'

'She doesn't talk, Mark. That's not alright. How can she go through life without speaking?'

'Frankie will get better, eventually. Isla loves Frankie. Frankie loves Isla and that's what matters.'

The words went right through her, like a punch. 'Frankie's *my* daughter. Can't you see what's going on? She's trying to get her feet under the table. With you and with Frankie. By the sound of it, she's succeeded.'

'Erin, I don't blame you for falling asleep and I don't expect Frankie to be a genius. I need you to do the same. Stop looking for reasons to be angry. It's the only way we're going to survive this.'

'You sound like you've swallowed the textbook, Mark. Why didn't you tell me sooner?'

'Because I could see you and Frankie liked her. I've forgiven her. I think you should too.'

Erin thought about the ladder shell. 'I don't think I can,' she said darkly.

Erin sat in the darkness for a good long time before she felt able to move. She thought about the three unnamed babies she had lost, that she had nearly lost Frankie twice. And now Mark. It seemed she was unable to hang on to anything for long, but she wouldn't let go without a fight. When she eventually rose from the table, her limbs were stiff as she shuffled her way into the kitchen to refill her glass. She didn't feel like being magnanimous. She was livid.

Chapter Forty-Four

ISLA

Tucked down a narrow side street flanking the Noel Coward theatre, Harrington's was a restaurant in Covent Garden that Isla had heard of but never visited. Black-and-white framed photographs of actors, dead and alive, interposed warm wooden panelling all over the walls. Crisp white tablecloths laden with wine glasses, old-fashioned silver cutlery and condiments stood out against the black-and-white mosaic floor. It looked both casual and posh at the same time. Isla glanced at the menu in the window, saw the prices and decided it was posh.

'I hope you like fish,' said Edward as he held the door open for her.

'I do. Never get tired of it.' Isla observed that Edward was known in here. They had received a warm welcome from the maître d' and been ushered to a table that provided more privacy than most. 'Is this your usual, then?'

'It used to be. A lot of my buyers were actors and it was easy for them to meet in here, particularly if they were working in the theatre district. I just kept up the habit when I retired, because the management treat me well and I love seafood. Oysters are a weakness of mine, but I'm too creaky to sit at the bar these days. I need a nice chair with a back to it in a draught-free corner.'

'Did you ever bring Astrid here?' Isla looked around at the elegant diners and tried to picture her amongst them.

'Good grief, no. She hated London and all that razzmatazz. She barely left the house. I think she thought she might turn to stone if she ventured out of the county. She was a nightmare to manage. Refused to do meet-and-greets with buyers. At the time I despaired, but I think eventually her reclusiveness added to her cachet and I probably made a few sales because of it. People love a mystery.'

'Well, she was certainly that.' She handed the menu back to the waiter and agreed with Edward that they should share a *Plateau de Fruits de Mer*.

'You do realise that if we have the *fruits de mer* we have to have champagne?' Edward remarked.

'Only if I'm allowed to split the bill with you. I can't be seen to be sponging off their favourite customer.'

'Oh in that case, dinner's off. I only invited you so I could spoil you.'

'I was hoping you could tell me a bit about my mother. And my aunt. Did Astrid ever tell you about her sister, Clare? Anything?'

Edward shook his head. 'Anything personal was implied by Astrid, never discussed candidly. But I did know more about Clare, or how Astrid felt about Clare, because of the painting Astrid made of her. She spoke through her work more than face to face.'

'Which painting?' Isla's heart thumped painfully.

'It should be in the house. Above a fireplace, if I remember rightly. She refused to sell it.'

'That's Clare? That scary, depressing painting?'

'Ah. I can see you haven't looked at it properly.'

'It's a picture of a woman drowning.'

'Correction.' He held his index finger up. 'It's a picture of a woman before she drowns. We don't know if she actually drowns, in the end. Do you know the Millais painting of Ophelia? Astrid always admired it. I think she had it in the back of her mind when she painted Clare.'

'You mean Shakespeare's *Ophelia*?'

'Yes. There's a beautiful passage in *Hamlet* describing how Ophelia sings before she drowns in the river, surrounded by flowers, completely unaware, or unconcerned, her life is about to be cut short. Maybe her joy comes from the simple fact that she will be happier in death. Who knows? You look more closely at Astrid's painting. I think your mother was exploring the possibility that Clare didn't suffer.'

'What am I supposed to look for?' Isla thought about the pale face and the swirling waters round it. It seemed full of suffering to her.

'I confess, the eye is naturally drawn to her face, just above the water. It brings terrific tension to the piece. The casual onlooker would see that and move on. But the real truth lies underneath the water. You have to look for it.'

'Look for what?'

'A change of state. From one thing to another.' Edward smiled at her encouragingly, waiting for her to get it.

'You've lost me, Edward.'

'Under the water, where her legs should be. Look closely and you will see . . . a flash of silver. Scales, in fact.'

'Fish scales?'

'Yes. In this picture, Clare isn't dying, she's metamorphosing.'

'Into a fish?' Isla felt utterly lost in the conversation.

'No. That would be too prosaic. I think Astrid thought Clare was capable of more remarkable things than that.'

Suddenly, Isla thought she understood. 'She imagined Clare changing into a mermaid?'

'Metaphorically. I can see I need to give you a lesson in art history. Try not to take what you see so literally. Astrid's talent lay in expressing the unspoken, in code. As an onlooker, you have to work a little bit to understand what she wanted to say. You have to crack the code.'

'And what was she trying to say by turning Clare into a mermaid?'

Edward sat back in his chair, clearly enjoying himself. 'I think Astrid was doing two things. She was pinning her hopes on Clare being utterly at peace with her fate, welcoming it even. There are many people who believe that just before a person drowns, they experience a kind of euphoria. I think Astrid was, in part, conveying this idea not just to the viewer, but also to herself. By painting Clare like this, Astrid was persuading herself that it was all going to be alright.'

'Because . . .'

'Because she couldn't bear to think of the alternative. It was the only way she could cope. By making it into something she could deal with.'

'And the second thing? You said there were two things she was trying to do with the painting.'

'Well, this is pure speculation and slightly supernatural. But I think she was inferring that Clare had two sides to her. And maybe when she died these two states were either reconciled, or Clare's true state took over.'

Isla thought about the drawing Astrid had made of Clare. A different Clare to the one everyone else knew. That word Penny had used: *beastly*. 'Do you think Astrid thought she was in some way . . . inhuman?' she asked.

'Not quite. I think Astrid and Clare had a deep appreciation of the sea. I think it was a place they both felt was their true home. And Astrid idolised Clare. Maybe, when she died, Astrid bestowed upon her some kind of mythical status so she could carry on living in a different form. So that Clare's death wasn't the end. It was the beginning of something else.'

'Astrid was a lot of things, but she wasn't superstitious.'

Edward raised his eyebrows. 'Wasn't she? She always used the same brushes for her paintings, the same water pot. She *had* to use them. There is a ritual in painting and she observed it every time she began a new piece. She told me this perfectly seriously. She didn't quite say a prayer before she started, but it wasn't far off. And then there's her subject matter. She thought of the sea as some kind of higher force that had her completely in its thrall. If that's not superstition, I don't know what is.'

'But she seemed so down to earth.'

'Superstition comes in all sorts of guises and Astrid wasn't big on telling everyone the detail of how she worked. And that painting of Clare was done for her own personal satisfaction. It was never for sale.'

Isla sighed. 'I feel like I didn't know her at all. Like I got everything about her wrong.'

'She kept a lot of things hidden. But maybe if I can tell you about the woman I knew, it might help you piece her together a little more?'

Isla leaned in. 'Yes, please. Tell me everything.'

Chapter Forty-Five

ISLA

Edward looked to the heavens briefly and began. 'I met your mother when she was a student. I was attached to a gallery in London – Porter's – we specialised in contemporary art and we had a showcase every year of up-and-coming artists. The owner, Bernard Porter, had ties to a few of the better art colleges and in exchange for hosting a show for hand-picked graduates, he would use the event to gauge the mood of his clients, see what was popular, that sort of thing. It also made him look like he had his finger on the pulse et cetera. He really was a pretentious old fart, but not many galleries would show graduate work at that time. Bernard knew that students are a great barometer.'

'Why?'

'They aren't afraid to try new things. They're not shackled by market forces and they don't have a lifestyle they need to fund, so their work isn't coloured by the kind of stress that more established artists have. And their work is cheap. So it was a win-win situation for the gallery and the artists.'

Edward continued his train of thought. 'Those that sold were signed up with the gallery and those that didn't were sent away.

Astrid was the youngest artist and she was the only one who sold all her work on the opening night. Bernard selected three pieces from her portfolio. They were displayed as a triptych. I still remember them because they were unlike any seascapes I had ever encountered. They were both menacing and beautiful at the same time. We signed her up immediately. When it became apparent that she was going to be very special indeed, the tables were turned.'

'What do you mean?'

He gave a wry smile. 'Like I said, students aren't afraid. But as soon as they're signed, the fear takes over. They have an expectation conferred upon them. They must sell, and sell consistently while they build up a reputation. They must produce work at a particular pace, depending on their technique, to sustain interest. Otherwise they're dropped back into anonymity by the very gallery that discovered them.'

'I can't imagine Astrid toeing the line.'

'Exactly. Astrid lacked the respect and obedience Bernard demanded from a new artist. She sold the rest of the paintings she had completed while doing her course and then dropped off the radar. There was a long gap where we didn't hear anything from her. Months, if I remember rightly. She didn't answer letters, and I don't think she had a phone back then. Bernard was doing his nut. He had a string of interested clients and no paintings to sell them. So he sent me up to see her.'

The seafood had arrived and they both tucked in. A helpful waitress tied a large white napkin around Edward's neck to protect his very expensive suit and Isla was reminded of a child being prepared for his supper.

'Well,' continued Edward, 'I eventually found the house. It took me all day to get there. I borrowed a car from a friend – a Morris Traveller, as I recall. Green with wooden panelling. Anyway, it was the devil's own job finding the entrance to the road. No sat navs in those days. The track leading down to the house nearly took my teeth out; the suspension was dreadful. It's a wonder I didn't pop a tyre.'

'No change there, then.' Isla smiled. 'It's still a bone-shaker.'

'I knocked on the door and, when Astrid finally opened it, I could see she was in a bit of trouble.'

'What do you mean?'

'Well, the house was a mess. Stuff all over the floor, dishes in the sink, that sort of thing. She looked like death. It must have been shortly after her sister had passed away, though she didn't mention that.'

'Yes.'

'And then I heard the baby. You. Wrapped up in a bundle and crying your lungs out. I had no idea she had a child.'

Isla nodded. 'What happened next?'

'Well, I stayed for the day and helped clean her house.'

'You didn't! That was very progressive of you.'

'I'm a very progressive man. Actually, I had to do something otherwise Bernard would have had my guts for garters. I needed to get her on side so I could squeeze another painting from her. It was all very self-serving.'

'And did you?'

'Yes, as a matter of fact, I did.' He smirked at the memory. 'She had an island painting lying against the wall in the hallway. Just sitting there, ready to be kicked by anybody passing, or crawling. Unbelievable. The price it would fetch now . . .'

He lost himself in a reverie and Isla let him. She drained her champagne and they both picked over some dressed crab in companionable silence. 'How did she manage it? To paint for you and look after me?' she asked.

'God knows. She was a remarkable woman, Astrid. I think I came as close to being a friend to her as anyone, but I still didn't know her, not really. I suspect she kept friends at a distance in case she lost her drive.'

'I don't understand.'

'Well, it's not an original thought, but the best paintings in my opinion have come from great pain or some kind of altered state. Astrid was no exception. She'd suffered before I met her and she used it as a kind of dark energy in her work. I suspect she was afraid that if she pursued happiness, she would lose that energy and therefore her livelihood. Actually . . .' He gave her a sidelong glance.

'What?'

'. . . I think she worked very hard at being unhappy. Whenever she had a sell-out show, she took the cheque without discussing the details with me. It's almost as if she were afraid of absorbing the praise. Anyway, it worked in her favour because she acted like she couldn't care less whether we kept her on or not. The only thing that gave her away was when I left Porter's to set up on my own. Then she revealed her cards.'

'Tell me.'

'Well, I'd been working for Bernard long enough to know that the real money lay in working for yourself. Astrid gave me a painting once for my birthday and said I could do whatever I wanted to with it. I chose to sell it so I could afford to leave Porter's and rent some gallery space of my own. When I told her, she said she wanted to come with me. It was the greatest compliment she ever paid me and it cemented our relationship for the next thirty years, until I disposed of the gallery and started working with Kate's father instead – you remember the lovely Kate from Cork Street, don't you? We always compare suits when we see one another; we have a friendly rivalry.'

'Bernard must have been furious.'

'Well yes, he was, but he always admired a bit of chutzpah and I think he respected the decision in the end. He used to call her *the harpy*. Nobody else could deal with her but me, so I don't think the relationship would have lasted if she had stayed with him anyway. The more famous she got, the more she took advantage.'

'Like how?'

Edward smiled at a memory. 'Bernard asked her once if she could paint a series of miniatures for an important client of his and she delivered mammoth-sized paintings we could hardly fit into the gallery. A punishment for Bernard for thinking he could tell her what to do.'

'And you didn't do that?'

'No, I left her alone and that's exactly what she wanted. It worked a treat.'

'Didn't you ever worry about her mental state?'

'I'm ashamed to say, I didn't give it a second thought. I was younger then and chasing the money.'

'I can't work out if she intended to die or whether it really was an accident.'

'Suicide?' Edward thought about it for a second and then shook his head. 'I can't see it, somehow. I know I said she worked hard at being unhappy, but she faced problems head-on – she was quite confrontational.'

'Confrontational enough to face her own death?'

'Well, when you put it like that. I don't know. She was volatile, unpredictable.'

'True. You seem to be the only person who could handle that side of her. She was lucky to have you.'

'Well we didn't make a habit of socialising, which won't surprise you. I had several other artists I was trying to develop, and Astrid was miles away from London. We seldom saw each other when she was established. That's why I only met you once. I had high hopes of incorporating a second Jarsdel in my stable, actually.

You showed real talent when she allowed you near her oils. She showed me a couple of paintings you'd done once.'

'Well, I have a talent for tax compliance now, so there,' Isla couldn't keep the edge out of her voice.

'I can't believe you're happy doing that.'

'It suits me.'

'That's not good enough, Isla. I'm sure your mother left all her equipment in the studio. You could give it a go when you get back.'

'She's left precisely zero. That's why I wondered about suicide. She cleared the whole lot out.'

'What? Not even her notebooks?'

'Nothing. I've turned the whole house upside down and there's nothing there. I'm amazed she was that unsentimental about her past. It doesn't fit. Her whole career was based on the past.'

'Have you checked in the eaves?'

The skin on the back of Isla's neck began to prickle. 'No,' she said slowly, 'I didn't know there were any. You mean in the studio at the top of the house?'

'Yes. When she had the roof excavated for the studio, there were odd pockets of space where the roof slanted down to the floor. Years ago, she had a kind of cupboard constructed, I think. I was always on at her to get a proper security system for the house when she became well known, but she told me all her precious things were hidden up there. When she painted over the walls, she told me, you couldn't see where the door to it began and the wall ended. It was completely camouflaged under all that paint.'

'Edward Mason, you're a genius.'

'Well, if you discover some long-lost Astrid Jarsdels up there, do give me a private view before you release them into the world, won't you?'

'You bet I will.'

Chapter Forty-Six

Erin

A bad night's sleep had solidified Erin's thoughts nicely. The anger had not abated. Those seconds . . . those wasted seconds when Isla could have been doing something were wisps of time that could never be clawed back. Isla had stolen them from Frankie. Mark had always taken the path of least resistance and it did not surprise her that he had swallowed everything Isla had fed him. Her disappointment in him deepened.

She would always blame herself for Frankie's accident. But Mark and Isla had their places too, in her mental court of reckoning. Can one apportion blame like so many bad pennies, divided up amongst the guilty? Or is it a solid mass, unable to be carved and split? It was impossible to decipher an answer. She was so blinded by the white heat of her own fury that it was almost a relief to turn to practical matters instead. Her own rehabilitation lay in salvaging herself, she was certain of that. She would deal with Mark and Isla when they returned.

A morning of phone calls focussed her ire. She would have to resume the climb on the career ladder a rung or two below where she left off. But the speed with which she could catch up with her former self could be more rapid than she supposed. An old boss was sympathetic; he remembered how well she worked in his team and he was prepared to take her on again if she was prepared to be patient. An alternative future began to open up in front of her, and, for the first time in many, many weeks, she felt she could breathe.

They arrived in the evening. Frankie was in the bath, listening to music on the radio. Erin was in the bedroom folding laundry. She saw the car climb up the hill, and when they got out they had the easy closeness of a couple. She watched Mark open the boot and find her bag for her. He made a joke when he handed it over and she laughed, nudging his elbow. Then they hugged. It was brief, but she had never been in the position where she thought Isla would accept a hug from her. They had only been together for a few days. She couldn't remember the last time her husband had hugged her.

They started up the garden path and Erin shook. If she thought she was going to come in and see Frankie, she had another thing coming. She darted into the bathroom. The air was thick with the smell of shampoo and the little radio on the toilet cistern filled the room with music. Erin turned it up.

'Frankie, I'm just going to answer the door. I'll be back in five minutes, OK?'

Frankie nodded, not looking at her. Her hands were covered in suds and she was trying to make a big bubble with her hands. She would be oblivious. Erin heard the door click as Mark turned the key and opened the lock. She raced down the stairs, her heat beating like a wild thing.

'Get out,' she hissed. 'Get her out of here.'

Mark was standing in front of Isla in the corridor. Their faces dropped in unison.

'Erin,' Mark said, understanding the situation immediately, 'please don't.' He turned to Isla. 'I'm sorry, I shouldn't have said anything, I . . .' but he stopped, because Erin pushed past him and thrust Isla out of the open door. Isla fell back hard, her backpack breaking her fall, but her head snapped back and hit the path with a satisfying crack.

'I never want to see you again.' Erin was shaking. 'Don't come near my daughter. Leave my husband alone. If you try and see her, I'll tell her what you did.'

Isla's face was white. She struggled to get up. Erin moved towards her but Mark caught her arm and pulled her back. 'Stop. Stop it. This is crazy.'

'Crazy? You think I'm the crazy one? Did you know that Frankie's been talking to her all this time, and she hasn't said a thing to us about it? We're her *parents*.'

Mark looked at her, confused.

'Oh, so she didn't tell you that piece of news when you were together, did she?' Erin lurched again, but Mark held firm. She fought against him; all her attention turned to Isla, who was still on her back on the ground. 'How could you? How could you? She was *drowning*! Six years old! Alone in a filthy cold lake! And you just carried on running . . . running *away*. I despise you. I don't know which is worse. You doing that or coming here and worming your way in with the very person you shat on. If Frankie knew what you did to her . . .'

'Don't tell Frankie. Please.' Isla touched her hand to the back of her head.

Erin saw there was a bit of blood, but not much. Not enough. 'The only reason I won't tell her is to save her from feeling like I do right now. Get up.' Erin watched her struggle like an upturned beetle on the path. Then she realised something. 'It's what you do, isn't it? You take things away from people. Things they love.'

'What? I—'

'You'll never see Frankie again. You won't contact her and you won't visit. If you try to come within fifty feet of her, I'll tell her what you did.'

Isla opened her mouth, but nothing came out.

Mark pulled Erin into the house and threw her onto the sofa. 'Stay there and don't move,' he muttered. She heard the door shut. She heard the car doors opening, closing. She heard Mark gun the engine, drive away, then nothing but the sound of the radio upstairs, blasting out pop tunes.

Chapter Forty-Seven

ISLA

Mark helped Isla into her house. Her head was ringing and she couldn't work the key. There was a struggle trying to open the door and, eventually, it swung open with its habitual reluctance. He put her bag down in the hallway and made her sit at the kitchen table while he got her a glass of water and looked for something to clean her head.

'What's all this about Frankie talking to you?'

Isla groaned as he touched her head with a wet tissue. 'She started saying a few words to me a while back. When she was painting at my place. I didn't want to make a fuss about it. The less of a fuss I made, the more she spoke. I was going to tell you before you left. But I couldn't be sure she wasn't talking at home anyway because I didn't want to ask her about it.'

'Well she wasn't. Erin's furious. How did she find out?'

'Frankie's Dictaphone. I think Erin was recording our conversations.'

Mark squeezed his eyes shut. 'Christ. This just gets better and better.'

'Frankie left it here, the Dictaphone. It's in the sitting room on the writing desk. You should take it before you go.'

'That thing's caused enough trouble. You can keep it. In the meantime, this cut needs a good clean.'

'She's not going to let me see Frankie again.' A miserable tear made its way down Isla's cheek. She felt empty and tired.

He dabbed the back of her head with the tissue. 'Look, Erin can be hot-headed sometimes, give her some time to cool down and maybe we can work something out. I don't support what she wants, if that helps.'

'But I can tell you're not going to go against it.'

'She's Frankie's mother,' he said simply.

'What am I going to do?' Isla tried not to sound like a child. *Frankie's all I have,* she wanted to say. But she couldn't, because she knew how it would sound. She got up and refilled her glass. She had, for the second time in her life, deviated from her own rules about becoming attached to others and the punishment was unbearable.

'She's angry because she's jealous,' Mark said eventually, throwing the tissue in the bin and washing his hands.

'What has Erin got to be jealous about?' Isla thought back to the girl on the beach, in a pretty dress that was new and clean, with two parents and an auntie who loved her. Now a woman with a husband and a child who was perfect. 'What more could she possibly want?'

'She wants Frankie to talk to her. She sees you two together. She hears you two together. That must be pretty hard to listen to.'

'Then she's denying Frankie, too,' said Isla sulkily.

'Is it so bad that she wants to mean as much to her daughter as Frankie does to her? She's hurting, Isla.'

'It's not fair on Frankie, what she's done. It's hurting Frankie.'

'Yes, I suppose it is. But this arrangement was never permanent. We live hundreds of miles away. We were always going to go back.'

She had known this all along, but when he voiced the thing she had been dreading, the violence of it caused her more pain than the cut on her head. A part of her hoped they might never leave, that they might see how good it was for Frankie to stay here. Now she realised it was ludicrous, thinking Frankie would come and visit. She was glad she'd never mentioned the possibility to Mark. 'Then you should go,' she said, turning away from him. 'Leave.'

'Isla, please don't be like this.' Mark squeezed her shoulder.

She spun round, angry. 'You just said this was never permanent. What is there to stay for now? I've ruined everything. There's nothing left.'

Mark took her into his arms and she clung to him, burying her head in his chest. 'If there was any way I could change things, I would,' he whispered, and he rested his cheek on the crown of her head.

'It was an accident,' she wept. 'Why do we always need somebody to blame?'

Mark sighed. 'People used to be more fatalistic. Accidents happened, end of. For what it's worth, I don't think it was anybody's fault any more. I used to think it was easier to hate you. Now I know better.'

He let himself out. She couldn't bear to say goodbye. She sat on the sofa and stared into the sea. It was raining and the wind was picking up. When the light finally departed and the stars filled the sky, there was nothing to look at but her own reflection in the black window. It trembled against the rain that hurled itself in gusts against the pane. The season was changing; it was cooler and less biddable. She shivered and decided to light a fire, for want of anything better to do. She held a match to the paper and watched it take, making sure the kindling was alight. When the flames began to reach, she stood up and put the matches on the mantlepiece.

She saw it then. The arrangement of her beach finds was all wrong. The stones weren't grouped as they should be and the driftwood was upside down. But, worst of all, there was a space in the middle where the wentletrap should have been. She looked on the floor in case it had been dropped, knowing it had not. She searched around the house, her understanding unfolding as she passed through the rooms. There was a glass of juice in the kitchen, half finished. The door to the studio was unlocked and open. The Dictaphone was gone from the writing desk.

Erin had been so very angry. Isla remembered how it was with her when they were children, how her desperation turned to fury as quick as a fish. This wasn't just about Frankie. It was also about another girl Isla had wronged.

Chapter Forty-Eight

ERIN

Mark returned eventually. She honestly didn't care what he'd been up to. She heard him talking to Frankie in the next room, reading her a bedtime story, turning the light off. He found her in the bedroom, sitting on the edge of the bed, a pillow in her lap, staring at the pile of laundry that still needed folding. He sat down next to her and gently took her hand. She was touched that he wasn't angry with her. She'd expected him to take Isla's side. She tried not to cry.

'Are you sure about all of this?' Mark asked. 'Frankie's pretty close with Isla. Have you thought about the effect this might have on her?'

'She's trying to take over, Mark.' She controlled the whine in her voice. 'I can feel Frankie moving away from me. I've always been so sure I was a good mother . . .'

'You are . . .'

'But that woman. She makes me question everything I've done. She makes me feel . . .' Erin grasped for the words and couldn't find anything to describe how seeing Isla and Frankie together made her feel. Like she was an outsider looking in; like they had made a world together she couldn't understand.

'What?' Mark said.

'I don't know. She makes me feel I've been doing it all wrong. She doesn't even have kids of her own, Mark. How could she possibly know what Frankie needs?'

'I don't think she has anyone else. All I know is that Frankie means a lot to her. And she means a lot to Frankie.'

'Just because she doesn't have a family – it doesn't follow that she can have mine.' She knew she sounded like a child, but she couldn't help it.

Mark spoke gently. 'What if it puts Frankie's recovery back? Isla's the only person Frankie's spoken to.'

'If she can talk to Isla, she can talk to me,' Erin said darkly. 'Has it occurred to you that Isla might not be what you think? There's something about her that's not right.' She thought about the room at the top of the house, the feeling she was being watched, and knew if she brought it up she'd sound deranged. She looked at him, pleading. 'We need a new start, Mark. At least, I do. Something has to happen. I can't go on like this.' She squeezed his hand sadly. 'We need to get out of here. And when we get home, I need to figure out what happens next.'

'What do you mean?' he asked, squeezing back.

She sighed. 'Even if Frankie hadn't had the accident, I think we would have fallen apart, sooner or later. You love the hotel. I don't. I need something else. I'm suffocating.'

'Are you going to leave us?' He sounded so sad, it wavered her resolve.

'I can't. Because of Frankie. But if you agree, I'll move into the suite when we get home.'

Mark looked away. 'I wish I hadn't told you.'

'You were right to tell me. I had a right to know what she did to Frankie.'

'What's going to happen now?'

'We are going to pack up this house and leave . . . I'm going to get myself a job. In fact, I already have a job.'

'Where?'

'In London. At my old firm. It's not as exciting as what I was doing before, but it's a start and I really need a new start, Mark. I've tried so hard, but I need to get out before I go mad.'

'Do I get any choice in this?' His voice was heavy.

'Yes. You get to choose where I live. I'll go if you want me to leave the hotel. I could try and find a cheap flat nearby.' They both knew that was impossible. They lived in the most expensive borough in London.

'I don't want you to leave. And I don't want you to go mad.' He sounded very sad.

'No,' she agreed. 'Neither do I.'

'How are we going to look after Frankie if you're holding down a full-time job?'

'We can manage between us and school. I can work flexi-hours. A lot of events are held in the evening so I can take some late mornings or come back early sometimes. I'll make it work.'

'And what about me? You're just throwing away our marriage?'

'I find it very hard to forget what you said to me, that day. I will always remember the way you looked at me in that hospital waiting room. I can't be with someone who looked at me like that.'

'But I forgive you, Erin. I love you!'

'And I love you. And I love Frankie. Which is why I'm going to stay with both of you and be some kind of family until we're ready to move on. But don't you see? I can't forgive myself.' She took her hand away gently and wiped away the tears. 'So how can I possibly begin to forgive you?'

Chapter Forty-Nine

PENNY

Penny saw the lights on in the house and knew Isla was back. She shrank into the sofa. She didn't want recriminations. Outside, a powerful gust of wind hurled debris against her windows. Penny lit a cigarette and listened.

'I had to write that letter,' she said at last, blowing the smoke into the air. 'Jacob didn't give me a choice.'

The curtains lifted and sighed.

She stubbed the cigarette out, ran upstairs and packed a few essentials. She pulled on her coat and prepared herself for the long walk to Jacob's house. It was more than three miles and it was getting dark, but if she arrived in the car it would be easier for him to turn her away.

When it started raining, she grew afraid he wouldn't be in. She didn't want to go back to the house alone, especially without a torch. She knocked at his door and crossed her fingers. It opened swiftly enough. She took this as a good sign.

'Hello, stranger,' he said with a wary look in his eye. He held the door fast in his hand, cocking his head to one side in an inducement for her to speak.

'I thought if I walked here, you wouldn't be able to refuse me.' She tried to make light of the situation, but the fear that this might truly be the last time they spoke threatened to overcome her. Begging wasn't her style. She wouldn't come here twice.

'A walk of contrition, then?'

'If you like.'

'I take it you've finally told Isla?'

'I imagine she'll be reading a full and frank explanation as we speak.'

'Hmm, I don't know if that counts, does it?'

'You didn't say I had to tell her face to face!'

'No, I suppose I didn't. And you do look very sorry for yourself here on my doorstep.'

'I'm wet and cold. And yes, I'm feeling very sorry for myself indeed.'

'You'd better come in then,' he murmured as he kissed her, 'let's get you out of those wet clothes.'

Chapter Fifty

ISLA

Penny was wrong. Isla had not noticed the letter. She had slept on the sofa, unable to get herself upstairs until the dawn light woke her up. It was only when she shuffled into the kitchen to make herself coffee that she saw the letter on the table. When she opened it, there was a disconnect between what her eyes were reading and what her brain could process. As she re-read Penny's words, it was impossible to undo the emotional knot that Astrid had tied. It was, though, a confirmation that her obsession with Clare came from a deeper place than idle curiosity. There was a bond between them that had endured, even after her death.

Bad things happened in threes. Isla counted them off in her head. She would never see Frankie again, Astrid was an imposter. Isla looked around the house, wondering what the next thing would be, expecting it to jump out and ambush her right there in the kitchen. If she included Astrid's death, maybe it had already happened. Isla tried feeling pleased she was free of the burden of Astrid, but she couldn't. Astrid was a person who didn't fit easily into any role that convention demanded. She had spent her whole life trying to navigate a world that wasn't welcoming to her and Isla had begun to feel she was owed some sympathy. She had gained and lost a parent in the space of seconds and that was something that couldn't be contained in a single emotion. She sat, motionless, at the kitchen table, filled with regret, anger and grief. But what she found the hardest to comprehend was why Astrid had lied to her and why Penny had been complicit.

Penny had done her best to explain in benign language what had seemed to be, in Isla's eyes, a monstrous deceit. She tried to muster up some more anger and found she was just too tired. She looked around her. Maybe she should sell this house and start again. It seemed to suck the joy out of everyone that lived here. But if she did that she would cut any remaining ties with her family, such as it was. Maybe one day Frankie would come to look for her. And what then? What if her departure prevented a reunion? The idea of starting again terrified her, anyway. Where would she go? She couldn't return to London and not be able to see Frankie. She would look for her in every girl she passed.

She felt everything more keenly now she had suffered loss. Maybe Erin was right; a person needed allies. She couldn't endure this alone, as Astrid had done. Penny had written that letter with good intentions. She was a friend Isla could not afford to lose. But when Isla knocked at her door, the house was empty. It occurred to her that perhaps she had gone away. She peered through the windows and saw no signs of life. It was another grey day, lowering with storm. The rain had fallen steadily all night and although it had stopped in the early hours, it looked like worse was to come. She would go for a run before it broke. A jog along the sand would make her feel better and Penny might be back by the time she returned.

The beach was empty and the bleakness suited her mood. She ran down to the shoreline. She had missed the sense of space that enveloped her now. She had not forgotten its perpetual, comforting rhythm. The place where Clare was pulled out of the water lay towards the end of the bay and before Isla had even been conscious of planning a route, her feet took her in that direction. This was always going to be the focus of her run, she supposed. She wanted to look upon that stretch of water with a new perspective.

My mother drowned here, Isla thought, trying out the unfamiliar words in her head. *My mother was called Clare. She died when I was a baby*. She paused at the mass of black water. It looked eerie in the dwindling light and the words brought her no comfort. As she ran on, it dawned on her why Astrid had always encouraged her to call her by her name. The word Mother would have been a lie that Astrid was not prepared to hear over and over again. Maybe it was some kind of tribute to Clare. She remembered what Penny had said once: *I think she found you hard to look at sometimes*. That remark had stung at the time, but now she grasped the reality of seeing the ghost of your sister emerging in the face of her child. It must have been bitter for Astrid.

A thunderous growl in the distance refocused Isla's attention to the oncoming weather front. The wind had gathered itself into a powerful gale and she could see the blackening cloud bank advancing over the sea towards the bay. She would run to the steps carved into the cliff that joined the path above and travel back that way. The ground would be firmer and faster up there, but the journey would be slightly longer. She calculated that the steps were a ten-minute sprint. They were not well marked out, even on a clear day, but she thought she remembered a pile of enormous rocks that heralded their presence. A theatrical crack of thunder tore through the heavens and the rain changed from a steady patter to a biblical downpour. It was impossible to keep her head up to locate herself; the water ran like a sheet down her forehead and into her eyes.

Just as she was beginning to despair that she had missed them, she saw three hunched black shapes crouched on the sand, like ancient creatures oblivious to the maelstrom around them. The sky had taken on an eerie, jaundiced quality now and a small niggle of panic welled up at the thought of climbing up the cliff in the downpour. She could barely see as she fought her way to the foot of the steps and grasped the rope that served as a bannister, hauling herself up onto a surface that was fast becoming slick with mud.

Halfway up, a cold stab of fear halted her progress as she wondered if this was the right thing to do. Should she turn back and run along the beach or should she carry on up a set of stairs that was fast disappearing? She cursed herself for not looking at the tide timetable. She had no idea if it was going out or coming in towards her. She couldn't risk going back along the beach if the sea came in. It would be too quick and she wasn't sure she could make it to the sea-wall before the tide did. She turned her head towards the bay to gauge the waves, but it was too chaotic to make out the direction of travel. The change in the water was frightening and she felt paralysed with indecision. Up and away from the sea had to be the sensible course of action. She turned back to the rope and resumed her climb, but the step below her foot crumbled and gave way under the deluge of water. She lost her grip on the rope and started sliding down. Terror flooded her body; it filled her mouth, her chest, her legs as she struggled in vain to stay upright. When she finally lost control, she thought to herself: *this must be bad thing number three.* Then she entered the darkness and the fear fell away.

'Isla!' Her name, half screamed in a howling wind. Penny's voice carrying over from the cliff path above. She had wanted to talk to Penny about something, but couldn't remember what it was. No matter. She was tired and wanted to sleep now. It wasn't important.

'Isla! Wake up!' A voice in her ear, a squeeze on her shoulder, the driving rain falling into half-closed eyes. Pulling and pushing of limbs. Impossible to sit up. Her head hurt too much. Better to lie down.

'Get up, get up! Or we'll both drown here! Can you move your legs? Put your arm around my shoulder! Shit. Jacob! She won't get up!'

A man's voice: 'Can you take her by the ankles and drag her to the steps? I can come down and meet you and we can haul her up together.'

'What if she's got a neck injury? Aren't I supposed to keep her still?'

'It's either dragging or drowning. There's no choice. Take your scarf off and wrap it around her neck like a collar. It might help. We need to get her up here before the tide comes in. Why the hell didn't she use the new steps instead of these ones? She must have known they were closed.'

'The sign's blown down. Maybe she got confused, I don't know. Oh, she's waking up! Isla! Can you hear me?'

Had she been to the dentist? Her mouth wouldn't work properly and seemed swollen somehow. Something gritty between her teeth. Salt on her tongue. Why was she so wet? It was freezing. And she couldn't move her head. There was something tied around her neck. A familiar voice nagging her, a face hovering over hers. 'Penny?'

'Yes, it's me. Sit up if you can, we need to get out of here.'

'Am I at the dentist?'

'What? No, you're on the beach and I need to get you walking up to the steps here.'

'Oh.'

'Not those steps, they're broken. These here. The wooden ones. Why on earth are you out in this weather?'

'Just wanted . . .' The wind, battering her eardrums, took away her words.

'Never mind. Can you walk up a little bit? Jacob's coming down to help. He's got the car parked up at the top for us. Why didn't you carry your phone with you? We saw you running along the sand and couldn't believe what a stupid girl you were. I tried calling you!'

'Hmm.' Her head was beginning to hurt now and her fingers wouldn't work properly on the metal handrail. Funny that, she could have sworn it was made of rope.

'Isla, grab my hand.' A large pair of arms, looming above her out of the rain. Better than a handrail. A push from behind. Steady as she goes. One step at a time. Pull, push, step. Pull, push, step. Then the calming warmth of a car and a blanket. And then darkness once more.

Chapter Fifty-One

PENNY

It was late when Jacob returned from the hospital and he made Penny jump when he poked his head round the door.

'Ah, still up, I see. That whisky looks good. Any left?'

Penny nodded towards the bottle on the side table and went to fetch him a glass.

'There's no need to worry,' he said. He lowered himself into the armchair opposite hers. 'Isla's going to be fine. I left her at the hospital. They'll make sure it's nothing worse than concussion. Panic over.' He leaned forward and looked at her as she came back into the room. 'Penny, what's the matter?'

Penny tried to speak, but the words deserted her. Her head was pounding. She touched her temple lightly, but even that was painful. 'I . . . I'm just glad Isla's going to be OK.'

'You don't look very glad. You look like death. Is it your head again?'

At this, her eyes pooled with tears. She could have let him believe it was just a headache, but she was sick of pretending.

'This isn't like you. What's going on?'

She shook her head and sat in the armchair opposite. 'I shouldn't have written that letter.'

'Why ever not?'

'If I tell you, it might make it worse.'

'Penny,' he sighed, 'we've been here before. No more secrets.'

'I can't.' Her voice sounded as she felt. Frightened, small, unstable.

Jacob leaned forward. 'How can we live like this if you won't talk to me? Shall I leave again? Give you some time to think it through?'

'No!' It came out as a shout. 'Please don't leave. I can't live here alone any more.'

'What is it?'

She shook her head in an attempt to fend off his questions, but the pain in her temple made her resolve melt away. When he softened his voice and knelt on the rug next to her, she crumbled.

'Penny, I promise I won't leave you if you tell me what's going on.'

'It's Astrid,' she admitted.

'What about her?'

'*She* did this.' Her voice dropped to a whisper.

'What did she do?'

'I think she did this to Isla. She hurt her. And I think she's trying to hurt me. And I'm beginning to wonder if she was responsible for Clare's death.'

'Whoa. Where did all this come from?'

How could she explain it to him without sounding like a lunatic? 'I *feel* her,' she said, 'everywhere in this house. Not when you're here, but when I'm alone. At first, I liked it. Her presence comforted me. But when Isla came, and we started getting friendly . . . She doesn't want me talking to Isla. She didn't like me writing that letter. And she never took that necklace off in the last few years. There was something going on.'

'Penny,' Jacob said gently, closing his hand around hers, 'Astrid died. She can't do anything to you now. It's impossible.'

Penny scoffed. 'Since when did a minor thing like death ever stop Astrid getting what she wanted?'

'What do you think she wants, Penny?'

'She wants me to keep quiet. She's angry that I told Isla about Clare. She wants Isla gone. I don't know.'

'Isla got caught in a storm, Penny. A storm that was well publicised ahead of its arrival. Clare drowned in a terrible accident. There's no evidence to suggest Astrid was responsible.'

'I knew you would rationalise everything.' She tried to wrench her hand away but he kept a firm hold.

'I'm just trying to understand and explain. There's no need to be frightened.'

'There is! She's here! In this house!' Penny gestured around wildly with her free arm.

'What makes you think that?'

'Little things. The palm, over there, tipped all over the rug. My coffee cup on the floor. Shadows. Salt water.' Penny cried as she relayed the details, knowing how pathetic it all sounded.

Jacob fished in his pocket for a tissue. 'That palm falls over when it's not watered. It's likely it fell because the pot was dry.'

'But I feel her here, Jacob!' Penny thumped her chest. 'She's out there too! In the wind! Waiting . . .'

'For what?'

Penny couldn't answer. All she could feel was a sense of foreboding that thumped in her chest as loudly as the thump in her head.

'Penny,' Jacob said, 'what's the point of keeping secrets? From what you're saying, Astrid was punishing you long before you wrote that letter. Surely it's better to get the truth out where it belongs? Being Astrid's secret keeper is making you ill.'

'Well I'm not her secret keeper any more, am I? She's angry with me for writing that letter. I shouldn't have done it. I promised her I wouldn't tell anyone about Clare. I let her down.'

'She's dead, Penny. You owe her nothing. You were a better friend to her than she deserved, if you ask me. I never understood what you saw in her.'

Penny sighed. 'There's something about living here, in this place. There's a division. It's like there's a separate set of rules for us. I know Astrid could be difficult, but she was my friend. As we got older, we needed each other more. I saw her for what she was. What's the word everybody trots out these days? Vulnerable.'

'Penny, I think you've got this the wrong way round. I think you were the only friend that Astrid had. I think she was afraid of losing you. She never liked it when I came over to see you. She relied on you. I think she was the weaker one in your relationship, not you.'

'I never thought about it like that,' Penny sniffed. 'I suppose it would explain that necklace.'

'What necklace?'

'The one with the hamsa motif. I think she was trying to protect herself from Clare. I think she was frightened, especially in the last year or two. Everything seemed to catch up with her. Whichever way you look at it, Astrid behaved badly. The way she raised Isla as her own, even if she didn't have anything to do with Clare's death.'

'There's not a shred of proof in any of this, Penny. It's just supposition.'

Penny persisted. 'The things that have happened to me since Astrid died; the same could have been happening to her. She had a haunted look about her this past year, Jacob. She looked frightened, sometimes.'

'People who carry a lot of sorrow in their lives and don't have many friends tend to die earlier than those who make the best of things, in my experience. It doesn't mean they come back and haunt their friends, though.'

Penny shoved him away. 'I'm not making this up. I sense something; her displeasure, I don't know. She fills this house when I'm alone. It feels like she has unfinished business with me. It scares me.'

'I know you're not making it up. But you feel her because that's what happens when people with whom you have a strong bond die. They don't just disappear. They live in your memory. Astrid was always in and out of this house and more often than not she was in a disagreeable mood. Of course you're likely to feel her here. It's a way of missing her, that's all.'

'I'd prefer it if she was a benign presence.'

Jacob stood up and scratched his chin. 'Then we need to do something about it.'

'Like what?' Penny asked.

'Did Isla ever scatter Astrid's ashes?'

'I don't think so. They were given to her, but she had no plans as I recall.'

'Maybe we could suggest it, lay a few ghosts? Do you think Isla would like to do that?'

'If there's anyone who needs to lay a few ghosts, it's her.'

Chapter Fifty-Two

ISLA

The house was both familiar and alien. She could hear the sea and the wind, so she knew she was at home. The view from her room was the same but a little skewed somehow. She was much closer to the lagoon. It was all wrong.

'Feeling better?' There was Jacob, in an armchair next to her bed. She didn't recognise the chair and wondered how he got in here. Then it struck her and she remembered she was at Penny's house.

'Headache,' she mumbled, her mouth thick with sleep.

'Yes, you will have, but I think you'll survive. Do you remember going to the hospital?'

'Sort of. It's all in pieces. My memory.'

'You have concussion and a few cuts, but nothing serious. They just want us to keep an eye on you for a day or two. What on earth were you doing out there?'

'I dunno. I knew it looked a bit stormy so I thought I'd go out before it broke and then I couldn't get up the steps. I didn't think it was going to be that bad.'

'It was all over the news and weather reports! Batten down your hatches! Stay indoors.'

Isla was suddenly struck by a thought. 'Oh God, is my house OK?'

'Penny went to have a look yesterday and apart from the disappearance of a few roof tiles and your telly aerial, everything seems OK. You should get the roof sorted out though, otherwise it will leak.'

Something nagged at her, something she felt she should remember about the roof, but it disappeared as quickly as it had appeared.

'Sorry. I'm such an idiot,' she said, 'I've put you both to so much trouble. I'll get out of your hair this afternoon.'

'One more night here and then we can let you go. The hospital didn't want to discharge you, but I persuaded them they could if you submitted to my care. I need to do my duty by you.'

'Thank you.'

'Are you hungry? Penny's making dinner. I can bring some up for you if you like?'

'That would be great. I'm famished.'

'OK. I won't be long.'

'Jacob? Do you think Penny would bring it up to me?'

'Of course! She's not been herself at all. She wasn't sure you wanted to speak to her.'

'I'd love to speak to her. I've missed her.'

'She missed you too. She's been anxious about the letter.'

'Tell her there's no need.'

The soft footfall on the stair gave way to a quiet knocking at her door.

'Isla? Are you awake? I brought you some soup.' Penny laid a tray on the dressing table and helped Isla sit up, moving the pillows round her back and smoothing the duvet. Penny sat down next to the bed and took Isla's hand in hers. 'I'm so very, very sorry.' She shook her head. 'I had no business keeping that from you.'

'It was Astrid's decision, not yours.'

'I don't know how you feel about her now, Isla, but I want you to know that for all her faults, she never meant to do badly by you. I know she was difficult. But she had nothing. No one. Mental illness is better understood now. Back then, you had to pull yourself together.'

'Why do you think she kept me? She could have handed me over for adoption. Why go to all that trouble of lying to everyone?'

'Because she really loved you even though she didn't show it very often? Because you were the last piece of her family? Because you were part of Clare? It could be any or all of those reasons. Doesn't have to be one. The fact is, she kept you.'

'You think? She just did it because she wanted to? She must have felt obliged to Clare. She must have felt trapped into doing it,' Isla said gloomily.

Penny shook her head. 'She probably hesitated at the thought, it's true. She wouldn't be human if she hadn't thought about what she was getting herself into. But once she decided, there was no question.'

Isla thought about this for some time. 'Do you think that if you hesitate before helping someone, you're a bad person?'

'If you jump straight into the unknown, it's foolhardy.'

'But what if, by hesitating, you damage that person's life?'

'What do you mean? Do you think she did that . . . damaged your life?'

'No. I'm just . . . thinking.'

'Ready for food?' Penny pulled the tray over and settled it before Isla.

'Jacob says the house has some storm damage,' Isla said.

'A bit. I know a good roofer in the village. He'll be busy the next few days, but I already phoned him and he said he might be able to squeeze you in tomorrow earliest, next week latest.'

'Thanks, Penny. It's amazing what these houses withstand,' Isla said thoughtfully as she stirred her soup, 'if I only lost a few tiles yesterday, it bodes well for the future.'

'Does that mean there is one? For you here, I mean?' Penny looked hopeful.

'Yes. Returning to London is impossible now. I guess here is as good a place as any to settle down.'

'Well thank God for that. I can't bear the idea of Astrid's studio being torn apart. I'd never been inside it until after she died and it broke my heart to see all those beautiful paintings all over the walls.'

A memory dislodged itself in Isla's mind.

'What's the matter?' said Penny.

'Something . . . something about the roof and the studio that I have to remember. What the hell was it?' Her eyes roved across the room, searching for the answer.

'The roof tiles? Like I said, I'm dealing with that.'

'No, it's got something to do with the paintings on the wall, about them being valuable.'

'Maybe you could get them insured? Though I don't see how they could be stolen up there.'

'That's it! How could I have forgotten?' She groaned and touched her sore head. 'I need to go up there.'

'Well not right now, you don't.'

'I do. There's something up there I need to check.'

'Can't it wait till tomorrow?' You need a bit more bed rest before Jacob will let you go. I can't have you running up to the loft.'

Isla sat up and pushed her tray away. 'It's important.'

'Well what about if I go up there for you?'

She considered this and decided against it. If there was anything up in that loft that had been damaged, it was already too late. She looked out of the window. The wind had dropped and it wasn't raining any more. A wave of fatigue enveloped her. 'No, it's OK.' She slumped back onto the pillows and closed her eyes. 'I guess it'll wait for one more night.'

'Sure?'

'Yeah.'

Penny took the tray. 'Then get some rest.'

That night Isla dreamed she was crawling in the roof space, picking her way through rafters and cobwebs, trying to find something that tethered her existence to the Jarsdel family tree. Like a blind thing, feeling her way along in the shadows, her fingers searched for clues, closing on form and texture that made her shudder. Finally she came upon a shape of metal reaching through oak, corroded and stiff to turn. As she worked the handle free of rust, it twisted and slipped out of her fingers opening into a vast room full of raging seas and blackened rocks. She smelled salt and sand, felt the whip of wind on her face. She closed the door and carried on crawling. Here was another handle, identical to the first. Again she coaxed the metal free of grit and dirt. Again it opened into a storm of water breaking over ragged stone, threatening to pull her in. When she woke, it seemed like she had spent the whole night on her hands and knees, searching for answers in a house that refused to yield.

She ate her breakfast in silence, brooding over the possibility that Edward was wrong and there might be nothing of importance stored in those eaves. The idea of finding nothing twisted uncomfortably in her stomach. This was her last chance for clarity. To come back from that house empty-handed would be a huge disappointment. In any case, she had to prepare herself for the possibility that whatever secrets those rooftop spaces held, she might end up wishing she had never looked.

Chapter Fifty-Three

ISLA

Penny and Jacob had both offered to come with her, partly out of concern for her general state of health – she had woken from a bad night's sleep looking particularly peaky – but really Isla could see they were burning with curiosity. She promised to tell them everything when she returned, even if there was nothing to see.

She walked down the lane, picking her way slowly over the potholes. The ground beneath her felt unfamiliar, the soles of her feet tender with bed rest. It was good, though, to smell the sea air and hear the gulls above her head. The effort it took to unlock the door prompted her body to remind her that she was still quite bruised from the fall. As it swung open and her eyes were drawn to the foot of the stairs, she realised she had been very lucky. If she was going to live here permanently, she needed to start paying more attention to her surroundings and that meant listening to the forecast and learning the tide timetable.

As she climbed the stairs and entered the room, the paintings on the walls loomed large. Through the windows the sea still looked restless and grey, so today it blended well with the theatre that Astrid had created. Isla felt she would never tire of looking at these images. They had lost their sinister edge somehow, now that she knew the truth. She still considered Astrid her mother, but something about knowing they were not so closely bound together had a freeing effect and Isla felt she could regard Astrid from more of a distance. That space of separation had brought about a tenderness for the woman who had tried to parent her and Isla was surprised at the urge she felt to talk to her in the place that Astrid felt most content.

'Astrid, I'm here to discover your secrets,' Isla murmured as she entered the room, 'so do me a favour would you and give me a hand?' Her words scattered and fell into the sound of the tide below her.

For a room in the roof, the walls still reached fairly high; there was plenty of eaves space behind them, she supposed, because the house was detached. It was unlikely that the handles to any hidden doors would be too high to use, yet nothing seemed to protrude from the wall, so Isla began by crouching down and peering closely for channels in the paint that might suggest the edge of a door. The surface was textured and thick with pigment. It would be impossible to see any kind of groove or fissure if the colour had seeped in and covered it. She might be here for some time. Reaching for her glasses in the pocket of her shirt, she lowered them onto the end of her nose.

Crawling on her hands and knees, she felt the tumble of the tides beneath her fingertips. There were worlds within worlds here. What had appeared as a large-scale seascape suddenly morphed into microcosms containing tiny details that simply disappeared when you stood back. She had not fully appreciated the level of detail that Astrid had factored into her work. Isla had assumed everything was applied in instinctive and expansive brushstrokes, but there had plainly been a time when Astrid had deliberately added in tiny elements that only she would ever know were there. Here, amongst the sinister rocks, a tiny pool revealed itself with fragments of sea-weed suspended in brine. An arch of spray transformed the light into a thousand tiny rainbows. Delicate shells and quick, silvery fishes appeared and disappeared amongst the gigantic sweep of the sea. The more she looked, the more Isla saw. Embedded in the violence of the elements, tiny islands of hope waited to be discovered. A murky mist obscured a small figure in the far distance picking her way along the sand, a cockling bucket swinging at her side. Was that figure a Jarsdel? Or a figment of Astrid's imagination? The regret at never knowing made Isla catch her breath. She remembered what Edward had said about the painting of Clare, the optimism it was infused with. She had misjudged Astrid. Her work wasn't all about loss and anger and violence. It was about the possibility of hope and beauty growing in a hostile environment. Isla thought back to the scent of roses, the sound of footsteps tracking across the studio floor, the nest of hair on the table. She had arrived here unwilling to believe in ghosts, but a part of her wondered whether it was all a bid from Astrid to be understood.

She glanced over the rest of the room. The expanse of wall she had yet to look at was daunting. This was going to take ages. Maybe she should search in a different way. Astrid was an artist, and she was clever. She clearly liked putting little hidden details into her work. Maybe she had played with the idea of hiding the handles of the door to the eaves? Isla looked around the room at the various seascapes and rock formations merging and transforming. She relaxed her eyes and scanned the scenery, trying to sense inconsistencies or details that drew her eye. Isla moved slowly around the room and stopped at a section of cliff. It was monolithic, painted in dizzying perspective. Two small figures stood at the top, looking down at her, so high up they were almost at ceiling height. She tracked the vertical structure of the strata down the wall and in a flash her eye was tugged back to a divergence. A small curl of an ammonite, low to the floor, tucked amongst the vertiginous line. It was the only thing that disrupted the rhythm. Marching over to the fossil, she could see the coil was also discordant. This was no Fibonacci spiral; it was instead the disguise of a perfect circle, three-dimensional, sunk into the wall. Isla touched the ring gently and saw it was hinged to a larger metal base plate, recessed into the wood. It would have been impossible for the casual onlooker to spot. But not to a curious little girl. Isla imagined Frankie in this room, trailing her fingers at just at the right height, coming across the handle, turning it as Isla was doing now, pulling back the door. The panel gave way and in an instant she understood why she hadn't discovered its outline before. It was not rectangular; it was cut in an irregular jagged shape to mimic the cliff that concealed it. It was completely camouflaged.

'I have to hand it to you, Astrid, you're all about the art. Even your storage is exquisitely constructed.' Isla pulled the panel wider. The space behind was dark, but she could see that it was large enough to stand up in and ran the length of the house. It was also full of objects she could not make out in the lack of light. Her heart lurched with excitement as she dashed downstairs to locate a torch. The beam was weak, but quickly illuminated a light-pull as she entered the eaves. It wasn't like her dream at all. The space had been insulated and boarded over so the rafters were hidden and there were no cobwebs to be seen. It was clean and dry. The perfect place to store paintings. Canvases leaned up against the roof, unframed but completed. Most were typical of her work, but there were some in the far end of the space that looked different in technique but still clearly Astrid's doing. She would have to get Edward here to look at them.

Then another canvas caught her eye. It was stored a little apart from the others, propped up against the eaves in a space of its own. The smudges of a seascape in blues and greys were still visible beneath the smeared and scraped crimson paint. Isla remembered the frustration she had felt, the desire for a connection with Astrid so brutally refused. It was a crude attempt, but now she looked at it more closely with adult eyes, she saw there was something there, within the paint, that spoke of her frustration; something that was entirely her own. But why had Astrid kept it all these years? Why had she not painted over it, as Isla had assumed? She put the canvas back, leaning it carefully against the roof.

A plan chest at the opposite end of the eaves revealed sketchbooks and some beautiful charcoal studies of a child squatting over a rock pool. With a jolt, she realised the studies must be of her. She turned them over and saw the date. It tallied with the age of the child in the picture. The representation was accomplished in only a few strokes, but it was done tenderly and with obvious warmth. The other drawers were filled with various paper stocks and on top of these lay a slender wooden box full of pencils and willow charcoal. Isla moved the box and took a pile of smaller sketchbooks of finely textured and rough-edged cream paper. The paintings didn't really interest Isla. She was already familiar with that style and subject matter. These charcoal and pencil drawings though, that was something new. The affection with which they had been executed touched her. She looked more closely and, with a stab of emotion, saw they were portraits of her as an adult. She looked at the dates scribbled in the corners. These were fairly recent, executed during a time they hadn't spoken for a while. For some reason, in her final years, Astrid had turned her focus from Clare to her.

She found you hard to look at.

Hadn't Penny said that? Judging by these images, that wasn't always the case. Maybe Astrid was more comfortable observing from afar, through the safety of willow and paper. The drawings she now slid carefully back into the plan chest were the most intimate things Astrid had ever said, and Isla knew she would treasure them.

As she prepared to exit the room, she looked around at a low table covered with a long muslin cloth. Its surface was clear of ornament. Why would a table be up here if it wasn't used for anything? There was no light with which to draw or paint by in here and the plan chest served any storage needs. Isla frowned and bent down to brush the fabric to one side. Instead of slender table legs, she confronted a solid mass of dark polished wood. Not a table then, but a chest of some sort. She put down the sketchpads and knelt to take the cloth away. The chest was very simply constructed and without any decorative metalwork. Isla was pleased to see there was no keyhole to confound her, just a heavy-looking lid to prise off. She prepared for another frustrating episode of old and stubborn hinges, but, to her delight, it opened easily. The lid rested against the pitch of the roof and she peered into the cavity, but the light in the room was not strong enough to illuminate the space. She fetched the torch and shone its beam into the chest.

From out of the gloom two faces smiled up at her. It was a photograph. A woman with long black hair ruffled by the sea wind, sitting on the sea-wall, legs dangling free. One arm circled a baby in her lap, her fingers splayed protectively against its chest, the other reaching out of the image, pointing at the photographer who must have been standing below on the sand. The expression on her face was comfortable, loving, and Isla realised it must have been Astrid behind the lens. Even at such a young age, Isla could see Clare's features were reflected in her own baby lips that parted to reveal a gummy smile to the camera, the same dark eyebrows arching high, the left a little straighter than the right. Isla could see Clare was in the middle of saying something to her, her mouth set in an amused 'O'. She would have given a lot to find out what that word was. Isla turned the picture over and pencilled in Astrid's hand: *Clare and Isla. A good day.* As if it had been important to write that fact down, because it could so easily be forgotten. Isla looked around the room, taking in the plan chest filled with sketches and the canvases covered in cloth. If the contents of the eaves were Astrid's heart, the contents of this chest were surely her soul.

Isla reached in and sifted through the jumble. The significance of what she saw; she couldn't believe it was all recorded on the most fragile of mediums – paper. It came in the form of letters, diaries, sketchbooks and newspaper clippings. It didn't seem right to disturb their contents in this dark and sombre space. Isla carefully laid the muslin out and gently placed the contents of the chest on top. She gathered up the corners and lifted the lot into daylight.

Chapter Fifty-Four

ISLA

Isla slept through the late afternoon and, on waking, ate a casserole Penny had left in her fridge. She cleared and wiped down the table with infinite care. She lowered the muslin cloth onto the wood and ordered its cargo, hardly knowing which bundle to unwrap first. She started with the letters and didn't finish until the sun came up in the small hours of the next morning. As she stoked up the log burner and made herself some breakfast, a knock at the door told her Penny and Jacob could contain themselves no longer. She took three cups down, settled them next to the kettle and let them in.

'Your light has been on all night. We were worried you might . . . oh!' Penny gasped at the display on the kitchen table.

'I see you found what you were looking for then,' said Jacob.

'And more. I've been reading all night. It's their whole life. Astrid and Clare. Everything documented. It's beautiful.' Whether it was the lack of sleep, being in the company of people who understood her, or the fact that some kind of gap in her psyche had been filled, Isla burst into tears and sobbed with relief.

'Where shall we start?' Penny put her arm around her, engulfing her in patchouli and tobacco, looking at a lifetime of documentation spread out over the table.

'Well, I put everything chronologically so it's easier to understand. There are diaries from Clare and Astrid. They begin before Alf, their father, died and they pretty much chronicle their lives here. Some of it's mundane, but, as historical documents, they are pretty interesting. They describe life by the sea, their schooling, their aspirations. I haven't read them in great detail, but, as far as I can tell, they're fairly typical diary entries from young girls. The significant stuff comes from when Nell, their mother, falls ill. So I guess this one first.' She handed Penny and Jacob a handwritten letter from Nell to Clare and Astrid.

> My Beloved Girls,
>
> I treasured you from the moment you were born. As I write this, I know that time is closing in. If I could stay with you I would choose to do it, but every winter I wonder if I will ever see the spring. Remember this: the grief at our parting is mine to bear. It must not sully your lives. Be happy that we had this time together. Look after one another, be strong, be kind.
>
> Your loving
> Mother

'That must have been an impossible letter to write,' muttered Jacob.

Penny didn't take her eyes off the page, now yellowed with age. 'I remember her a little. It was typical of her to do something like this, telling them not to be sad. She was a lovely woman. The girls missed her terribly.'

'Well yes, that brings me on to the next letter. The diaries stopped after Nell died. I imagine running a house and working didn't leave them much time to write.'

'Or maybe they didn't feel like it,' suggested Jacob.

'True.' Isla handed over another letter to Penny. 'I still don't know if you kept this from me or whether you didn't know yourself. Either way, it's pretty hard to read,' she said.

'*Dear Astrid,*' Penny read and then looked up at Isla and Jacob. 'Dear God, this is a suicide note. From Clare.' She pulled out a wooden chair and sat down with a thump. 'I had no idea. Astrid never told me. Poor Clare. How awful.'

'I knew something wasn't right about her drowning like that,' said Isla.

Penny nodded. 'I felt the same as you,' she said, 'but there was shame in a suicide back then. Maybe that's why Astrid kept it to herself. I could have helped her if only she'd told me. It would have made things so much easier.' Penny put her head in her hands and Jacob rubbed her back.

'I'm sorry, Isla,' he said. 'This must have come as quite a shock for you, too.'

'I couldn't take it in when I first read it. I was angry with Astrid for keeping it from me, then I read it again and . . . Look, Jacob, read it out loud.'

Jacob cleared his throat and read the letter in a steady voice.

Dear Astrid,

I fear I am continuing a family tradition of letter writing before one's passing and I am so very sorry I have not been able to speak to you about this in person. I am too much of a coward and I am afraid you will try and save me once again. Mother's letter asked us to look after one another; be strong, be kind. I am unable to do any of these things. I can't even look after my own daughter. You are already a better mother to her than I could be.

I have tried, Astrid, and every day is a trial through which I cannot put myself any longer. I am poisoning this house and I am poisoning my child. This is a sickness for which there is no cure. Father had it, I believe. I have it and I will not infect the rest of this family with it.

I have thought hard about what I should write to you. I have felt Mother's wishes strangling me when I have been unable to fulfil them. I will not do the same to you. Live your life however you choose. I am departing mine, so I have no right to ask anything of you. Take the necklace if you want it, it might help you. It brought me comfort when things were bad. It might bring you comfort too.

I love you both dearly.

Forgive me, forgive me.

C x

'Do you see the significance of this?' Isla wiped her wet cheeks, smiling at Penny and Jacob who looked blank. 'Clare told Astrid to do as she pleased with her life. She didn't beg her to look after me. She explicitly told her to live life however she chose.'

'Which means she chose to bring you up herself instead of sending you away?' said Jacob.

'Exactly,' said Isla, 'the point is, Astrid had a choice. And she chose me.'

'I always knew that Astrid loved you, Isla. I tried to tell you that,' Penny said, sadly.

'I know, Penny, but don't you see? Now I have it documented here in black and white.' Isla gestured to the contents on the table. 'You can't imagine what a difference it makes when it's all written down like this. Look, here.' She pulled out a brown envelope with elaborate red printed script and black inked signatures. 'Clare's death certificate. Here . . .' She stretched over the table and collected a group of newspaper cuttings in her hand, 'newspaper reports about Clare's death, about Astrid's art shows. There's a pile of my school reports over there. And in that blue envelope are some of my baby teeth and a lock of my hair.'

'Good grief,' said Jacob.

'Astrid's whole life was about putting things down on paper. She drew and painted endlessly, documenting what mattered to her. I have that same need, to see things in front of me, not verbalised. It becomes real. The fact that Astrid took the trouble to keep these too shows that she cared. And that's all I ever wanted to know. That she cared about me.'

'She certainly did.' Penny squeezed her arm.

'Look, here's a letter from Astrid's art school begging her to come back.' Jacob put the paper back into its envelope. 'It's dated just after Clare's death. What a mess.'

'It doesn't matter.' Isla took the envelope from him. 'She got what she wanted. All she ever needed was to paint and she was able to do that, college or not. I've come to the conclusion that if she did decide to take her own life, that if her death wasn't an accident, it's something I'll have to come to terms with.'

'Talking of which,' Jacob said, 'Penny and I were discussing Astrid's ashes. Do you still have them?'

'Yes, they're up in the studio.'

'What do you plan to do with them?'

'I hadn't thought, really. But I suppose she can't hang around here for ever.'

A look passed between Jacob and Penny. He said, 'Have you thought about scattering them? Maybe here, on the beach?'

'I suppose I could,' said Isla. 'I'd like to scatter them where Clare died. So they can be together in some way. I'll get them now, shall I?'

'I'll get them,' said Penny. 'I'd like to see the hidden cupboard Astrid made.' Penny made her way out of the room and could be heard treading slowly up the stairs.

Jacob turned to Isla. 'Between you and me, Penny hasn't been herself for a while.'

'You said that yesterday, is she OK?'

'Generally, yes, but I think she's finding it hard being on her own now Astrid's gone. I hadn't appreciated how much until recently.'

'Is it something I should be worried about?'

'No, no, I'll do the worrying. But I think you could help by letting her have Astrid's ashes for a little while before you scatter them. I think it would be good for her, to say goodbye.'

'I'm not scattering them by myself. We'll do it together.'

'I didn't want to presume anything, but, yes, I think she would like that very much.'

Jacob pulled out a bundle of cloth containing several rectangular canvases. 'What's this?' he said.

'These are the paintings that bookend Astrid's life. Some very early ones that pre-date Clare and Nell's deaths. Look at them, they're so joyful. They're in watercolour too, so they must be early. She switched to oils before she got into art college, I think.'

'They're absolutely beautiful.' Jacob picked one up and stared at it.

'They're the best work she's ever done, as far as I'm concerned. It's like they've been painted by her true self, before everything turned sour.'

'Are you going to keep them?' asked Jacob.

'Yes, I'm going to give them pride of place above the fireplace.'

'But there's already a painting there, isn't there?'

'Not for long.' Isla grinned.

'And what are these?' Jacob pointed to the larger canvases.

'I didn't think they were hers, until I saw the signature and date. She did them in the last couple of years.'

'Extraordinary,' said Jacob, crouching down to inspect them. 'It's a completely different style.'

'Yeah. The rest of her stuff was so full of detail. But these are almost like Impressionist paintings and the colours are incredible.'

'I wonder what precipitated the change?'

'I don't know. But the fear has all gone. They're more melancholy than sinister. They're actually rather beautiful.'

'And quite similar, in colour at least, to the early watercolours. Just without the detail and on a much bigger scale.'

'Yes, I suppose they are,' Isla said. 'I hadn't appreciated that.'

Penny came back holding Astrid's ashes in one hand and a small plastic bottle in another. 'What's this for?' she asked. 'I didn't know Astrid was taking medication.'

'They're just eyedrops. She had some in the bathroom too,' Isla replied, still looking at the large canvases.

'But there's a prescription sticker on them,' Penny insisted.

'Is there?' Isla peered at the note. 'I can't read it. Where are my glasses?' Isla rooted through the mass of drawings on the table.

'Jacob?' Penny asked. She handed the bottle to him.

He read the label. 'Ah. This explains a great deal.'

Isla and Penny looked at him.

'This is medication for glaucoma,' he said.

'You mean her eyesight was going?' Isla asked.

'Yes. Poor Astrid. That must have been a significant blow to someone like her.' Jacob gave the bottle to Isla.

'Why on earth didn't she say anything?' Isla said, putting her glasses on and reading the label. 'I could have helped her.'

'That's precisely why she never said anything, I imagine,' Penny replied. 'Can you imagine Astrid asking you to move in with her to help? She would have rather chewed her own arm off.'

'Do you think that's why she fell down the stairs?' Isla mused.

'And why she seemed different, the last few years. She couldn't see properly, poor thing.' Penny sounded upset.

'It must have been terrifying for her,' Jacob agreed, nodding.

A few months earlier, Isla had felt certain there were more clues about Astrid scattered around the house, and there had been. She had thrown away a bottle of eye drops just like this one from the bathroom cabinet, and another from the bedside table. The house was full of magnifying glasses. It took Penny and Jacob to put two and two together, but she should have done it sooner. The answers had been right under her nose.

Chapter Fifty-Five

PENNY, OCTOBER

Astrid's ashes occupied a rather pedestrian grey plastic container, which seemed to Penny to be completely at odds with the woman she knew. Isla had insisted on giving it to her for a few days before they scattered them. Penny had been puzzled, but Jacob had exhibited uncharacteristic enthusiasm for the responsibility. She had brought the container home to humour him and put it on her mantlepiece. It caught her eye every time she walked past and when she began talking to it she found the act of focussing her thoughts on a singular object quite comforting.

'Jacob thinks you're a figment of my imagination,' said Penny as she looked at the jar. 'Maybe he's right. What do you think?'

A breeze blew in through the house as the back door banged open and snaked through the loose strands of her hair. She breathed in and caught the faint whiff of roses on the air before it disappeared and turned to salt.

Penny rattled the jar and felt the soft shift of the ashes within. 'Do you need some closure, Astrid? Well, you're getting some today whether you want it or not. You're leaving this afternoon.'

The last few days had been transformative. When she'd read the letter that Clare had written all those years ago, she'd finally understood that the necklace was a token of love, intended to protect Astrid from the terrible lows that her sister suffered. It all began to make sense. Something inside her fell away; it was the only way to describe it. Her spirit had lifted, the feeling of pressure that had filled her head over the past year suddenly cleared. The few days she had spent with Jacob in his house on the other side of the village made her realise there was more to living here. Her eyes had been nourished by the green of his garden, the lushness of it. She was so used to seeing the browns and greys of the ocean it was as if she had forgotten there was an alternative. When she woke up every morning, she had missed the noise of the sea but delighted in the sound of birdsong, her ears ready to hear something other than the mournful cry of the gulls. Jacob had occasionally asked her about living together properly and she had always been reluctant to alter an arrangement that seemed to suit them both, but now things felt different. She had begun to imagine summers spent away from tourists in Jacob's comfortable house, spending time in his beautiful garden, digging the earth. Planting flowers that wouldn't grow in her own garden, perhaps. There was even a new yoga class for OAPs starting up in the village hall. She could try that, sort her balance out. She imagined herself walking the sand at night, taking her shoes off without fear of falling over. She would always return to the sea, she was certain of that, but the ties that bound her to this place were slackening and she saw that as something not to mourn, but to be celebrated.

'Ready?' Isla called from the porch. She was wrapped up in waterproofs and wellingtons.

Penny shook herself out of her reverie. 'We could delay it until the weather improves?' she suggested.

'If it's not raining, I don't care. Today's as good a day as any. Is Jacob coming?'

'No. He thought it best if we did it together. *Three's a crowd*, I think he said. My guess is he would rather fall asleep in front of the rugby.'

'OK, let's do it.'

Penny picked up the plastic bottle and handed it to Isla while she pulled on her anorak.

'Well, don't we look the part!' said Isla, her words muffled by an enormous scarf obscuring her face.

'How is one supposed to dress for ash scattering, I wonder? Is there a dress code?' They tramped onto the sand and walked in an easy silence down the beach. The sand was empty save for a couple of discerning anglers digging for lugworms. Several gulls were eyeing their progress, hovering above them, ready to swoop. Isla looped her arm through Penny's.

'Do you think Astrid would have approved?' said Isla.

'You mean the manner of her departure?'

'Yes. I wasn't even sure if she wanted to be cremated. Maybe she would have preferred a burial?'

'Bit late for that,' snorted Penny, and they both started laughing. 'Here's the spot,' she said eventually. 'Do you want to do it?'

'Why don't we both do a bit?' Isla and Penny waded into the water as far as their wellingtons would allow and unscrewed the container. It had a wide neck and Penny could clearly see the grey granules inside. It didn't look like ash from a fire; the texture was different. Isla tilted the bottle and the ash poured in a thin stream into the grey of the water. 'Do you want to say something?' She cocked her head to Penny.

'You first,' said Penny.

'OK. Then I'll just say this.' Isla turned back to the sea. 'Astrid, Clare wrote that you should live life however you choose and I've decided to take her advice. I choose to be happy. So if you're listening, thank you for choosing to look after me. Thank you for leaving me your life's work. I'm sorry we didn't get along better. You did the best you could. If it's forgiveness you're looking for, you have it. I forgive you, Astrid, and you too, Clare.'

Penny took the bottle from Isla and tipped the rest of it into the sea. 'Did you hear that, Astrid? She forgives you. We all do. Now get along, will you? I want my house back.' At that moment, a part of Penny believed the wall between this life and the next was so permeable, the sensation she felt was the embrace of her oldest friend, but it was probably the wind. As the last of the ash fell into the water, the wind dropped. The storm was finally leaving them behind.

They walked back across the beach together and stopped at Penny's steps.

'Do you want to come in for a drink?' Penny offered. 'I think we deserve one after that.'

'Actually, I have plans,' Isla said shyly. 'I'm meeting some old school friends at the White Lion.'

Penny felt a surge of pleasure, as if Isla were her own child. 'Well that's a much better option, I think.'

Isla shook her head. 'No it's not,' she said with sincerity, 'but I've been meaning to go for ages and today is the day, that's all. Danny – from Astrid's old art shop? He's been on at me to go.'

'Well, you could do worse than Danny Atherton. He's a lovely man.'

Isla rolled her eyes. 'It's not like that. It's just . . . old friends, catching up.'

Penny gave her a look and tried not to laugh. 'Whatever you say.'

They hugged, tightly, promising to take an evening walk together sometime. Penny climbed the stairs to her house and as she reached the top, she turned to look back across the sand. She could see the journey that she and Isla had made together. Years later, she still maintained that three sets tracked up the beach but only two returned.

Chapter Fifty-Six

ISLA, NOVEMBER

Isla had a picture in her head of Edward rushing up the stairs to the studio, but the train journey had tired him out. When Isla had picked him up from the station, she'd been struck by how stately he looked, a graceful reed amongst the crowds. He had refused to take her arm, but had allowed her to carry his bag and together they made their way in a leisurely manner to the car. It wasn't until well into the afternoon that he mustered up the energy to climb the two flights to the roof.

She watched with alarm his slow progress up the steps to the studio. 'I should have brought the paintings down for you to see. It was stupid of me. I could still do that, you know.'

'Nonsense. I have always wanted to see where Astrid worked and she always refused me. Wild horses couldn't keep me away.'

'I'd never forgive myself if you fell down my stairs though.'

'Well I have no intention of doing that. I'm quite capable of climbing a staircase or two. I just need a little more time, that's all. Astrid's private life has been just that for more than half a century. A few more minutes won't make any difference. Oh my!' He reached the top and gasped as he saw the paintings on the walls. 'This is stupendous!'

'I know. Pretty dramatic, isn't it?' Isla couldn't help feeling proud of Astrid.

'Let me sit down so I can appreciate it fully.'

Isla reached for the only chair and moved it into the middle of the room. She positioned its back to the window so Edward could see all the paintings together. He remained quite still for some time. Then he got up and slowly walked closer to observe the smaller details. 'It's extraordinary. I recognise some of these elements in paintings I sold many years ago. She must have used the walls to experiment.'

'Or she liked details and replicated them here perhaps?'

'Unlikely. Once she finished a painting she immediately lost interest and didn't want to look at it or discuss it again. It was almost as if she hadn't had any part in it. These walls show her development as an artist. I can see decades of change here; it's fascinating. What do you plan to do with it all?'

'Honestly? I have no idea. I can't see how it could be preserved.'

'Well if you wanted to do that you would need to remove the walls.'

'I'm not doing that. Somehow I think Astrid would have wanted to leave them as they are, not put them in an art gallery. That's not why they were painted. This feels private.'

'I agree. But they will deteriorate eventually. You should get them photographed and properly documented by someone who knows what they're doing.'

'Do you know someone who could do that for me?'

Edward's mind flitted to a man he had loved and lost. 'I used to, but he passed away. I'll dig around and see if I can find someone else.'

'Do you want to see the pictures now?'

'I can hardly tear my eyes away from the walls, but yes, let's examine the pictures while the light is good.' Isla took out each canvas in the order in which they had been stored. After some time the entire collection surrounded them both, tilting against the walls of the studio.

'I think I'm running out of superlatives,' said Edward.

'Why do you think she kept these?'

'There is only one reason Astrid kept these. She liked them too much to part with them.'

'How do you know it wasn't the other way round? She might have hated these.'

'Astrid was not known for her sentimentality. She destroyed work she disliked. She would never have kept a collection of sub-standard art in her studio.'

Isla's thoughts turned to the painting still in the roof space not ten feet from where she stood. 'Are you sure? I ruined a painting she criticised once and she kept hold of that.'

'A painting she made?'

'No. It was one of mine. We had a disagreement about style, so I obliterated it with her least favourite colour. I found it in the eaves.'

'Let me see.'

Isla ducked into the roof space and brought it out.

Edward looked at it for a long time. 'I can see why she kept it,' he said eventually.

'Why? It's pretty awful.'

'It's not a sophisticated painting, it's true, but there is something there. Something visceral. It's very raw.' He touched the contours of the dried paint very gently with his fingertips, as if he might bruise the canvas and smiled. 'She wouldn't have kept this if it didn't hold significance for her. She was a pragmatist. We both know that.' He looked at her and chuckled. 'I always knew you had something in you. And here it is.'

Isla felt her face heat up and put the painting back. 'We aren't talking about me. This is about Astrid. Why did she keep these paintings in particular?'

Edward surveyed the room, his eyes roaming from one canvas to the next. 'This is a vanity collection. I'm beginning to think I was played.'

'What?'

'Well, judging by these, I was given the more commercial stuff and all the while she was producing this, which never saw the light of day. It's far superior, more experimental. She must have rattled off a painting to keep me sweet and then spent time developing her technique without any pressure.'

'Why wouldn't she sell them?'

'Conceit. She probably thought they were too good for the general public. She could be quite a snob at times.' He turned to her. 'She was right actually, some of the buyers we had could be pretty crass . . . people who just collected art that was trendy. They had no interest in fine art, just the kudos. There are some, though, who really would have appreciated what she was trying to do and I include myself in that. It's a pity she didn't feel she could share this with me.'

'Wouldn't you have wanted to sell it to the highest bidder back then?'

Edward gave a little grunt. 'I'd like to think not, but, at the time, I was younger, trying to build up a business . . .' He sighed. 'She was probably right to hide it away from me.'

'Well, it's hidden no longer.'

'The question is, Isla, what are you going to do with it?'

'That's why you're here. Some of them I want to keep, but I'll sell what I don't want.'

They spent the evening looking at the charcoal studies and Astrid's sketchbooks in the dining room.

'Her deviousness knows no bounds,' Edward declared over a glass of wine that evening. 'I feel quite aggrieved, actually. I thought I knew her, but clearly I didn't.'

'Nobody knew Astrid. I only just found out she wasn't actually my birth mother. She was my aunt.'

'What?' Edward was aghast.

'It's a long story. I'm too tired to go into it now. Let's keep tonight's topic art-related and tomorrow we can go into parentage. I want to talk to you about that.' Isla gestured to the large painting of Clare above the fireplace.

'What about it?'

'I wanted to get rid of it as soon as I moved in, but since you told me the significance it held for Astrid, I can't bear to sell it to someone she would disapprove of. Is there a museum, somewhere she felt attached to, that might like to buy it? I've tried very hard to like it and I just can't shake off the childhood associations that come with it. Do you think you could find a suitable buyer for me?'

'I can do better than that.' He leaned towards her. 'I have wanted that picture since the day Astrid painted it. If you'll sell it to me, I'll give you a fair price and I'll make sure it goes somewhere suitable when I meet my maker if you don't want it back.'

'But here's the problem: I have to get a good price for it because I need the money.'

'Can I help, perhaps? Financially, I mean.'

'No, thank you. But I have an obligation.' It was then that Isla decided to tell Edward about Frankie.

Chapter Fifty-Seven

ISLA, MARCH

ONE YEAR AFTER ASTRID'S DEATH

Isla had given up texting Mark to ask him how Frankie was. He never replied. She supposed Erin had given him instructions and he was too spineless to disobey. But this was different. This time, she wasn't going to take silence for an answer.

Call me. We need to talk, she wrote. It didn't take long for him to reply. She had never demanded a conversation before.

With monumental effort, she let the phone ring three times before she answered it. 'Mark!' His voice threw her back to those few days in the hotel, conversations into the night and a sense of companionship on the car journey home.

'Hi,' he said shyly.

'I can't believe you called back so quick.'

'I thought it might be important. Erin's at work. The hotel is dead. So . . .' His voice sounded flat.

'How are you?'

'I've been better. Erin's still in the suite. There hasn't been a reconciliation. It's over.'

'I'm sorry.'

'Don't be. It's all very amicable, actually. Civilised. I think we did all our shouting when we were still together. We've both run out of steam. I don't think we've got anything left to argue about.'

She could hear the sadness in his voice. 'How's Frankie?'

He sighed. 'She's doing fine.'

She didn't believe him. 'Really?' Isla said. She imagined Frankie's puzzlement that she hadn't come to say goodbye.

'I think, with all the changes, she's been distracted. She's only just started to say a couple of words. Not much, but it's progress.'

'Oh. That's great. Really, really great. Will you say hi from me?' She fought to conceal the pain in her voice.

'You know I can't do that,' Mark whispered.

'So no change with Erin, then?'

'No. She's pretty set on the arrangement.'

'Implacable Erin.'

'Yeah.'

'She's lucky you're still so loyal to her.'

'I owe her. She didn't want to take on the hotel in the beginning. My parents left a lot of debt and I couldn't have cleared it without her help. She gave up a lot for me.' His defence of her was automatic.

'You still love her, don't you?' Isla asked.

'Yes. Unfortunately.'

'And what about Frankie? How do you think she feels about all of this?'

'I'm doing what's best for Frankie, I promise.'

'I don't believe she doesn't miss me.' Her voice was small.

'Look, Isla, if there was a way we could work this out, I would. But Erin is Frankie's mother. She has rights. And I believe she'll turn Frankie against you if you try and get in touch with her. You know what she's like when she gets an idea in her head.'

'What if I told you there was a way through this? Some way I could keep in touch and help Frankie without involving Erin?' She had the feeling of teetering off a steep cliff.

'Go on,' he said slowly.

'I have a proposal. I'm selling some paintings belonging to my mother and I want to set up a trust fund for Frankie with the proceeds.'

'A trust fund?'

'I want Frankie to have a pot of money so she can live her life however she chooses. I know that sometimes cash flow at the hotel . . .'

'I can support my own daughter!'

'I didn't mean it like that. Look, I'm doing this for selfish reasons. I want to atone for hesitating and I want to keep some kind of bond with Frankie so I know she won't want for anything throughout her life.'

'Erin won't accept it.'

'Erin won't have to know. We could keep it secret. An arrangement just between us.'

'Come on, Isla, I can't conceal that kind of cash from her. She's bound to find out.'

'Then tell her if she doesn't accept it I will come and visit Frankie regularly. I'll meet them in the street as they go to school and I'll call into the hotel when she's at work. I'll buy a bloody flat on your road.'

'Yeah. That would probably do it.' He laughed quietly.

'I'm coming to London next week. There's an auction of some of Astrid's paintings. I'll meet you with the documents and we can sign them and then you'll never hear from me again.'

Isla got to the cafe first and waited for him in a quiet corner, back to the wall, facing the door. At two o'clock exactly, he showed up looking nervous. But when he saw her, his smile was automatic and filled with warmth.

'Hello, stranger,' he said, and reached out to hug her. 'How did the auction go?'

'Surreal. Apparently Astrid's work is still very much in demand. I'm glad some of them stayed in this country though. It would have been a shame if they'd all ended up abroad.'

'So am I looking at a rich woman then?'

'Let's just say that there's certainly more than enough for me – and for Frankie. Did Erin agree to everything?'

'She's allowing Frankie to benefit from the fund, if that's what you mean. I haven't told her we were meeting today. I think she would rather not know the details.'

'So she's not changed her mind then?'

'No. I'm sorry.' He touched her arm in sympathy. 'Are you sure you want to do this?'

'Utterly.' She brought out a plastic sleeve filled with various documents. 'All you have to do is sign. The money will be put into trust for Frankie. You'll have power of attorney until she's older.'

'What's to say we won't squander it on new hotel fittings and flash cars?'

'I trust you. It's obvious she comes first. Saying that, there are a few clauses about it having to directly benefit Frankie. So don't get any ideas about retiring to the Caymans.'

'Damn. You read my mind. Seriously, though. I don't know what to say. This is very generous.'

'It's the least I can do. There's one more thing though.' Isla reached down into her bag and pulled out a familiar wooden box.

'The watercolour set,' Mark said.

By the look on his face, she could tell Frankie had missed it.

'Will you give it to her?' she asked.

'I'll have to talk to Erin.'

Isla nodded, disappointed.

'I have a farewell gift for you, too, before you go,' said Mark, putting the box into his bag.

'What is it?'

'Come with me. But you have to promise to be discreet.'

Chapter Fifty-Eight

ISLA

The school was a Victorian red-brick affair: white painted windows and a mean playground typical of central London. Mark walked through the gates and Isla waited, as instructed, on the pavement. She could see a crowd of parents surrounding a door to the classroom. At the entrance a teacher stood, acknowledging each parent and calling the children, one by one. Frankie was almost last, struggling to get her coat on, her arms clutching sheets of paper and a black book bag. Isla caught her breath as Mark started walking with her towards the gate and she could see her lovely face unobscured by others.

Frankie had altered in the time of their separation. Her features looked a little wider, she was taller. The dull ache of knowing she had not been there to witness these changes shifted painfully in Isla's stomach. When Frankie smiled to see Mark, her front tooth was missing. Isla wondered who had crept into her room as she slept to slip some money under her pillow. She suddenly had a vision of birthday presents waiting to be unwrapped, stockings being hung up by trembling fingers, the wonder of a sparkler in careful hands. All those little rituals she would never be part of stretched out before her. As Mark approached, he put his arm around Frankie and pulled her towards him as they stepped onto the pavement. It was important that she did not see Isla, but he need not have worried. The little girl listened happily as Mark told her about his day and didn't look round to see who was following close behind.

Isla could hear Mark speak and she could see Frankie nodding and smiling as she turned her face up to him. Isla breathed in her profile like an exotic scent. Frankie's hair had grown and the colour was beginning to darken into a burnished chestnut. Her curls bounced as she walked. Isla tried to take in every detail of her, knowing it would be the last time. She savoured the way Frankie's feet slowed and then took a few skipping steps to catch up with Mark so she could hear the narrative of his day; the way she pushed her hair away from her face with the back of her hand, the dimples of her knuckles still soft and round. It was all she could do to stop herself from catching those curls in her own hands, sniffing Frankie's familiar smell and burying her face in the warmth of her downy neck. Ten short minutes slipped by and Isla knew they were almost there.

They had both agreed how it would end.

Mark and Frankie would enter the hotel by the front door and Isla would walk past them, head down, just another stranger on the street. At every crossing she edged nearer, able to see each individual hair crowning that delicate scalp. Isla feasted on the details she had grown to love: a rounded cheek, dappled with freckles sloping to a crest of dainty eyelashes. She willed time to slow and cursed every light that obligingly turned in their favour.

As they rounded the final corner, Isla put her fist in her mouth and bit down hard. With just a few steps left, the battle to keep the tears from obscuring her final few moments could not be won. She would for ever berate herself for transforming her last view of Frankie into a shifting, watery blur.

Isla left the hotel as she had found it, baffled by crowds she had no desire to be part of, stumbling amongst people who neither noticed nor cared. She would always associate London with the Baker family. As long as they continued to reject her, Isla could not imagine ever wanting to return.

Chapter Fifty-Nine

Isla

THREE YEARS AFTER ASTRID'S DEATH

The first few weeks had been difficult. Time had stretched out like a prison sentence, but over the months – busy with the contents of Astrid's estate – the pain of losing Frankie had dulled and Isla felt the house begin to lean towards her. After two years it felt as if it were, finally, her own. Three years to the month of her death, the only place that remained Astrid's was the studio in the roof.

Managing Astrid's estate had become a full-time job for a while. The missing paintings had created a lot of excitement, and Isla had become used to talking to the press about Astrid's technique and how she had discovered her lost work in the eaves. Isla had made a conscious decision not to reveal their biological relationship to the wider world. It seemed a betrayal, somehow. Astrid had made a decision to adopt her, and Isla felt it would be a rejection of that commitment if she cut their emotional tie in public. She had come to understand Astrid in a way a middle-aged daughter understands her mother. She loved her despite her flaws. Selling some of Astrid's work did not trouble her. It was the drawings and watercolours that Isla wanted to keep. The paintings that had not been sold were being prepared for a travelling exhibition and would then go on loan to various galleries. If Edward had been younger, he would have managed everything, she supposed, but when Isla asked him, he initially declined the job.

'I'm too old for that sort of thing now,' he said.

'Oh come on, you'd love it.'

'You're right, I would. But it might involve a lot of travel and I'm rather attached to sleeping in my own bed these days.'

'What if I helped? Did the travelling for you?'

'Well, it's possible. It's not a huge collection of paintings. Once they're framed it's just a question of liaising with the various galleries who are displaying them. And there's the paperwork. Never my favourite bit of the job. There will be a lot of insurance forms to fill in.'

'I love paperwork! I could come and see you regularly and bring a bundle with all the stuff I don't understand and you could tell me what to fill in and where.'

'Well, I suppose so . . .'

'And now that you're finally using email we can write and Skype. It will be like you're in the room with me.'

'I find the laptop more tiresome than you can imagine, Isla. I don't know why I ever let you buy me one.'

Despite his protestations, she could see that Edward was delighted to be involved once more with Astrid's work. He finally agreed to provide all the information she needed from his armchair and everything else would be achieved with the help of Kate and her father. It would work out somehow.

Isla had taken Edward's advice about getting the studio photographed. They had begun to enquire about who could do it until a publisher had expressed an interest in documenting the lost paintings and the house they were created in. Although Isla was not directly involved in the book, she answered questions about Astrid and their shared history. It was fascinating delving into Astrid's past and Penny, freed from her role as secret keeper, was a willing source of information about their childhood together, though she was careful to avoid mentioning Clare.

Dealing with Astrid's estate had been a welcome distraction from the fallout with Erin, but the heavy thud of loss would beat in her chest when she least expected it and it didn't diminish as time progressed. Families came in all sorts of shapes and sizes, and she was not alone any more. She met Danny regularly for a drink in the White Lion. Through him, she was slowly reacquainting herself with the classmates who had chosen to stay or come back. Penny and Jacob were never far away and the particular affection she felt for Edward had only become stronger. The one person who mattered to her most, however, lay out of reach.

Today was particularly painful, because it was Frankie's birthday. She would wake up as a nine year old. Isla didn't know why, but the fact that it would be her last year of single digits seemed poignant. She was shedding her childhood and the Frankie that Isla had got to know was beginning to slip away. Erin had not changed her mind. Although the trust fund had been given solely to protect Frankie's future, she couldn't help wondering whether it might have softened Erin's attitude. It hadn't.

Mark, at least, wrote Isla a Christmas card every year. She kept them all and stored them with the paintings that Frankie had asked her to keep. Tucked inside each card was a recent school photograph of Frankie, which Isla immediately compared to the year before. She was growing up. Her freckles hadn't disappeared; her adult teeth were beginning to emerge and jostle for room. The gaps only made her look cuter. Her hair was a bit shorter every time and Isla wondered if this was Erin's influence or Frankie's decision.

Isla had stopped working to concentrate on managing Astrid's estate. Now that the initial flurry of activity had died down, she had more time on her hands and didn't like what her mind did with the freedom. Running still provided the solace it always had, but today exercise had only taken the edge off her bad humour, not quashed it entirely. She sat at the writing desk and looked out at the view beyond, considering what to do with the day. Her fingers tapped the metal drawer pulls rhythmically, a tuneless beat. She pulled the drawer open and saw a sheaf of papers she needed to go through. The exhibition of Astrid's work was about to commence and she should finish off the paperwork involved. As she gathered the forms together, her fingers brushed a soft synthetic smoothness she did not recognise. Moving the papers away, she ducked her head to look into the back of the drawer.

There it lay, completely forgotten until now, a clear Ziploc bag of Astrid's hair. Suddenly she was plunged back into those first few weeks of grief: the dirty dishes, the lethargy, and the loneliness. She wondered how different it would have been had she known about Astrid and Clare before Astrid died. She pulled the bag out and placed it on top of the desk. The whorls of hair were no less fascinating; they still held a certain pull. They could be gathering storm clouds or plunging waves. She peered more closely and was reminded of Edward's description of the dark energy that drove Astrid's work. Looking at these fragments of her mother was like looking into a different world. You could lose yourself in it; just like a painting.

She stood up and took the bag with her. As she crossed the living room and mounted the stairs, she wondered if she was mad to try it. But each step she took brought her closer to the studio and the pull was irresistible. It was almost as if there was something willing her up the stairs. Although she had spent a lot of time there, it was invariably Astrid's room. Isla had always entered as a guest. But as she turned the silver key with the initials 'AJ' entwined at its head, she ascended the steps in a different capacity.

Chapter Sixty

Isla

Isla had a peculiar feeling she was being accompanied when she mounted the stairs. It was as if Astrid were walking alongside her, not crouched in the corners, watching, but guiding her body. Penny was right. This house was a Thin Place, the walls barely able to separate one world from the next. She could almost feel the past and future converging as a physical sensation. The notion that this was solely Astrid's space receded. It was passing to Isla now. It had taken her whole life to try and understand Astrid, and now she felt she did, she had finally begun to understand herself.

Over by the windows, the wide wooden table ran underneath the span of glass and Isla placed the bag of hair upon it. She knew this was going to be the beginning of a very long journey, yet she could see it mapped out in front of her with a clarity so startling she wondered if the vision had always been deep inside her, waiting to surface. It would begin with the contents of that bag, but, eventually, Isla knew it would be about Frankie. The photographs Mark sent every Christmas were not enough. There had to be another way of keeping Frankie near. There *was* another way.

Isla pulled out the images of a growing girl and mounted them on the wall. There was a reason she had always kept these photographs here and not on display in the rest of the house, but it was only becoming apparent now. The little ammonite turned willingly under her fingers, strangely familiar as the handle to her own front door. There was the plan chest, sitting quietly in the shadows, as if it had been waiting for her to return. She opened the drawer and the wood moved smoothly; the smell of the paper stock as familiar as Astrid's breath upon her head. She remembered Astrid teaching her to paint as a child. She remembered sitting on her lap, holding a brush with Astrid's hand over hers, moving through the canvas together. The memories released themselves and fluttered freely like moths in moonlight.

A loose stack of assorted watercolour paper lay in the third drawer down. Her fingers moved towards the correct weight, governed by something other than her own instincts. She drew the paper out. It was thick, creamy and slow to bend. She reached further into the recess of the chest and felt for the flat wooden box she knew would be there. Her fingers closed over the shape of it like a familiar handshake. It opened with a slow, intimate squeak. The contents were desiccated, but she knew that the darkened squares of cracked colour would be coaxed into life under a gentle stream of warm water. As she moved to the sink and did this, Isla rubbed each square with a damp cloth to reveal vivid shades of cobalt, ultramarine and viridian and was temporarily paralysed by nostalgia, though she couldn't remember seeing them before now.

She should have stretched the paper first, but she didn't want to wait for it to dry. She was anxious to begin, lest the feeling ended with nothing to show. She placed the sheet of paper on the table and sat the watercolours to the side. A collection of ceramic and glass vessels gathered at the end of the table. Isla selected a wide-necked glass jar, dull with age and paint flecks, knowing somehow it was Astrid's favourite. She sluiced it out, emptied it of water and filled it twice more, a ritual she knew would be performed at the beginning of every new piece of work. A large brown jug filled with brushes jostled for her attention. She selected one instinctively, sure it was right. She drew it out as a conductor draws a baton. The fine bristles flexed on the palm of her hand and she noticed a faint thumbprint, the same size as her own, on the handle; indelible in oil paint. She immersed the brush in water and watched the filaments swell and relax. Lightly, she touched the brush to the colours she knew would blend and settled her fingers around the wood. The grip felt familiar and right.

As she swept the colour over the paper and watched it flood the surface, she knew she had finally come home.

Epilogue

She came across the name by accident, quite innocently; Frankie was no snoop. The owners had told her to make herself at home and encouraged her to use the library. She had a project to do before her college course began in September and this was the perfect place to think about it. The fact that she was being paid to be here was a happy bonus. All she had to do was water the plants, keep the place ticking over and walk the dog. Ollie was prone to hiding from her when it was time. He was old and tired and although they liked each other very much, a house-sitter was no replacement for his real family.

'There you are.' She crouched down on the thick wool carpet and ducked underneath a colossal oak writing desk. Ollie had several beds scattered throughout the house. This one was tartan with a thick fleece lining and smelled of warmth and sleep. Frankie scratched him underneath his elegant chin and his brown eyes stared up at her and closed slowly as she hit the right spot. 'Don't you fancy a walk, Ollie? Walkies?'

The dachshund opened his eyes but remained resolutely still. It always amused Frankie how a dog as small as Ollie could still appear to look down his nose at her.

'Can't say I blame you. It's raining out there. Shall we wait and see if it stops soon? Then go? What do you say?'

He licked her wrist in gratitude and closed his eyes once more. She left him to sleep and looked around the room. This was Martin's room, really, and Ollie was Martin's dog. Near to the chesterfield, there was an expensive-looking cigar humidor and a drinks cabinet displaying cut-glass decanters filled with various types of port. The combination of leather and smoke permeated the atmosphere. Most of the wall space was filled with hefty-looking law books, with titles she found impossible to understand. The section in the far corner of the room near to the window was different, though. This area overlooked the vast garden and Frankie knew it must belong to Rosemary, Martin's wife. The books were more colourful, most of them devoted to gardening. Frankie ran her fingers across the stack. None of the titles interested her, but the pictures on the covers were filled with blooms and greenery. Frankie idly trailed her fingers, enjoying the sensation of her fingertips bumping across a vast landscape of knowledge.

Then she saw it. A large hardback, the biggest, really, on the shelf above her eye-line. It was surprising she hadn't noticed it from across the room. A collection of letters in large Helvetica capitals, running up the spine: ISLA JARSDEL. A memory swam forward in Frankie's mind and she knew this was a name that held significant personal importance for her. She reached up and carefully freed the book from its neighbours, inspecting the cover. It was a book about art. Paintings, by the look of it. Strange, because she didn't recognise the work. She did know this name, though, she was sure of it. As sure as she was of her own.

A vague memory of struggling to spell it out in fat crayon gathered and firmed in her mind: I.S.L.A. Like the beginning of the word *island*. She always found it difficult to get the shape of the S under control. She remembered warm fingers on her shoulder, a kiss on the top of her head, being told it was OK to make the top curve smaller, the lower one fatter, *like the belly of Mr Greedy. See?*

Had she just made that memory up? It seemed so pure, it couldn't be fiction.

Frankie opened the book and began to read. The paintings were abstract, colourful swirls that seemed to move when she stared at them. Another memory surfaced: a beautiful watercolour set, the colours like jewels, a deep desire to sit and paint. What had happened to that paint set? She had loved it like a sibling, choosing which colours to use with confidence, never unsure. She remembered the feeling of absolute certainty, knowing what she wanted to accomplish. A feeling she had lost after the accident, but this woman had helped bring back. Her attention returned to the book. The paintings had a pleasant energy that drew her in. She kept reading, hoping for some clue, another memory to surface, but nothing happened. When she reached a chapter called 'Early Work', the mood changed completely. Here, she saw watercolours filled with pathos. Indistinct figures, misted and drab, lost in a fog of grey and brown. She flipped the page and was suddenly confronted by an image so shocking she almost snapped the book shut.

Her own face. Younger, but unmistakeable, filling the page, staring out of a Stygian gloom with such sadness it made her afraid. Frankie searched for the title, certain she would see her name, but the label read 'Untitled VII'. The next few pages contained a variation on the same theme: a snatch of her hair, the curve of her cheek, indistinct fragments appearing and disappearing into a mist, like the fleeting image of a dream. All of the paintings were untitled and all of them were of her; she knew it with a certainty that hammered her chest. She flipped through the book until she found what she was looking for. A black-and-white photograph of a face that she had loved briefly, passionately, and then forgotten entirely until this day. How could she justify such a lapse?

Frankie was transported to a stone patio, a view of the sea, islands breaking the water like the backbone of a huge beast. She remembered a room in the roof of a house, full of beautiful and mysterious paintings, a secret door that she had discovered and told no one about. This woman had loved her, she was sure of it. Then nothing, a blank. Her parents never mentioned her. Was she dead? Frankie's heart lurched at the thought. She frantically flicked through the book until she found the information she was looking for. Isla was still living and the book was a recent publication.

So why the silence? It was impossible to piece together a time frame. In her mind's eye, it felt as if Isla had been a part of her life for years, but Frankie knew her memory was unreliable. An image of herself, walking across the sand, holding Isla's hand bobbed up. She remembered knocking on a red wooden door and slipping in, waiting to open the box of watercolours. A wiry arm patting her shoulder, a warm encouraging smile. That feeling of safety, of having her hair stroked and her opinions sought; she dreamed about it sometimes but she had never realised it was an image rooted in fact.

Frankie thought hard, willing the past to swim near enough to rescue it. She couldn't have been a relative. Maybe she was a family friend. She thought about asking her mother. They had only found a better footing with one another recently. Erin had not approved of Frankie leaving school at sixteen to work as a house-sitter. But now she had decided to take up this college course, things between them had begun to thaw out. Frankie didn't want to jeopardise that by asking about something her mother had purposefully kept from her.

Her dad, then. He must know something.

Frankie picked up the phone before she gave herself a chance to think what she was going to say. 'Dad?' She smiled when he picked up.

'Frankie! How's it all going? Are you still at the Fitzroys'?'

'Yes, three more days and then I'm coming back down to London.'

'Marcia was telling me that you're the sitter with the most repeat bookings. I think you must be her favourite employee. She's going to be beside herself when you leave for college.' He could not keep the pride out of his voice.

'Oh come on. She knows I'll be back every holiday. She totally has a thing for you, Dad. You should put her out of her misery and ask her out.'

'I thought she was buttering me up because she wants to do some kind of partnership with the hotel. She mentioned something about advertising here.'

'You should still ask her out. She's suffering.' Frankie giggled.

'Hmm. Maybe.'

'Listen, I have a question for you. And I want you to answer it honestly. Do you promise?' Frankie's heart jumped as she said the words.

'That sounds ominous, Frankie. I hope I always try and answer questions that you ask me honestly. What's the dilemma?'

'Who's Isla Jarsdel?'

The silence stretched out between them.

'Dad?'

His voice completely changed. 'What on earth made you ask me that, Frankie? That went on years ago.' The words came out breathless and unsteady. It thrilled her to know she was on to something.

'I saw her name on a book and I suddenly remembered. I want to know what happened to her.'

Mark paused once more. 'I don't know if this is a conversation we should have over the phone.'

'We don't have much choice. I want to find her as soon as I've finished here.' Frankie hadn't been aware of this impulse, but, as soon as she articulated it, she knew it was something she would do with or without her father's help. 'The project I've been set?' she continued. 'We have to interview someone who's important to us personally – a family member or a friend. After we've researched their life, we have to make a portrait of them or a collage. A photographic biography in pictures. I've decided it's going to be her, if she lets me.'

'You're going to find her? Have you spoken to your mother about this, Frankie?'

'Not yet.'

'I don't know if that's a good idea.'

'If you don't tell me what the big secret is, I'll have to ask her all about it, won't I?' She felt sorry for her dad. She had rattled him, but she knew that if she didn't push it now, he would have time to compose himself and fob her off.

'Look, Frankie, I'll tell you everything if you promise not to let Erin know.' There was another silence.

'I'm waiting, Dad. And I'm not promising anything. What's the big deal?'

'It's not as easy as you think to explain. I can't just . . . parcel it up in a neat sentence. It's a long story.'

'Then tell me.'

She could hear him take a breath, and then he began.

It had been an unspoken rule in the Baker family that the details of the accident were not to be picked over, so her knowledge of that holiday had been scant. Frankie made Mark tell her everything. There were no photographs of that week in the family album. The memory card was still in Erin's possession and on the way to the train station, Frankie went to her mother's flat to retrieve it. She expected a refusal, but Erin had been unusually compliant. She had changed since she met James. She was more relaxed, her edges were softer. It seemed that finally she had stopped looking beyond what she had, and had begun to appreciate what was in front of her. Middle age suited her, Frankie thought as she opened the door.

'I should have told you my side of the story before now,' Erin said, a tinge of regret in her voice.

'I have to get my train, Mum.' Frankie looked at her watch.

'Come over when you get back and I will.' She hugged Frankie goodbye. 'I'm glad you're doing what you want to do with your life. I hope it makes you happy.' Erin handed over the memory card and Frankie put it in a small pocket in the case of the camera that was perpetually slung round her neck. Then Erin gave her something else, wrapped in tissue. 'If you do manage to find Isla, give her this. It's about time she had it back.' She dropped the object into Frankie's palm and closed her daughter's fingers around it gently.

'What is it?' Frankie asked, peering into the tissue.

'Something I borrowed. I can't imagine why I thought I needed it. It's been in the back of a drawer for the best part of a decade. Whatever you do, don't break it.'

Frankie nodded and pushed it gently to the bottom of a pocket in her rucksack.

The journey from the train station was a five-mile hike. She had considered getting a taxi, but opted for a bus that dropped her in the village. The walk from there helped her gather her thoughts. As she crested a hill and made her way down to the beach, the sky opened up and the sea lay before her, flatly obedient, reflecting the sunlight. She started taking photographs, eager to begin the project she hoped to complete. Only the islands broke the surface of the water and the sea birds diving for fish. She could hardly equate the scene before her with her own near death. It seemed preposterous.

As she drew closer, she smelled the sea, the briny seaweed left behind by the tide and the popcorn machine outside the sweet shop by the lagoon. She stopped and bought an ice cream, eating it while she looked at the great sea-wall curving away from her and onto the beach. She decided not to walk along it and she didn't take pictures. She would stick to the road. That other, trickier route would keep for another day. As she picked her way past families returning to their cars and makeshift bucket and spade stalls packing up for the day, the holidaymakers thinned out and she saw the single track that signalled the beginning of Isla's lane. It was just as Mark had described it: potholed, neglected and overgrown with weeds.

There were only two houses. The first looked, for all intents and purposes, like someone lived there, but as she approached she saw it had been transformed into a small art gallery devoted to Isla and Astrid's work. A curator sat in the porch, reading a book in the early evening sunshine. Frankie peered in through the open door and recognised the paintings hanging on the wall. She was familiar with them now, after all the research she had done.

'I'm shutting in a minute, but you're welcome to have a look.' The curator shifted in his chair, putting his book down, eager for a chat.

Frankie considered entering, but she knew she had procrastinated enough with the ice cream. 'I'm actually on my way to see Isla Jarsdel, in the house down there?' She felt a fool. The curator would know this already. 'I'll look around another time, when you're not about to close.'

'Fine by me. Is she expecting you?'

'We used to be friends a long time ago.'

'You've chosen a good time to see her.'

'Have I?'

'She usually finishes painting at this time.' He looked at his watch. 'She'll be fixing herself a drink about now and sitting on the veranda with Archie. Like clockwork, she is, except on Fridays when she's in the pub.'

'Archie?'

'Her lurcher. Lovely dog.'

'I thought she might be married.'

'She's only ever been married to her work, far's I know. If she's not painting then she's teaching, or doing talks. Are you the student who wanted to do the podcast?'

'No. I'm doing a portrait. Of sorts.'

The curator eyed the camera around Frankie's neck. 'She loves working with students; they're in and out of here all day long. She funds the Jarsdel scholarship, see, helps young artists who can't help themselves, that sort of thing. Are you one of those?'

'No. I'm just here for a day or two. Is this all of her work?' Frankie gestured to the paintings on the wall.

'Gracious, no. It's just a small selection. The rest of the rooms aren't open to the public. It's actually someone's house in the winter months. This is only open for six months of the year, for the tourist season.'

'Oh, I see.'

'The owner lives with her boyfriend in the summer on the other side of the village.' He jerked his thumb in the direction for the town. 'They both come back when everybody goes home.'

'Huh.' Frankie could see through to the back of the house and onto the beach beyond. The sea-wall was close. She averted her gaze. 'Well, I should go, I guess.' She said goodbye to the curator and continued down the lane.

The house stood right at the end, on the furthest reach of the spur of the land, obscured by tall clumps of marram grass that yielded to the warm evening breeze. The air carried the sharp tang of salt. Frankie could make out the studio in the roof, an obvious addition to the original building but the rest of the house seemed to sink into the landscape, unwilling to be discovered. The houses here were back to front and she didn't know whether she should have approached from the beach, but the gallery had opened onto the lane so she assumed this was the right side to use.

She halted, suddenly feeling shy, a child again, desperate to get things right. She felt her words desert her. The door was closed, and she peered through the stippled glass that obscured the view of the rooms within. Frankie cocked her head and listened, but all she heard was the cry of the seagulls and the restless sigh of the marram grass. She felt as if she were in some kind of limbo, treading water between the past and the future. She stayed like that for some time, paralysed by hope, numbed by fear, until she saw beyond the glass the ghost of a shadow, slowly moving down the stairs. It didn't seem real, but it paused as if it heard her heart beating, not ten feet away from where she stood.

Frankie crossed her fingers, took a breath and found her voice.

ACKNOWLEDGEMENTS

They say it takes a village to raise a child and the same can be said about publishing books. I am indebted to Oli Munson, who kindly passed the manuscript for this book on to Rebecca Ritchie. Becky, thank you for taking a chance on me and for your detailed and thoughtful feedback. Thanks also to Victoria Oundjian and Sophie Wilson for your collective skill and insight and for making my work the best it could possibly be. Claire Baldwin edited a very early version of this manuscript. Thanks go to her for her help. My admiration and gratitude go to Nicky Lovick and Sarah Rouse for a forensic copy-edit, and to Emma Rogers for designing the cover.

There are several brave friends and family members who read early versions of this book before it was ready to go out into the world. Thanks to them for their feedback, friendship and time: Beth Davies, Nicola Fox, Louise Morriss, Lyn Sherwood, Jill Trevellick, Jenny Edwards, Anna Brown, Alka Tailor, Fran Littlewood, Laura Ashton, Diane Snyder.

Special thanks to my mum, Gill Edwards, for reading this book almost as many times as I have and heartfelt thanks for your belief, support and medical advice – not just for this endeavour, but throughout my life. If ever there was a mother who deserved a book to be dedicated to them, it is you. To my brother Jim, I'm so happy you came back to us after so many years away and that I will get to see your first book in print later this year.

To my Curtis Brown writing buddies, who individually and collectively made me a better writer; sincere thanks to Tim Adler, Daniel Baker, Bella Dunnett, Brenda Eisenberg, Michael Goldberg, Sadiq Jaffery, Sarah Masarachia, Sophie O'Mahony, Michele Sagan, Chris Steer, Claire Tulloh, Alex Wall, Christopher Wakling and Margot Wilson. Louise Doughty taught the first writing course I ever signed up for when I had the idea for this novel and she was a skilful and generous teacher who took me seriously, despite my inexperience. Thank you.

Thanks to Old Gold for all the laughs and friendship you have given me over the years, but particularly Emma Tait for publishing advice and Rosie Ruddock for smuggling me into writerly events. Thanks also to my Crouch End book club buddies for widening my reading horizons, particularly Anna Wise for her support. Sincere thanks to Frank Tallis for taking me seriously and sharing wisdom. Love and affection to Sian Hurst and Maggie for the fresh air and friendship. To my oldest friend, Lizzy Walton, thank you for the adventures through the years and for being such a loyal friend.

Lastly, thank you to Satish, Milly, Ruby and Luna. You are the scaffold that holds me up. I really don't know where or who I would be without you. Love, always.

ABOUT THE AUTHOR

Photo © 2021 Rob Rowland

Hilary Tailor is a design consultant, and has worked with clients including adidas and Puma as a colour and trend forecaster. She was raised on the Wirral Peninsula and graduated from the Royal College of Art. *The Vanishing Tide* is her first novel.

READING GROUP QUESTIONS

1. Isla blames Astrid for her inability to make a family of her own or keep her friends. Do you think this is fair?

2. Do you think Astrid was haunting Penny and Isla or do you think it was in their imagination?

3. Was Erin's anger justified when she found out Isla hesitated before saving Frankie?

4. When Erin and Mark were arguing about their domestic and business responsibilities, who did you feel the most sympathy for: Mark, for keeping the business afloat single-handed, or Erin, for bringing up Frankie without much help from Mark?

5. Do you think Erin and Mark would have split up anyway, even if Frankie hadn't had her accident?

6. Do you think Penny was right to try and keep Astrid's secrets, even after she had died, or do you agree with Jacob?

7. Do you have any sympathy for the way Astrid behaved when Isla was growing up?

8. Who do you think was the rightful owner of the wentletrap shell?

9. Isla began to see parallels between Erin and Astrid's parenting and personality traits. Do you agree with her?

10. Which character do you have more sympathy for: Isla or Erin?